A SCANDALOUS AFFAIR

A SCANDALOUS AFFAIR

A DAUGHTER OF SHERLOCK HOLMES MYSTERY

LEONARD GOLDBERG

PEGASUS CRIME

NEW YORK LONDON

A SCANDALOUS AFFAIR

Pegasus Crime is an imprint of
Pegasus Books, Ltd.
148 West 37th Street, 13th Floor
New York, NY 10018

First Pegasus Books cloth edition March 2025

ISBN: 978-1-63936-835-8

10 9 8 7 6 5 4 3 2 1

Printed in the United States of America
Distributed by Simon & Schuster
www.pegasusbooks.com

For Mia and Jackson,
both of whom continue to sparkle

The higher the rank, the greater the scandal.

Love and scandal are the best sweeteners of tea.
—*Henry Fielding, Love in Several Masques*

CONTENTS

1

THE PHOTOGRAPH

As twilight fell, not a cloud was to be seen over Southern England, which was an ominous sign, for the clear sky was an open invitation to German bombers. Only the evening before, a thick fog covered much of London and thus shielded the area from a terrifying air raid. Having been denied their target, the bombers were certain to return at their earliest opportunity. Yet, despite the impending threat, Inspector Lestrade visited our rooms at 221b Baker Street to provide us with the important pieces of a most puzzling case whose resolution had escaped Scotland Yard as well as the keen mind of my dear wife, Joanna, the daughter of the Great Detective. At this point, I should mention that my father, John H. Watson, M.D., the close colleague and friend of the long dead Sherlock Holmes, had also contributed his medical expertise to this unsolved case, but to little avail. Whilst Lestrade summarized the details of *The Lloyd's of London Forger*, I reached for pen and paper to jot down any new findings which might merit inclusion in my latest chronicle on the Daughter's adventures.

"You must give the forger credit, for he chose the perfect victim to fleece," Lestrade remarked. "Here she was, a wealthy, elderly woman, who was ill and losing her senses."

I had written down those very facts earlier when penning the initial notes on the adventure. John Morton Harrington, a high-ranking manager at Lloyd's of London, had been assigned the task of conservator for the considerable fortune of Lady Jane Wellesley. Her holdings were valued at over two hundred thousand pounds and consisted of bonds, stocks, real estate, and interest-bearing cash deposits. With enviable skill, Harrington, over a number of years, had moved substantial amounts of Lady Wellesley's holdings into hidden accounts at other banks for his personal use. And he would have gotten away with it had he not made a mistake in transcribing her initials. Yes, her initials! For the elderly dowager was suffering from Parkinson's disease, which caused an uncontrollable tremor and necessitated her signing off on each transaction by scribbling her initials.

"It was quite remarkable for you to detect the change in Lady Wellesley's handwriting," Lestrade was saying to my wife. "Not one in a thousand financial experts would have noticed it."

"Oh, they would have had they followed the money trail," Joanna said, deflecting the compliment. "Here we have stocks being cashed and despite being used to supposedly buy more profitable stocks and bonds, yet the newly acquired stocks and bonds were nowhere to be found."

"Perhaps they were placed under a different name or account," Lestrade countered. "The very wealthy have a habit of attempting to hide their money."

"But to what end?"

"To avoid paying income tax, of course."

"But only the profit and not the transfer itself would be taxed," she said. "You will note that there was little profit in these transactions."

"You raise a fine point."

"Moreover, why would a lady of such abundant, stable wealth consider transferring her holdings around with such frequency? Surely her current income was more than enough to allow for a life of comfort. Why would she take unnecessary chances?"

"She was no doubt following the advice of her conservator."

"That was the reason given, but why expose herself to such risks? And once again, where are the stocks and bonds which were supposedly purchased in the process? Then we come to the forgery itself," Joanna continued on. "The poor lady's hand was shaking so badly, she could not even scribble her signature, and was thus forced to place only her initials on legal documents. And with her terrible tremor, it would have been most difficult to make those legible."

"Which the conservator attempted to forge."

"And that was his singular mistake, Lestrade, for he forged her initials from a set she had used during the earlier stage of her disease. When her tremor was not so pronounced, the W had a very small, complete circle at its very end. The forger continued to place the circle on the initial W, even though the progression of her tremor would have never allowed her to do so."

"And with the onset of her dementia, which at times accompanies Parkinson's disease, she would have been easy to manipulate," my father added.

"It was easy, indeed, to the tune of ten thousand pounds which has mysteriously disappeared," said Joanna.

"All of which was probably deposited into deeply hidden accounts," Lestrade surmised.

"That is not a sufficient explanation," my wife challenged. "And without the money being found, his guilt can never be established."

"But surely his suicide when confronted by Scotland Yard points strongly at his involvement."

"Yet, as you well know, Inspector, dead men cannot be convicted unless the most convincing evidence is presented. For our forger to be charged, you must demonstrate beyond any doubt that funds from Lady Wellesley's accounts were transferred into his for personal use."

"That is no simple task, for no such accounts seem to exist."

"Oh, they exist, but I suspect they were cleverly hidden under a fictitious name or entity which he alone controlled. And once those newly acquired accounts were drained, he closed the accounts."

Lestrade's brow went up. "Are you suggesting that the ten thousand pounds has already been spent?"

"That is a distinct possibility."

"But to what end?"

"That is the question which has to be asked, for the answer will lead to the money."

"Could it not have been spent on wine, women, and song?" my father proposed.

The inspector shook his head in response as he consulted his notepad. Now in his middle years, Lestrade was a tall man of medium frame, with a pleasant face except for his eyes which seemed fixed in a perpetual squint. Other than a fringe of hair about his ears, he was totally bald and kept his head covered with a worn brown derby. According to the newspapers, he closely resembled his father, who was the well-known inspector chronicled in the Sherlock Holmes mysteries. At length, he looked up from his notes and continued on, "He was a confirmed bachelor who resided at the Diogenes club on Pall Mall and appeared to live a prudent life which showed little luxury. His personal bank account revealed that he spent mainly for the necessities of life and little else."

"Were there any debts?" Joanna queried.

"None that he wrote checks for."

"That does not exclude the possibility."

"We kept that in mind, for gentlemen who live a solitary existence will at times search for readily available forms of excitement, such as gambling. Thus, we inquired at the major casinos whether Mr. Harrington was a regular player. No one knew of him. Nor were the high-end bookies aware of such a serious bettor." Lestrade flicked his spent cigar into the blazing fireplace and reached for his derby. "I was afraid, Mrs. Watson, that Lady Wellesley's money has disappeared."

"Money does not disappear, Inspector, it gets spent."

"Perhaps so. But Scotland Yard considers the matter closed, with the most likely perpetrator having met his just end. As you are no doubt aware, we have far more serious cases to pursue and must devote our limited resources to bringing those to a satisfying resolution."

"Do let us know if the money turns up."

"I shall," said Lestrade and, with a tip of his derby, bid us a pleasant good evening.

Once the door closed, I remarked to my wife, "You seem most concerned with the purpose of the stolen money."

"It is a loose thread which must be tied," she said. "It is in fact the crux of the matter."

"But it will certainly lead to John Morton Harrington alone."

"Do not be certain of that." Joanna strolled over to the window overlooking Baker Street and watched the Scotland Yard vehicle drive away in the dwindling light. "We must admit that Inspector Lestrade is coming along rather nicely. You will note how doggedly he pursued the destination of the stolen money, even going to the extent of questioning high-end bookies. He realizes very well indeed how important the money trail is."

"But it appears he will no longer pursue it," I said. "Which shows an obvious lack of interest."

"Oh, the interest is there," Joanna insisted. "For that was the purpose of his visit. He wishes for me to find the money and thus bring the case to conclusion."

"Will you do so?"

"Perhaps, but for the present my mind is focused on the Belgrave murder which was headlined on the front page of the *Daily Telegraph* this morning. It would appear that a fine gentleman was bludgeoned to death whilst he slept, yet no one in the household heard a sound."

"Have you been consulted?"

"Not as yet."

There was a brief rap on the door and Miss Hudson looked in. "I am sorry to disturb you, but an envelope was just delivered by special messenger. It is addressed to you, Mrs. Watson."

"Thank you," Joanna said, reaching for the sealed mail. "We should like supper served shortly, if your oven permits."

"For three?" Miss Hudson asked, eyeing the letter.

"For three."

My wife waited for the housekeeper to depart, then quickly opened the envelope. It contained only a calling card which we read over her shoulder. It was engraved and stated:

William Radcliffe, KBE
11 Downing Street
On the back was a handwritten note:
7:30 P.M., if convenient

All of our eyes were focused on the address, 11 Downing Street, for it was the official residence of the Chancellor of the Exchequer, the second most powerful position in the British government. Of particular importance, he occupied a seat in the War Cabinet where his advice was highly valued and much needed.

"Allow me to explain," Joanna said, adding a log to the fire, for a frosty chill had set in, promising a light snow later in the evening. "This morning I received a phone call from one of London's most prestigious lawyers whose name will not be mentioned at his request. He informed me that a crime was being carried out and that my services would be required. It involved a very senior member of His Majesty's cabinet who would inform me of the details. I was to make myself available at our Baker Street address, with the exact time of the meeting to be determined later in the day."

"It cannot be more mysterious," my father concluded.

"Or more grave," my wife noted. "The Chancellor of the Exchequer, who answers only to the king and prime minister, is somehow involved in a crime which can only be spoken of in the confines of our Baker Street parlor. And he employs London's most savvy barrister to arrange the meeting."

"I would think some basic elements could have been given during the phone call," my father thought aloud.

Joanna shook her head at once. "Phone calls can be overheard."

"Then by special messenger."

She waved away the notion. "Any message sent by post or special delivery can occasionally go astray. It is obvious Sir William wishes to take no chances that might occur."

"Moreover, the meeting is being scheduled on a night when all London is bracing for another bombing raid, which denotes the gravity of the matter."

"Quite so."

"Have you no idea what dire situation would require such secrecy?" I asked.

Joanna strolled over to the shelf that held a Persian slipper and extracted one of her Turkish cigarettes. After lighting it, she began pacing the floor of our parlor, leaving a trail of white smoke behind. The answers to whatever questions were in her mind must have come easily, for she did not mumble to herself as she usually did when faced with a complex problem. "There are several conclusions to be reached," she said, nodding firmly to herself. "First, this is not a governmental matter nor anything related to the throne or cabinet, for were that the case we would have been summoned to Downing Street. Secondly, this surely is a personal matter, for Sir William has engaged the services of a barrister who is known for his expertise in criminal cases. And all this is done under the cloak of extreme secrecy. Thus, I think we can safely say that either Sir William or a close member of his family is somehow entangled in a crime which, if brought to the surface, would cause immeasurable harm to the family name and could well jeopardize his position in the War Cabinet."

"Do you have any notion as to the nature of the crime?" I asked.

"I would be guessing, which is a bad habit, for it all too often leads one down a false road," she replied. "Nevertheless, the act is so despicable that it cannot be spoke of outside his barrister's ears, where client-barrister confidentiality exists."

"Of course he does not dare go to Scotland Yard," my father assisted.

"Unless he wishes it to be on the front page of every London newspaper tomorrow morning."

"What could it possibly be?" I wondered, more to myself than to Joanna.

"We shall find out soon—"

A shrill whistle sounded outside, which caused us to momentarily freeze in place as a chill ran up and down our collective spines. We raced for the window to watch a constable passing by on his bicycle and shouting, "Take cover! Take cover!" It was a dire warning that German bombers were approaching, now no more than a few minutes away.

We quickly closed the curtains, then switched off the lights and moved the sofa in front of the fireplace to block out the blazing logs. These maneuvers dimmed the various lights in the parlor in hopes that none of their rays would escape through the window and thus act as a target for the bombers soon to be overhead. Only then did we reach for our topcoats and dash down the stairs to Miss Hudson's kitchen, where large timbers had been recently installed to brace against explosions. Our housekeeper was waiting for us, her hand on the light switch.

"Hurry over to the timbers!" she directed, her voice calm despite the peril we were about to face.

We huddled against the reinforced wall where we would be safest and listened in the dimness for the dull drone of overhead bombers. Our ears remained pricked, but all we heard was an eerie silence. Toby Two, the keen-nosed hound who now lived with us and was Miss Hudson's constant companion, detected our anxiety and stood motionless by the hot oven whilst awaiting our next move. Then the dog began to whine, and I wondered if she now sensed the impending danger. Yet the silence continued.

"Perhaps they will bypass London tonight," Miss Hudson whispered.

"Let us pray," my father added, which we all did, now bowing our heads in silent pleas.

But our prayers were not to be answered, for we heard the thunder of far-off explosions, and soon thereafter came the hum of overhead bombers. We pressed ourselves against the thick timbers, and awaited the hell that was sure to come.

The thunderous explosions came nearer and nearer, which caused the oven and icebox to rattle noisily. Despite the precautionary lips placed on the shelves, glasses and dishes slipped off and fell to the floor where they shattered into pieces. Joanna and I held onto each other tightly, wondering if this was to be our last moments together on earth. I heard my wife utter a brief prayer for her son Johnny, now a student at Eton, to be looked after. Toby Two desperately searched for a place to hide, but none could be found, so she dashed across the kitchen and flew into Miss Hudson's arms. Then came a deafening blast which shook the room with such violence that large layers of plaster were torn from the ceiling and rained down upon us. My ears rang as another bomb exploded and yet another, but the latter, although quite loud, seemed further away. We waited anxiously until the explosions were far off in the distance, then stood and, after catching our breaths, switched on the lights. The oven and icebox had tilted noticeably, but both by good fortune were still upright. The entire kitchen had a ghostlike appearance, with everything covered in a fine, white dust. Miss Hudson swept aside the broken glass, clearing a path for us to venture into the alleyway. Again, good fortune was with us, for the exterior of our building, as well as those nearby, had suffered no significant damage. As we gazed out into the distance, it appeared that half of London was ablaze, with the inferno so intense it lighted up the landscape of the city. Trucks from the Fire Brigade raced by, bells clanging, followed by yet more trucks. They would have a long night's work, for the damage was beyond extensive and the number of people trapped in the burning rubble impossible to count.

"Why do they continue to take so many innocent lives?" Miss Hudson asked dolefully.

"They wish to break our spirit," my father replied. "They want us to accept an inevitable defeat."

"I would rather die a thousand deaths in Hell before bowing to some bloody German," she responded resolutely.

Which summed up all of our feelings as well, thought I, and had no words to add.

Miss Hudson swept aside the remaining debris and brought order back to the kitchen, with her unhappiness now focused on the tilt of the oven which had tossed her roast beef onto the red-hot coals and thus soiled our supper. But our ever-resourceful housekeeper assured us she could trim enough of the roast to make excellent sandwiches, particularly when creamy horseradish was applied.

Joanna glanced at her wristwatch and said, "Please delay supper, Miss Hudson, for we are expecting a visitor to arrive shortly."

"At this dreadful moment?" she asked, in surprise.

"I am afraid so."

We retired to our parlor and moved the sofa back to its original position. The fire in our hearth had dwindled into red ashes during our absence, so I added two sturdy logs to ward off the deepening chill. Then we waited. But the seven thirty hour came and went.

"Perhaps, due to the circumstances, Sir William will wish to reschedule his visit," my father proposed.

"The gravity of the matter will not allow for delay," Joanna assured. "And the circumstances work in his favor, for the streets will now be empty, with people huddled up in their homes. Thus, his visit will go unnoticed."

"You seem so certain it is a family matter," I said. "And one that involves an unspeakable crime, no less."

"There is no other explanation," she responded. "How else can you explain the need for secrecy, the services of a noted criminal barrister, and now a concealed visit to 221b Baker Street?"

Fifteen minutes more were to elapse before we heard a motor vehicle draw up to our doorstep. Joanna hurried over to the window and parted the curtains ever so slightly to steal a peek at who had arrived.

"He comes in an unofficial vehicle, which no doubt is an official one in disguise," she said.

"What is the tell?" I asked.

"The driver who opened the rear door has a noticeable bulge on the left side of his jacket."

"Sir William is a very careful man."

"Which is a prerequisite for being a Chancellor of the Exchequer."

Moments later, William Radcliffe, KBE, was ushered into our parlor by Miss Hudson who gave him a curtsy, as she was obviously aware of his social standing. Everything about the gentleman spoke of high status. He presented as a tall figure, erect in posture, with silver gray hair and strong, chiseled features. His attire was perfect for his post, for he wore an elegantly fitted dark suit, accompanied by a neatly knotted maroon tie. His stride was confident and showed no sign of weakness, but there were dark circles beneath his eyes.

"Thank you for agreeing to this rather clandestine meeting," he said in a steady voice.

"It is our honor to meet you, Sir William," Joanna greeted him. "With me are the Watsons, who I believe you are aware of."

"I am."

"They are of great assistance to me and have helped bring the most difficult cases to resolution. Thus, you must speak freely in their presence."

"I shall."

"Then pray tell what is the purpose of your visit?"

"I need your advice."

"Easily gotten."

"And your help."

"Not as easily gotten until I hear of every particular in your troubles."

"I do not mince words, Mrs. Watson, so I shall get directly to the threat. My family is being blackmailed."

"Is the dagger pointed at you?"

Sir William shook his head slowly and sadly. "It is directed at my dear granddaughter and her future happiness."

"I must have every detail, no matter how sordid."

"Why do you presume it is sordid?"

"Because on learning of your request for my services, I took it upon myself to review your family history. You have only one granddaughter who not that long ago was listed on the society pages as a sought-after debutante, whose loveliness and adventuresome spirit had attracted a number of suitable bachelors. She is now engaged to the son of the Earl of Marlboro and a late summer wedding is planned, which of course is the future happiness you mentioned. With this is mind, the blackmail or extortion no doubt revolves around some escapade which threatens her upcoming wedding. Such an adventure must involve sordid behavior to merit blackmail at the highest level."

"I can see why the tales of your talents are so well placed," Sir William said, and took a deep breath as if to ready himself for the exposé. "My granddaughter, Anne Atwood, is the apple of the family's eye. She is sweet and kind and lovely, but has an exuberant side and happily participates in activities we may not approve of."

"Pray be specific of this exuberant side," Joanna interjected.

"She finds clever ways to escape the attention of governesses or chaperones, and can disappear and reappear as if by magic, and always with a cheerful explanation. Men adore her and are easily smitten by her looks and attitude. Occasionally, she is known to slip away from our eye and enjoy a glass of champagne with friends and potential suitors, but never did she cause us embarrassment. Never . . ." Sir William's voice cracked momentarily, but he swallowed and quickly regained his composure. "Never, until now."

"And the cause of this embarrassment?"

He reached inside his coat and extracted a black-and-white photograph which measured five-by-five inches. After giving it a long, unhappy stare, he passed the photograph over to Joanna.

She studied it at length before continuing the study with her magnifying glass. Up and down, then side to side, my wife examined every detail, never showing the slightest emotion. Finally, she turned the photograph over, but its back was white except for a scribbled note that read:

Another 5000 pounds
Instructions at noon tomorrow

"Do you have any idea as to the identity of the man who is holding her with such affection?"

"Sadly, I do not," Sir William replied. "Nor does my granddaughter, for she was obviously intoxicated during the event, as evidenced by her glazed expression."

"Has she any recollection of place or person?"

"None whatsoever. Her last memory was attending a play, but only after somehow managing to escape unnoticed from the family estate in Hampstead Heath. Once the performance was concluded, she went backstage to congratulate the actors and was welcomed with champagne, for she had visited them in the past. My granddaughter recalls being escorted to a waiting carriage and little else thereafter."

"A carriage, you say?"

Sir William nodded. "And one which was horse-drawn."

"Was she accompanied?"

"Not that she could recall," he replied. "Her next recollection was returning to the estate later that evening, complaining of a bitter headache. She went directly to bed."

Joanna arose from her chair and, with an iron stoker, poked at the logs in the fireplace, all but ignoring the elder statesman. She continued to do so whilst gathering her thoughts on what appeared to be a misadventure on the part of an immature young woman. But obviously, to my wife, there was much more to it than that. She placed the stoker aside and gave our visitor a long, studied look. The bright light from the fireplace seemed to define every aspect of my lovely wife. She was tall, just a few inches shorter than I, with soft, patrician features and sandy blond hair pulled back and held in place by a silver barrette. She had inquisitive brownish gray eyes that seemed to study you rather than look at you. Her figure was trim as ever beneath a deep blue dress. I could not help but marvel at how little she had changed in our seven years of marriage.

"Is there a remedy?" he asked, breaking the silence.

"You have presented a most tangled problem, Sir William, for your granddaughter has committed a serious indiscretion which may be impossible to undo," said Joanna, and passed the photograph over to me and my father.

It revealed a quite attractive woman, in her late teens or early twenties, wearing a low-cut dress and sitting on the lap of a handsome, young man who was seated on a mat of some sort. He had a hand placed around her slender waist, and appeared to be exchanging a happy smile with her. In his other hand was a white pipe whose bowl had an ornamental cover. Her shoes were off and lay next to her open purse.

"I take it this man was entirely unknown to her," Joanna queried.

"Quite so."

"Does she recall his name?"

"Unfortunately, no."

"On the reverse side of the photograph, it states, 'another five thousand pounds,' which indicates that blackmail payments have been made in the past."

"Regrettably so," the elder statesman admitted. "Three weeks ago we received the initial photograph which revealed Anne arm-in-arm with this very same man. But in that picture she had her head nestled against his shoulder, and her hand in his. The blackmail was brought to my attention because her father, Captain George Atwood, is currently at sea in command of the *Prince Valiant*. I dared not bother him with this family disaster, for he is entirely occupied chasing down German U-boats in the North Sea. So I paid the blackmail which in retrospect was a stupid mistake."

"May I see the initial photograph?"

"It was destroyed."

"Another stupid mistake." Joanna again studied the second photograph with her magnifying glass. "Do you recall if he was similarly dressed in the initial photograph?"

"Are you referring to one particular item of clothing?"

"The sleeves on his shirt."

Sir William furrowed his brow in thought. "I assumed it was the same in both."

"Assumptions will not do here," Joanna admonished. "Were there others in the family who viewed both photographs?"

"Only my wife."

"Then ask her about the sleeves."

"I do not see its relevance."

"I do," she said, and left it at that. "I have one further question. Does anyone else, other than your wife and your barrister, know of the blackmail?"

"No one."

"Please see that it stays that way."

"I have and will continue to do so," Sir William pledged before sighing deeply to himself. "I take it you will have to interview my granddaughter?"

"I must, for she may unknowingly hold the key to this mystery."

"Should I in any way prepare her for your visit?"

"Say nothing until prompted to do so."

"Very well, then," he said and glanced down at his timepiece. "I must hurry off for a most important meeting unless you require something further from me."

"Only that you leave the photograph with us."

"And what of the second blackmail demand?"

"Ignore it."

Once Sir William departed, Joanna again closely studied every centimeter of the photograph, first by gross examination, then with her magnifying glass under the brightest of lights. There was something about the bottom of the picture which seemed to merit her intense interest.

"What so captures your eyes, Joanna?" my father asked.

"The calling cards left by the blackmailer," she replied and gave the photograph a final inspection before turning to us. "The clues tell us who he is and where they were."

My father and I exchanged the most puzzled of glances. I quickly reached for the picture and held it up so both my father and I could study it at length. All we could discern was a young couple posing in a romantic manner. She was intoxicated, and he perhaps so.

"Well?" Joanna asked, smiling mischievously at our bemusement.

"We see nothing which points to your conclusion," I replied.

"That is because you see, but do not observe," she said. "Allow me to draw your attention to the young man's puffed sleeves and somewhat ruffled collar. That speaks of the Shakespeare era, does it not?"

"So it would appear that the young man was an actor in a Shakespearean play," I deduced.

"And he may still be performing at that very play," she added. "We shall need the exact date Anne Atwood disappeared from the family estate, and then search for Shakespearean plays being performed in London on that very day."

"Could we simply not ask Anne for the name of the play and theater she attended that fateful night?" I asked.

"I think it best we not reveal ourselves to her at this juncture," she responded. "Anne is obviously involved to some degree with this actor and might be tempted to tell him of our entrance into the case, which would alert the fox that the hounds have picked up his scent. Thus, it serves our cause to take the longer route to discover the locale of the theater."

"There may well be more than a few, if one considers professional as well as amateur playhouses," my father said.

"There are ways to narrow that number and determine if our young man was amongst the actors in a given play," said Joanna. "But of immediate and more importance is the white pipe in the photograph. You will notice that he is *not* holding the bowl between his thumb and index finger, as most smokers do, but rather has the stem clinched in his fist. And on closer inspection, you will observe that the stem is exceptionally long and extends beyond his grip for the length of at least two more clenched fists. Now, think back and tell me where we have seen pipes with such long stems before."

"Opium dens," my father answered at once. "There the clients recline and position their lengthy, opium-filled pipes directly over lamps that heat the drug until it evaporates, thus allowing the smoker to inhale the vapor."

"That also explains the straw mat the couple was seated upon and the dazed expression on Anne Atwood's face," Joanna denoted. "So, we have our very young debutante with a handsome Shakespearean actor in an opium den on the night of her disappearance."

"It would appear that the young actor is an active participant in the blackmailing scheme."

"Undoubtedly, for he led her every step of the way," she concurred. "And now there are two avenues by which we can identify this scoundrel—the play he was in and the opium den he visited with her."

"But the second of these avenues might well prove to be the most difficult, for there are dozens and dozens of opium dens in London, many of which are hidden in the darkest corners."

"Tsk, tsk, my dear Watson! Would you expect this villain, who arranges magical carriage rides, to escort his princess into a dangerous, lower-class den?"

"Hardly."

"He would only venture with her into the very best of the lot, where untoward experiences never occur," she said. "Now, I would like you to think back to our past visits and tell me who would be the owner of such an establishment."

"Ah Sing," I answered promptly.

"Mr. Ah Sing indeed, who also happens to possess a very keen set of eyes," my wife recalled and reached for the phone.

2

THE SCENE

O nly an hour had elapsed before we found ourselves in a taxi traveling
to a meeting with Ah Sing, the owner of a prosperous string of opium
dens in East London. As we rode through the darkened neighborhoods,
it was obvious that the German bombings had done even more extensive
damage than we had anticipated. Block after block of brick houses and
stores had been reduced to smoldering rubble. Only a scattered, few individuals could be seen on the footpaths, making me wonder how many
more lay trapped in the devastated ruins. Our driver apologized repeatedly
for the length of our journey, for alternate routes had to be taken to cir-
cumvent the streets which had been badly cratered by the bombing raid.
It was only as we approached the dark district of Limestone that Joanna
spoke of the pipe in the photograph.

"Do you recall the white pipe which was in the grasp of the Shakespearean actor?"

"Are you referring to features other than its length?" I asked.

"I am," she replied. "In particular, its peculiar design."

"It seemed ordinary except for its elongated stem."

"Think back to the pipes we saw in the opium dens and describe them
for me," Joanna prompted.

My mind returned to our last visit to Ah Sing's and our walk through the haze-filled den. The reclining smokers were holding tubular pipes which appeared unadorned and made of brown wood. Then it came to me. "They did not have bowls at their ends."

"Spot on, John. They were simple, wooden tubes, with an opening for a small container into which opium could be packed and heated," Joanna depicted. "But in the photograph we have a nicely carved, white pipe, with a rounded bowl at its end, which tells us that it is quite expensive and not one provided by the opium den."

"So the culprit brought along his own pipe," my father reasoned. "Which proves beyond a doubt that he was an active participant and not some innocent bystander."

"Oh, it proves a great more than that, Watson."

We came to a stop at a storefront that had Chinese characters written on its window. Lurking in a nearby alleyway, I could see shadowy figures in the dimness, all of whom I knew worked for Ah Sing and assured the safety of his customers.

The taxi driver glanced around at the ominous surroundings and asked, "Are you certain of the address, ma'am?"

"I am, and you are to remain parked across the street awaiting our return," my wife instructed. "You will not be harmed, for the man we are visiting controls this area with an iron fist and will see to it you are free from danger."

"Very well, ma'am," the driver said hesitantly, obviously not convinced.

Joanna reached into her purse for a five-pound note which she tore into halves. Handing one half to the driver, she told him, "You will receive the other half on our return."

The driver took the half, but I had my doubts he would stay once we disappeared from sight.

Joanna led the way to a thick, wooden door and rapped twice upon it. Almost immediately the door opened and a young, sharp-featured Chinese woman looked out and briefly studied us before saying, "I, of course, recognize you from your previous visit. My honorable father awaits the presence of the famous daughter. He is pleased to see you once again."

"I look forward to seeing him as well."

"This way, then, please."

The woman escorted us through a smoke-hazed den, where beds and mats took up most of the space. Upon them rested Englishmen and Asians, all puffing on lengthy pipes held over lamps that heated the opium into vapor. Many of the customers appeared emaciated, with sallow skin, which indicated they were chronic users addicted to the drug.

A stout Chinese man attired in expensive Oriental garb of blue silk hurried over to greet us. Now well into his middle years, Ah Sing seemed to have aged considerably since our last visit. His face appeared heavily lined and the braid that extended halfway down his back had turned entirely gray.

He bowed respectfully to the three of us, but his eyes stayed on Joanna. "It is an honor to be visited by the Watsons again."

"Thank you for making the time to see us on such short notice," she replied.

"It presented no problem whatsoever," Ah Sing said in perfect English, which one might expect from his colorful past. As he guided us to a quiet corner, I recalled Joanna's account of his remarkable history. Whilst still a youngster, the Shanghai native arrived on our shores as a stowaway on a tramp steamer and immediately entered the world of crime. At first he worked for a Chinese syndicate as a runner or messenger before rising up to the rank of extortionist. After numerous arrests, he served a brief sentence at the Hammersmith Prison where he mastered the English language from a cellmate who was a former aristocrat. Upon his release, Ah Sing settled into the opium trade, initially being part owner of small opium dens. But his partners all seemed to mysteriously disappear, and he became the sole owner of a large string of opium dens that was said to reach every corner of London.

Our initial encounter with Ah Sing occurred four years ago whilst we were tracking the trail of a high-ranking British cryptographer who had gone missing. The den owner was at first reluctant to supply us with important information, but agreed to do so when Joanna informed him we would return shortly with Inspector Lestrade at our side. I was to mention Ah Sing's assistance in *The Disappearance of Alistair Ainsworth* which pleased him greatly, for he believed it put him in good stead with Scotland Yard.

In the brighter light Ah Sing gazed at my wife's face and commented, "How is it that you do not age, whilst I find myself slipping down that inevitable slope?"

"With all due respect, I do not believe your vision is as keen as it once was," Joanna replied.

"Oh, it remains quite good, unlike other parts of my anatomy," he insisted. "Pray tell, do you use a special lotion that defies aging?"

"I do not, but should I encounter such a remedy, I shall be glad to notify you of its existence."

"I shall look forward to that happy day," said Ah Sing. "Now, let us speak of the purpose of your visit."

Joanna produced the photograph of the smiling couple sitting on a straw mat. "Do you recognize either or both?"

Ah Sing reached for a pair of reading spectacles and carefully studied the individuals. "I have never seen them, and were they regular customers I would have surely been aware of their presence." He examined the photograph once again, squinting at the images. "When was the pair supposedly here?"

"A little over three weeks ago," my wife replied.

He gave the matter considerable thought before nodding, ever so slightly. "It is possible they were present at that time, for I was inconvenienced by a harsh bout of bronchitis which kept me housebound. My daughter, Mei Ling, who is my second in command, assumed all duties during my absence." He motioned to the young, sharp-featured Chinese woman who hurried over.

"Yes, Father?" she said, her voice submissive.

Ah Sing passed the photograph to his daughter and inquired, "Have you any recollection of this couple?"

Mei Ling studied the photograph briefly. "They were here for a short visit several weeks ago, both being inexperienced users."

"One pipeful, then?"

"At the most."

Joanna inquired, "Were you at the door when they arrived?"

"I was, Mrs. Watson," Mei Ling replied. "They came in a carriage, which was most unusual."

"How so?"

Mei Ling smiled faintly at the obvious answer. "Because the visit was at night, during which time the bombing raids might have occurred and spooked the horses. Should that happen, all in the carriage would be at great peril."

"You mentioned *all* in the carriage," Joanna queried at once. "How many were there?"

"Four. The couple, the driver, and another man seated next to the driver."

"Did the latter man keep his face hidden?"

"He was smoking a large pipe he held close to his lips."

"Which would have served that purpose."

"Most assuredly."

"Very good," Joanna praised the observation. "Let us return to the couple. Were they intoxicated on arrival?"

"She more than he, for the woman had to lean heavily on her companion, so as not to stagger."

"Was it opium-induced?"

"More likely alcohol."

"Why so?"

"Because she giggled, which is something opium users rarely do."

I watched Joanna nod appreciatively at the young woman's astuteness, for the daughter was proving to be the most valuable of witnesses. With her keen eye and mind, I was certain Ah Sing had no reservations leaving her in charge during his absence. But beneath that lovely face, I wondered if she was as dangerous as her father.

"Where in the den did they situate themselves?" my wife asked at length.

"They demanded the private room," Mei Ling replied.

"Demanded, you say?"

"Yes, madam, for they waited impatiently for more than a half hour for the room to be vacated and swept."

"How long did they occupy the private room?"

"Thirty minutes at most, which in itself was strange, as they had paid a fee for the full hour."

"Are you certain of the exact time?"

"Quite certain, madam."

Joanna smiled humorlessly at the answer. "I take it there is a secret aperture through which the occupants of the room can be viewed."

Mei Ling hesitated, with her eyes quickly going to her father, as if asking permission to respond.

Ah Sing stepped forward, obviously pleased with his daughter's reluctance to answer. "You may return to your duties, Mei Ling."

He waited for his daughter to depart before speaking in a low voice which could not be overheard. "Such an opening is required so that we will be aware of any disreputable activities."

"And if there are?"

"The occupants are summarily dismissed."

"Thus, we can conclude that the couple was periodically viewed by your daughter."

"That is an accurate statement."

"There is one further question I have of Mei Ling."

Ah Sing gestured to his daughter who quickly returned. "Mrs. Watson has one last question which you should feel free to answer."

"Of course, Father."

"Whilst you were viewing the couple, please describe their activities," Joanna requested. "And I need the particulars."

"They were seated arm-in-arm, both fully clothed, and puffing on a single, ivory pipe," she recalled. "There was no kissing or embracing."

"Were there any signs that they were lovers?"

"None that I could see."

"Simply friends, then?"

"Perhaps," Mei Ling said noncommittally.

With a nod that only another female could interpret, Joanna came back to Ah Sing. "Are cameras ever allowed in your den?"

"Never," he said sharply. "And if one is discovered, it is destroyed in the presence of its owner who is forcefully evicted."

"Which is a stern warning to others who may be tempted."

"It serves that purpose as well."

"May we see the aperture in the private room?"

"Of course," Ah Sing replied and guided us to the very rear of the opium den, then over to the side where a thin wall awaited us. He opened a small, well-hidden panel and stepped away. Joanna was the first to gaze in, followed by me and my father. The private room was small, no more than ten feet in length and five feet across, with good lighting and a straw mat that was stained from years of use. There were no windows and only a single door.

"Was it busy that night the couple appeared?" Joanna asked.

"Very much so, with eager customers standing on the footpath," Mei Ling replied. "There was even another, older man waiting to use the private room."

"Can you describe him?"

The daughter shrugged indifferently. "He was middle aged and working class, and a first-time customer to our establishment."

"Did he wait by the door for the room to be vacated?"

"As I recall, he stood nearby."

"Very good," said Joanna and turned back to Ah Sing. "Your daughter mentioned a white, ivory pipe which the couple used. Certainly, your den does not provide them."

"No opium den would, for they are far too expensive and would be stolen in the blink of an eye."

"How expensive?"

"Twenty-five pounds or more, for they have to be hand-carved from an elephant's tusk."

"Only for the well-to-do, then?"

"Only the very well-to-do."

"Where might one purchase such a pipe?"

"It would be available at Fielding and Marsh, a very fine tobacconist's shop in an arcade near Marble Arch."

"Only there?"

"There alone, for they have connections in China where the ivory pipes are made."

Joanna paused a moment to docket the information, then tapped a finger against her chin, as if considering another question, but decided against it. "Thank you for your time. I know it is quite valuable. But before we go along our way, I have one final request."

"Which is?"

"Since this case involves an individual at the highest level, it would be best if our meeting this evening is never mentioned."

"It will be as if it never occurred," Ah Sing said, and gave his daughter a signal which promised their lips would be sealed.

We departed the opium den and walked out into an unseasonably cold night, with a light snow beginning to fall. We turned up the collars of our topcoats as we strolled toward our waiting taxi that was parked across the street, well past the alley where the shadowy figures presided.

"It all comes together nicely, doesn't it?" Joanna said, whilst we stopped for a passing motor vehicle. "Everything was planned by a mastermind who personally saw to the smallest detail, beginning with the horse-drawn carriage."

"But why a horse-drawn carriage?" my father queried. "Mei Ling herself brought up the distinct possibility that a German bombing raid would have spooked the animal, which would have resulted in a disastrous ending for the occupants of the carriage."

"Tut, tut, Watson. I will wager you a guinea that on the night of this adventure a heavy fog shrouded London, and thus made it most unlikely that the German bombers would make an appearance."

"But why not use a taxi or personal motor vehicle for comfort and safety?"

"Because all motor vehicles have licenses which are obvious to the eye and can be easily traced," Joanna replied. "Furthermore, a taxi driver can be a witness. And then there is the romantic, fairy-tale aspect to this escapade. Here we have a highly spirited young woman who sneaks away from her confines to see a play and meet with the actors afterward. She had done this in the past, obviously, for she knew her way around the theater and backstage, where she made merry with the actors, one of whom may have added a drug to her drink. In her intoxicated state, she was easily persuaded to go on a carriage ride through London, with a handsome companion by her side."

"But not to an opium den," I interjected with certainty.

"Never, for she may well have been adventurous, but not stupid."

"I see a flaw here," my father pointed out. "The carriage had a driver who could serve as a witness."

My wife quickly shook her head at the notion. "The mastermind behind the blackmail is a man of wealth, as evidenced by the remarkably expensive ivory pipe, which even the upper middle class could not afford. He, in all likelihood, owns the carriage, and its driver is a manservant of long duration who he trusts implicitly. And I suspect it was the manservant who

27

surveyed the den and provided the mastermind with the necessary details, including the private room and its secret aperture." She paused to smile at our bemused expressions. "I can see by your faces that you are wondering how the manservant became aware of the secret opening."

We both nodded simultaneously.

"It was a simple task," she said. "All that was required was for him to watch Mei Ling periodically employ it."

"Thus, it was the manservant who took the photograph, then."

"I think not, Watson."

"Then who?"

"The fourth person in the carriage who is the mastermind," Joanna replied, as we slowed our pace. "He directed every phase of the blackmail, including entering the den in disguise and waiting in the haze-filled room for the opportune moment to snap the most compromising photograph of the couple. It was the coup de gras of the evening which he would only entrust to himself."

"And this mastermind remains closed in secrecy."

"But not so his accomplice, the actor, who will be the key to this lock," said Joanna.

As we approached the taxi, she quickly brought a finger to her lips, for past experiences had taught us that taxi drivers had sharp ears and loose tongues.

3

THE AGENT

Our carefully crafted disguises added ten years and fifteen pounds to our images. After donning grayed wigs and making certain they fit securely, we had placed mounds of padding beneath top and lower under-garments, all for the sole purpose of presenting ourselves as an upper-class, well-to-do couple at the office of Aaron Edelstone, a theatrical agent of some note, who represented a goodly number of Shakespearean actors. Whilst seated and awaiting our appointment, we gazed around the reception area whose walls were adorned with large, framed posters of plays with which the agent had been associated. The receptionist was a stern-looking woman, with lackluster auburn hair and suspicious eyes that seemed to be intermittently measuring us, like a Roman centurion guarding her post.

Joanna and I ignored her glances and used the quiet moment to silently rehearse our upcoming presentation to the theatrical agent. It was of the utmost importance that he have no notion we were seeking the name and identity of a singular actor who may have recently played the role of a young male in a Shakespearean drama. Were such a peculiar search mentioned to the actor in question, he might relay the information to the mastermind behind the blackmail, which would surely work to our disadvantage.

"Mr. Edelstone will see you now," the receptionist called out and opened the door to the inner sanctum.

We were warmly greeted by a smiling, stout man of middle years, with a round face and rosy cheeks. He stood briefly behind a large Victorian desk and gestured to two comfortable chairs which were before him. Clenched between his jaws was a lighted cigar that gave us a pleasant, spicy aroma Joanna immediately recognized. She was to later tell me that the cigar was a costly Havana, telling of the agent's considerable success in the theatrical world. Like the reception room, the walls of his office were covered with large, framed pictures of actors and actresses whom Aaron Edelstone represented.

"Thank you for being so prompt," he said, without introduction, for he had spoken with Joanna by phone earlier. "It is a manner which is disappearing from society."

"Sadly so," Joanna agreed.

"Indeed," Edelstone said and rubbed his hands together, as if preparing for a pleasant encounter. "Now, Mrs. Harrison, I must say that your request is most unusual. Would you be kind enough to once again give me the particulars?"

"Of course," my wife replied. "Our twin daughters adore the works of William Shakespeare and are about to celebrate their fifteenth birthday, for which we are planning a gala event. As a surprise, we thought it would be an enchanting delight to have in attendance an accomplished actor, who could recite lines from their favorite play, *Romeo and Juliet*. It must be a young actor, say in his twenties, for this would be most appropriate for a Romeo."

"That should present no problem," the agent said. "But I should ask whether the quality of the actor is a consideration."

"Most assuredly, for he must be convincing in the eyes of our daughters."

"For top quality, the cost could be substantial."

Joanna flicked her wrist dismissively. "That is to be expected."

"And he must have the looks of a Romeo," I added. "Only a handsome face will do."

Edelstone nodded his response, then puffed gently on his Havana as he gave the scene further thought. "The presentation should last for no more than ten minutes or so, for beyond that time boredom may set in for the young ladies."

"And he must be appropriately attired."

"Without proper attire, sir, there can be no worthwhile performance," the agent noted. "And of course someone off-stage must recite Juliet's most famous line, 'O Romeo, Romeo, wherefore art thou, Romeo?'"

"Which is an absolute necessity," Joanna concurred.

"I would anticipate a cost of twenty pounds."

"Done."

"Very well, then," Edelstone said, reaching for a thick stack of photographs, which included headshots. "These are the candidates who would best serve your purposes."

Joanna and I carefully studied each photograph, as if all details mattered and all the faces new. We went through the stock ever so slowly before purposefully placing one of the headshots aside, although it bore little resemblance to the actor we were seeking. Then we chose another, but his facial features seemed too hard to be a persuasive Romeo. Near the end of the stack we came to our man. There he was beyond a doubt and wearing a white shirt with puffed sleeves. We added him to the wanted stack and passed the three photographs over to the agent.

"These are the ones who seem the most suitable," Joanna declared.

Edelstone gave the three only casual glances and, with a firm nod, said, "Quite good choices. Do you favor one over the others?"

"All appear quite fitting, but we must insist on auditions before a final choice is made."

"Which can be done here, if you wish."

"In this rather confined space?" Joanna objected.

"No, no, madam," the agent responded quickly. "You should hear and see auditions at a distance which would be similar to that between the actor and the guests at your party. To meet this requirement, the audition will be held in a large conference room just down the corridor. Such an arrangement will allow you to judge the range and quality of the actor's voice."

"And what of the lighting?" Joanna asked. "I neglected to mention that the actor will be performing in a shady gazebo, whilst the audience will be seated on the lawn of our garden."

"We shall lower the light in the conference room, so that it matches that of your gazebo," Edelstone proposed.

"That should do nicely," my wife agreed with the setting. "When can such auditions be arranged?"

"The day after tomorrow," he replied. "Mid-morning would be best, say half past ten, for the actors will not be occupied at that time. I shall schedule the actors to appear individually, with their performances clearly separated from one another."

"Then all is settled."

"Quite so."

We bid Edelstone a pleasant good day and strolled out into a dreary, gray afternoon. Although traffic was heavy on Edgware Road, not a taxi was to be seen, and thus we decided to walk the relatively short distance to the tobacconist. Ordinarily, we did not speak of cases in public, but the noise of the traffic was such that it would drown out our conversation to even the curious passerby. Still, we kept our voices low.

"That went well enough," I said.

"Agents can be very accommodating when it serves their purpose," Joanna replied.

"I fail to see how a fee of twenty pounds would attract a high-profile agent who smokes expensive cigars. And of that fee, he collects only a small percentage."

"It is not the fee which draws his attention, but the possibility of expanding his clientele," she explained. "Most actors are a poor lot who are always seeking openings. Word would spread that Aaron Edelstone looks after young actors and at times provides them with a source of income."

"And if there is a real talent among the lot, they hear of and seek out such a caring agent," I added.

Joanna nodded at my conclusion. "It is the way the game is played."

"Would it not be ironic if the actor we are pursuing turns out to have some heretofore hidden talent?"

"Then he will soon have the opportunity to perfect his skill whilst serving time at one of His Majesty's most uncomfortable prisons."

"You make him sound as if he is inexperienced."

"Most young actors are, but there is a chance he knows his way around the stage, which is why I insisted the auditions be held in a large, shady room, where we could not be seen close up."

"How would that work to our benefit?"

"Keep in mind that even an inexperienced actor would be aware of disguises, for that is an integral part of their trade. Can you imagine his response, as well as that of Aaron Edelstone, when they learn they are dealing with a disguised couple?"

"They would demand we reveal ourselves, which we would not do."

"But all would still be lost, particularly if word of the disguised intruders reached the ear of the mastermind."

We came to Oxford Street and, passing Selfridge's department store, approached the signage of Fielding and Marsh. Joanna slowed our pace and spoke in an even lower voice. "We must be very careful with this white pipe business, for it is a clue of immense value."

"I find it bothersome that our clever mastermind would leave such an obvious clue in clear view."

"As do I, but there is only one explanation as to why he would do so," she said, as I reached for the door to the tobacconist. "It was used to woo our dear Anne Atwood into the opium den."

"How would it do so?"

"It would serve as part of the enchantment, dear heart."

We entered the store, with its rich mahogany paneling, and gazed around, as if unaccustomed to being in such a shop. The delightful aroma of fresh tobacco filled our nostrils, whilst we appeared to take in the surroundings. Before us was a section devoted to cigarettes and freshly cut leaf, and beyond that a large, glass-covered showcase containing the finest of cigars. Joanna paid momentary attention to the carefully rolled Cubans, then gravitated to the pipe display, where she was approached by a neatly attired clerk of thin frame, with short gray hair and a pleasant smile.

"May I be of service, madam?" he inquired.

"We are here to purchase a pipe, as a present for my father-in-law."

"Do you have a particular make in mind?"

"He seems to favor cherrywood, but lately I have heard him speak of briar," she replied innocently. "Is there a difference?"

"Not initially, madam, but with time a difference will be noted," the clerk elucidated. "As the pipe is smoked, the briar will soak up the moisture from the tobacco and thus absorb its flavor somewhat better than the cherrywood. However, if your father-in-law has a preference for cherrywood, then that should be your selection."

Joanna nodded as if the information was new and an important consideration. "I take it there are cherrywoods of various quality."

"Indeed so, madam, but I would recommend the black cherrywood because of its more pleasant-tasting flavor and beautiful grain."

"May I see one?"

"Of course," he said and went to a wide display of pipes that was suspended on a nearby wall.

"Oh, look, John!" my wife exclaimed, pointing to the handsome display. "This white pipe is remarkably similar to the one we saw at the party not long ago."

"It could pass for its twin," I affirmed, not certain where my wife was taking her observation.

34

"But that white pipe had a far, far longer stem," Joanna recalled, and demonstrated its length by holding her hands a good foot apart.

"What you witnessed was an ivory pipe used by the Chinese to smoke opium," the clerk informed us.

Joanna spun her head around in surprise. "Opium, say?"

"Opium," he repeated.

"Allow me to assure you that was not the purpose of this particular pipe, for the owner is a fine gentleman," she said firmly. "It was on display with many others, and appeared to have never been used."

"Ah!" said the clerk, now understanding. "It would seem that the gentleman you are referring to is a collector of unusual and perhaps antique pipes."

"I believe he is indeed, for he was obviously well educated on the subject," Joanna continued with her fabrication. "As a matter of fact, he is in all likelihood a member of your clientele, for it was he who recommended your fine shop to us."

"Ah!" the clerk uttered yet again. "You must be referring to Mr. Eric Halderman. He purchased that very rare ivory pipe from us some months back."

"I am, and let me assure you that Mr. Halderman's display would make your fine shop proud."

"And of course his magnificent home was the perfect setting for such a remarkable display," I appended, taking my wife's cue.

"As one would expect of a home situated in Hampstead Heath," the clerk remarked.

"Well, enough of this idle chatter," said Joanna impatiently. "May I see the black cherrywood pipe you mentioned?"

"Of course, madam," the clerk replied and held up the polished pipe for inspection.

"Most handsome," Joanna approved. "But here I will require your assistance. Pray tell, how can I question my father-in-law about such a pipe without arousing his suspicion that a gift is on the way?"

The clerk considered the matter at length before giving us a concealed approach. Glancing in my direction, he inquired, "Is the man we are speaking of your father, sir?"

"He is," I replied.

"Then, in a casual fashion mention that you were in attendance at a meeting of some sort, and the individual seated next to you was smoking a black cherrywood that gave off a most pleasant aroma. Inquire of your father if he was aware of that particular pipe. I am certain he will have a most favorable response."

"Excellent!" I approved. "Once we know he favors it, we will return and make our purchase."

"Please call if you have any questions at all."

"We shall."

I took Joanna's arm as we departed and walked out into an even darker afternoon that promised an evening thunderstorm. We were able to hail a rare hansom and climbed into the back compartment just prior to a clap of thunder, which fortunately, did not frighten the horse.

"That went better than expected, did it not?" asked I. "We obtained both the name and address of the owner of the white pipe."

"His address may well have added significance," she said.

"How so?"

"Because the estate where Anne Atwood resides is also situated in Hampstead Heath."

"Do you believe they are close together?"

"I would wager a guinea that is the case."

4

ANNE ATWOOD

The target of the blackmail was petrified with fright. Any semblance of her social standing or adventuresome spirit had long vanished. She bit down on her lower lip to hold her composure as we strolled through the expansive garden of her family's estate.

"I have made a mess of things, haven't I?" said Anne Atwood in a soft voice.

"That you have, and it will take some doing to straighten out this most unpleasant matter," Joanna replied. "But for this to be accomplished, you must disclose every detail of your adventure, not leaving out a single happening despite the embarrassment it might bring."

"I have already done so to the best of my ability," she asserted.

"No, you have not," my wife challenged. "And without your complete honesty, the blackmailing will never end and your family may well be driven into bankruptcy."

"Why are you so convinced I have been less than honest?"

"Because it is my business to know what others wish to conceal," Joanna said in a neutral tone. "With that in mind, let us begin with your first mistruth." She waited for an elderly gardener pushing a small wheelbarrow to pass by before stating, "You visited that very same theater more than once, did you not?"

"On several occasions," Anne admitted.

"Exactly how many is several?"

The granddaughter of the chancellor counted mentally, but her lips moved. "I was there three times."

"Did you go backstage on every visit?"

"Only on the last two, for I was accompanied on my initial attendance."

"By whom?"

"A chaperone."

"On your subsequent returns, did you encounter the young man in the photograph on each occasion?"

"I did."

"Here we require particulars, and you are to give me every detail without exception," Joanna insisted. "What might seem of little matter to you may be of great consequence to us. Do you clearly understand?"

"Yes, madam."

"Did you and the young man exchange names?"

"We did."

"We need to know his name."

"Hugh."

"And his surname?"

"He did not give it, nor was his name listed in the program, for his role was quite minor."

"On your first meeting, did he approach you?"

Anne considered the question before speaking. "Our eyes caught from across the backstage."

"But your initial visit was not to see him, but rather one of the prominent actors," my wife went on. "I suspect you sent a note to that particular fellow, in which you praised his fine performance."

"That is so."

"And thus, your meeting with Hugh was happenstance."

"So I believed."

"There was mutual attraction, I take it."

Anne blushed noticeably whilst she nodded. "I found him to be strikingly handsome."

"So much so that you arranged to sneak away from your confines in Hampstead Heath to visit him yet again."

"It was inordinately foolish of me," she admonished herself. "But he was so charming and dashing."

"The best of scoundrels usually are," Joanna said. "Yet I find it surprising that you threw all caution to the wind and agreed to a carriage ride with a man you hardly knew, and at night, no less."

"I am afraid my reckless behavior was caused by champagne which flowed so freely backstage," Anne recounted. "My dear grandfather is of the opinion that my drink was drugged."

Joanna gave the former debutante a long, stern look. "I do not share your grandfather's opinion, for I believe you were fully aware of what transpired that evening."

"But I can assure you—"

"Stop the nonsense!" my wife interrupted sharply. "Your mistruths are little more than convenient excuses to spare your father embarrassment. But please keep in mind they greatly hinder my investigation which is the only hope to save your fine family name."

Tears suddenly came to the young woman's eyes, telling us the truth was about to be revealed. She dabbed at her cheeks with a lace handkerchief, then sniffed back the remaining tears. "I did have a glass or two of champagne backstage and was perhaps a bit tipsy, yet still in control of my actions. Near the end of the celebration, Hugh mentioned he had a surprise in store for me, and led the way through a side door to a waiting horse-drawn carriage."

"You must have looked up at the driver," Joanna prompted.

"I did, but the light was dim and he was bundled up against the cold," Anne recalled. "I can only state that he seemed to be a quite large man, for he occupied most of the driver's seat."

"Do you recall if there was another individual situated next to the driver?"

Anne thought back before nodding slowly. "There was a much smaller, shadowy figure beside him, whom I took to be an assistant of some sort."

"Very well," my wife encouraged. "Pray tell, go on with your adventure."

"I had reservations about entering the carriage, but Hugh assured me the ride would be short and great fun," she continued, with an expression which now showed a flash of anger. "It was so foolish of me, but off we went, with a bottle of champagne in hand. Our ride took us around Hyde Park, then through Knightsbridge and on to Buckingham Palace where we stopped and raised our glasses to toast the king. All seemed innocent enough at that point. It was as if I was in some sort of fairy tale. Here I was, sipping champagne with a handsome escort in a horse-drawn carriage outside the gates of Buckingham Palace.

"Then the champagne began to run low, but Hugh knew of a place where we could obtain more and off we went." Anne stopped her narrative for a moment as tears again welled in her eyes. "I should have known better when the carriage left the westside and entered the dregs of East London."

"Was the prospect of opium mentioned?"

"Not until we reached the storefront in Limehouse," she replied. "When I saw the Chinese coming and going I immediately knew of its purpose and wanted no part of it. But all the drink I had consumed weakened my resolve, so I agreed to a brief visit, particularly when Hugh explained the function of the beautiful ivory pipe."

"What function was that, may I ask?"

"He stated that it purified the opium and diluted its effect, thus preventing the user from becoming addicted."

"So you participated."

"I did, ashamedly so," Anne confessed. "It was in the den that my consciousness faded, but I do recall a straw mat which had to be positioned in a particular way."

Joanna's brow went up. "Can you be more precise on the positioning?"

"Hugh insisted the mat be placed facing a front wall where the ventilation would be better."

"Was it?"

"I am not certain, for it is here that my memory faded completely."

My wife and I exchanged knowing glances; it was obvious that the placement of the mat allowed for a most illustrative photograph of the couple to be taken.

"I am being entirely truthful," Anne asserted, no doubt misinterpreting our momentary pause as one of disbelief. "I have no recollection beyond that dreadful encounter."

"I believe your statements are indeed accurate, but I do have one final question which is most personal, and one you must answer."

"Ask your question," Anne said, without hesitation.

"I need to know how close you were to this handsome fellow," Joanna queried. "Were there embraces?"

"None, other than the arm around my waist in the photograph," she replied at once. "And I can assure you that was not encouraged."

"Were there kisses?" Joanna asked directly.

"Only on our first introduction when he bowed and kissed the back of my hand," she answered, without having to give the matter thought. "If you are referring to facial kisses, I can promise you there were none."

"Very good," my wife said. "Your honest responses could prove to be helpful in bringing this case to a successful resolution."

"Please do so, madam, for the very last thing I wish to do is embarrass the fine name my family carries," she implored.

"We shall do our very best."

"And thank you for being so patient with a rather foolish young woman."

"You held up well under the most trying of circumstances," Joanna praised.

"I shall be at your disposal should other questions arise," Anne offered.

"Very good," my wife said again, then held up a finger, as if recalling another matter. "One final question comes to mind, then we shall take our leave. Are you familiar with the Haldermans who reside in this lovely neighborhood?"

"His place is just next to ours, but I know little of him, for he keeps mainly to himself," she replied. "He is believed to be of considerable wealth."

"Are you aware of how he built his fortune?"

"That is unknown."

"Great wealth at times brings about necessary seclusion."

"So it would appear."

"Well then, we shall not take up more of your time, but I must insist that you do not mention a word of our conversation to anyone, including your family members."

Anne's expression brightened noticeably, even bringing forth a faint smile. "So my family will not learn of my further exploits on that most regrettable evening?"

"Our lips are sealed on the matter."

We bid Anne Atwood farewell and strolled out of the lovely garden whose flowers were just beginning to bloom. The nearby gardeners followed us with their eyes, as did the faces at the windows of the multistory limestone mansion. Apparently, word that the daughter of Sherlock Holmes was visiting had spread through the estate, which was a bad sign, for servants tended to gossip, and thus our involvement could reach the ears of neighbors in Hampstead Heath.

Once we were well clear of the manor, I asked, "How did you know that Anne Atwood had passed a note to the actors?"

"Because gaining entrance to the backstage of a reputable theater is most difficult," Joanna replied. "You cannot simply walk in, but must be invited or request an invitation, the latter of which Anne did."

"But surely the request was not made to the handsome, young actor."

"Of course not, for she did not know his name which was not listed in the program."

"Thus, the note must have been directed to one of the lead actors," I deduced. "He no doubt allowed for her entrance."

"But only after a background search," Joanna said knowingly. "It did not require much effort to determine that Anne Atwood was the granddaughter of the Chancellor of the Exchequer."

"So she was welcomed in."

"With open arms, and of course the cast was told of the impending visit of the high-profile guest."

"And that is where the plot was hatched."

"Perhaps, but not by the handsome, young actor who was no doubt the go-between." My wife paused to light a Turkish cigarette and exhaled smoke in the direction of our waiting taxi. "A struggling actor would not have access to an impressive horse-drawn carriage nor to an expensive ivory pipe. Nevertheless, we must keep in mind that there is no evidence he was and remains an active participant in the blackmail. He would claim he was an innocent bystander who agreed to escort a lovely woman on a journey through London. He was hired like an actor in a play, with all the props provided."

"Which included a most unusual white pipe which the silly girl believed would purify the smoked opium and thus prevent addiction."

"I am afraid she goes beyond being silly, for here is a young woman who is both naïve and adventuresome, which is a combination that can lead to the most unmentionable of follies."

"Are you suggesting the interplay between Anne Atwood and the handsome actor went beyond an introductory kiss on the hand?"

"We had better hope that is not the case," Joanna said in a most serious tone, as she flicked her cigarette away. "For if it is so and there are photographs to prove it, the blackmailing will never end."

5
THE AUDITION

We arrived at the theatrical agent's office thirty minutes before the scheduled auditions to assure the appropriate settings were in place. The conference room itself was quite spacious, measuring at least twenty feet in length. Most of the space was taken up by a long, polished conference table which was surrounded with leather upholstered chairs and fronted by a waist-high podium. The curtains were drawn in such a fashion that the light which entered was directed mainly at the podium. We were seated in comfortable chairs at the rear, where it was shades darker than the remainder of the room.

Aaron Edelstone stood by the door and rubbed his hands together, in what apparently was a habit of his that indicated a theatrical performance was about to unfold.

"I take it all is satisfactory," he said.

"Indeed so," Joanna replied. "But I do have a few questions which are of some importance. I trust you can answer them."

"I shall do my best, madam."

"First, have these actors performed in front of small audiences previously?"

"Most certainly, madam. They all began acting either in school or at small, amateur playhouses where the audiences would not exceed a hundred.

44

Moreover, their prior auditions would have occurred in the presence of very few."

"Secondly, will they arrive at the gala in costume or will a dressing room be required?"

"They will come in costume, but the actor should be kept out of view from the children if it is to be a surprise. Perhaps you might provide a room to serve that purpose."

"That can be done, and when given the signal, our actor can make a grand appearance."

"Capital!" the agent approved enthusiastically.

"Will assistance be needed for makeup?"

"That will be done prior to his arrival."

"And he of course will arrange for his own transport."

"That presents no problem."

"Then let us begin the auditions."

"It shall go in the following manner," the agent instructed. "I will escort the actor to the podium which he will stand beside. His name and an account of his most recent performances will be given prior to the audition. You may ask questions if you wish."

"That will not be necessary."

"Then, on with the auditions."

He rapped gently on the door which was opened immediately by his secretary, whose expression remained stern, as if pasted on her face. In walked a tall man, in his mid-twenties and of medium frame, who had a most confident stride. He was clever enough to attend in a white shirt with puffed sleeves, as one might expect of a Romeo.

"Allow me to present Mr. Jason Bates," Edelstone introduced. "He is currently performing in Shakespeare's *Macbeth* at a highly regarded theater in Surrey. You should know he has played the role of Romeo in the past."

The agent stepped aside as Bates cleared his throat audibly and began his recitation. His voice was soft, but easily heard and perfect for a Romeo.

The role was well played, but was highlighted when Edelstone took on the words of Juliet, as he uttered in perfect pitch the famous question, "O Romeo, Romeo, wherefore art thou, Romeo?" The actor's response was so mesmerizing that we were tempted to applaud.

The next performer, whose name was Charles Hightower, was not nearly as impressive, for his voice did not seem to carry well in the conference room. Moreover, he was dressed in jacket and tie which did not set the appropriate mood. He bowed deeply at the end of his performance which I considered out of place.

The third actor, named Hugh Marlowe, drew our intense scrutiny, for he was the young man in the blackmailing photograph. He was taller than expected and so strikingly handsome that he could have passed for a matinee idol. His acting experience was limited to small theaters, other than his current, minor role in a play on St. Martin's Lane. But he carried himself well and was canny enough to wear a shirt with puffed sleeves and a ruffled collar, which set the desired tone. It was also identical to the one he wore in the photograph. He obviously had talent, for his response to Juliet's ". . . wherefore art thou, Romeo?" was superb.

When the door closed behind Hugh Marlowe, the agent hurried over to us. "Well then, who is your choice?"

"I think we can exclude the second performer," Joanna replied, with a dismissive flick of the wrist. "He seemed to be of lesser quality."

"Not of the best," Edelstone agreed. "I expected more from him."

"The other two actors were quite impressive, however, and we find it difficult to choose between them."

"They are the most experienced, particularly Jason Bates."

"Yet the third actor, Hugh . . . ah . . . Hugh," Joanna stuttered, as if she had forgotten his last name.

"Hugh Marlowe," the agent reminded.

"Yes, Mr. Hugh Marlowe, seemed to be on equal footing with Mr. Bates."

"I think either would serve your purpose rather well."

Joanna tapped a finger against her chin, as if she was contemplating a choice. "My husband and I shall give the matter our closest attention before reaching a decision."

"That would be most wise," Edelstone concurred.

"Please allow us some time to decide whom we favor."

"There is no rush, although I think it best you reach a choice by the weekend."

"It may require a bit longer, for the background of both actors must be looked into."

Edelstone gave my wife a most puzzled look. "May I inquire why such a search is necessary?"

"We must make certain neither has a criminal past."

"That would be most unlikely."

"Perhaps so, but I will not allow anyone with such a record into my home," Joanna said forcefully. "And if they appear clear of such misdeeds, they may have friends who are not."

"Our neighborhood has been plagued with recent robberies, and that is why we must be so cautious," I joined in the fabrication.

"One cannot be too careful," Edelstone conceded.

"In order for a thorough search to be carried out, I shall need the addresses of the two preferred actors."

"Give me a moment, then," the agent requested and hurried off, leaving the door open, where his secretary remained, as if standing guard. We chose not to speak in her presence and waited in silence for Edelstone's return. Nearby, we heard Big Ben beginning to loudly toll the onset of the noon hour. On the eleventh ring, the agent reentered and handed us a slip of paper which listed the addresses of the two actors.

Only after we were well clear of the agent's office on St. Martin's Lane did we read the addresses. Jason Bates lived in St. John's Wood, a thriving, middle-class district, northwest of Charing Cross. Hugh Marlowe, on the other hand, lived in Canary Wharf, a tough, lower-class neighborhood in Central London where crime abounded.

"Do you believe Hugh Marlowe is simply a hired hand?" I asked. "On the surface, it appears he was paid and sent on his way."

Joanna shook her head in response. "I suspect he remains more deeply involved."

"But to what degree?"

"That is what we must discover."

6

CIRCUMSTANTIAL EVIDENCE

B efore returning to Baker Street, we shopped at several costume stores for garments that were more suitable for our upcoming visit to Canary Wharf. Our current attire was far too rich for a working-class district and would be certain to draw unwanted attention. We also had to purchase wigs which showed less gray and were more unkempt, for well-styled hair-cuts were rarely seen in those who resided near the docks of London. On our ride home we remained silent, for all the details of the case, new and old alike, would soon be discussed with my ailing father. Although still mentally sharp, age was catching up with him, and he was being bothered more and more by an arthritic knee which was currently swollen and tender.

"Should we stop at the chemist and obtain an additional supply of salicy-late cream for my father's knee?" I suggested.

"I overheard Watson placing such an order by phone earlier today," Joanna said. "Another layer of cream, together with the application of heat, usually brings considerable relief."

"But that combination does not appear to alter the frequency of the attacks."

"Has he tried it as a preventative, such as applying it when his knee is asymptomatic?"

"Not to my knowledge."

"Perhaps he should."

Our taxi arrived at 221 Baker Street just as a sudden downpour began. We hurried in, then up the stairs and into the parlor where my father was seated in his comfortable chair, with his leg resting on a cushioned ottoman. He was attired in a tattered, maroon smoking jacket that was so badly worn it was threadbare at the elbows. He refused to replace it, even when offered a new one as a present, as it was the last vestige of his happier, exciting days with Sherlock Holmes.

"How is your knee, Father?" I asked.

"It is improving, but not as rapidly as I would like," he replied.

"Have you considered using the salicylate cream as a preventative?" I inquired. "Joanna believes it might be worth a trial."

My father, ever the astute physician, smiled at the suggestion. "Has she considered the possibility that its chronic, daily application might lessen its effectiveness when a painful flare occurs?"

"You must direct your question to my dear wife."

"What say you, Joanna?"

"I say I should keep my focus on crime," she said, returning his smile.

"At which you excel," my father noted, then pushed the morning newspaper from his lap and onto the stack beside his overstuffed chair. He religiously read all of London's daily newspapers in a most careful manner, searching for crimes which might merit our attention.

"Is there anything of interest in the dailies?" my wife asked.

"Only the dreadful news from the Western Front, with ever mounting losses on both sides," he replied. "There is not the slightest inkling of a blackmail in progress, if that is your question."

"Let us hope it remains so, for its exposure would bring appalling consequences for Sir William's family."

"And the blackmailer would be none too happy," I thought aloud. "For he would be deprived of a small fortune in revenue."

"He would lose little sleep over the exposure, for it could yet work to his benefit," said Joanna.

"How so?"

"I suspect our blackmailer has other similar cases maturing, which is evidenced by his considerable wealth that comes from obscure sources," she replied. "If it became known to those being ransomed that this would be their fate should they choose to resist the blackmail, I can assure you those so affected would pay up at the earliest moment."

"And the ransom demand would no doubt increase considerably."

"That, too, for professional blackmailers are a merciless lot, who will only cease when the victims are drained dry or dead."

"The second demand on Sir William's family for five thousand additional pounds shows this to be the case with our current blackmailer as well," said my father.

"I am afraid this progression will continue, for there may be even more disreputable photographs in store," Joanna predicted.

My father raised his brow in surprise. "How do you come to that most unpleasant development?"

Joanna walked over to the shelf holding her Persian slipper and extracted a Turkish cigarette which she carefully lighted. Then she began her customary pacing between the fireplace and the window, which indicated her brain was shifting into a higher gear.

"Think of the evidence which has already shown itself, Watson," she elucidated. "We know with certainty there are two compromising photographs that have thus far been presented to Anne Atwood's family, one of which paid off handsomely, as the blackmailer knew it would. And I further believe that the second photograph was even more suggestive than the first, and thus the demand for an even greater ransom."

"So?" I asked impatiently.

"Those two may have only been appetizers," she went on. "Put your minds on the setting in which the photographs were taken. Here we have an intoxicated, foolish, young woman in the company of a dashingly hand-some young man, and all taking place within the confines of a private room where both are enjoying the vapors of an opium pipe. Is it not the perfect setting for behavior far less delicate?"

"Such as?"

"I leave that up to your imagination."

My father shook his head in disgust. "Could he be so evil?"

"Even more so, I am afraid."

"Then you had best make haste and bring this case to a rapid conclusion."

"That is easier said than done."

"Was the audition not revealing?"

"More so than I expected, for we now have the name and address of the young man in the photograph," she said. "Assuming we were not given an invented stage name and a false address, we are dealing with a Mr. Hugh Marlowe who resides at Canary Wharf."

"Then you have a most promising lead."

"But all the evidence around the lead is circumstantial and will not hold up under even modest scrutiny," said Joanna, puffing absently on her ciga-rette. "Take for example the white ivory pipe. We assume it was provided by Eric Halderman, but we have no proof to back up that assumption. The pipe may be rare, but it was instantly recognized by Ah Sing which showed he was familiar with it."

"Thus similar pipes had been used in the past in his opium dens," I reasoned.

"Precisely the point, dear heart, which indicates they are not priceless rarities and could have multiple owners," my wife continued on. "Further-more, Fielding and Marsh is not the only fine tobacconists in London, and there are more than a few who could arrange such a purchase. Eric Halderman is certainly not the sole possessor of a white, ivory pipe, but simply one amongst a select several."

"But still an important clue," my father insisted.

"No doubt, but one which is shrouded in a mist."

"As is the reason the blackmailer chose to include it in his malicious scheme," I thought aloud.

"That is not so hidden," Joanna responded. "The pipe was a perfect prop to entice the young Anne Atwood into an opium den, where she was told it would have magical powers to ward off the evil side effects of the vapor. Moreover, I am of the opinion that the actor was instructed to conceal the pipe, which he attempted to do by grasping the lengthy stem of the ivory pipe. And you may recall that it required a magnifying glass to reveal the stem of the pipe extended well beyond the grip of Mr. Hugh Marlowe. Thus, the blackmailer was concerned with the white pipe in the photograph." My wife discarded her cigarette into the fireplace before continuing on. "The other clues at our disposal are even less convincing. The fact that Eric Halderman resides in the same neighborhood as Anne Atwood, and that he has considerable wealth of unknown source, are of interest but prove nothing."

"But surely the actor is involved," my father asserted.

"Where is the proof?" Joanna countered. "He will simply say that he was hired by a mysterious individual who knew of Anne Atwood's visit and wanted to surprise her with a magnificent gift, including a horse-drawn carriage ride, with exciting stops along the way."

"But you realize that the actor is intimately involved."

"Of course, but proving it is another matter."

"Somehow, my dear Joanna, you must bring all these circumstantial clues together."

"I plan to."

"Pray tell, how?"

"By connecting Hugh Marlowe to Eric Halderman."

The phone rang loudly, which interrupted our conversation at a most important juncture. With effort, my father pushed himself up from his overstuffed chair, then, noticeably bent at the waist, limped toward the phone with measured steps. The advancing years had taken their toll on this fine man, with his hair and mustache now deeply grayed and his once strong jawline partially hidden by hanging jowls. Unhappily, I knew the same fate awaited me, for my thick brown hair and moustache were already showing flecks of gray and the lines in my forehead appeared deeper than they should be as I approached my fortieth year. But for now, my jawline remained strong and my face unblemished except for a somewhat misshapen nose and a few patches of scar tissue about my brows, compliments of my boxing days at Oxford. Because of the last two features, my wife considered me ruggedly handsome, which I thought a bit of an exaggeration.

On the fifth ring, my father reached for the receiver and, whilst listening intently, spoke only a few words. After placing the receiver in its cradle, he looked directly into my wife's eyes. "I am afraid you were correct, Joanna."

"How so?"

"That was Sir William, bearing more bad news."

"Which is?"

"A third, most disreputable photograph has arrived, and the blackmailer is demanding yet another five thousand pounds."

7

CANARY WHARF

We departed from our rooms in full disguise and strolled to the Baker Street underground where we boarded a train to Canary Wharf. Our schedule was such that we would reach our destination at twilight and thus have enough light to view Hugh Marlowe's abode and perhaps have an idle conversation with a nearby neighbor who might provide us with much needed information. We assumed Marlowe would be absent, for he would in all likelihood be performing at a matinee elsewhere.

The ride to Canary Wharf was rapid and we disembarked into a crowded underground station which carried the heavy aroma of the sea. We were given directions to nearby West Indies Avenue by a helpful station conductor, and took the moving staircase into a gloomy late afternoon. With the fading light, it was difficult to see the addresses, but the avenue seemed to consist mainly of large warehouses and scattered, closed stores. But eventually we came to an area of weathered brick houses whose addresses were more clearly displayed. We approached the five hundred block, then continued on to 585 West Indies Avenue, which was the residence listed by Hugh Marlowe. Our spirits dropped as we read the faded sign above the large glass window at that address. It signified the presence of a pub called The Hidden Duck.

"It seems Mr. Hugh Marlowe has given a false address," I growled.

"Perhaps his post or telephone messages are received here," Joanna wondered aloud. "Remember, he is a struggling actor who probably cannot afford a telephone, yet he must be notified when possible positions become available."

"Such as for his audition, in which he had only one day advance notice."

"Precisely," she said, taking my arm. "Now you must keep in mind that our questions should be low-key and nonintrusive, so as not to arouse suspicion. And do not mention his name unless we have no other recourse."

We entered The Hidden Duck which had all the characteristics of an English pub. There was a long, wooden bar, with occupied stools pushed up against it. The air was clouded with tobacco smoke which gave off a stale aroma that was mixed in with the odor of overcooked food. Booths and tables lined the walls except for a space for a busy dartboard. A big-busted barmaid with a thick frame hurried about as she served drinks to noisy customers.

We found two empty stools at the end of the bar and were immediately approached by a bearded, stout barkeep, with an abdomen so protuberant it entirely overlapped the top of his trousers.

"What'll you have, then?" he asked.

"A pair of half and halfs for me and my sweetie," Joanna said.

"Want the Guinness?"

"Yeah, it's my birthday," she replied, explaining her request for the pricier brew, which was a mixture of two beers, one of which was of less density than the other.

Whilst waiting for our drinks, we surveyed the crowd gathered under the hanging lights. They all appeared to be working class, attired as I was, with heavy woolen garments that were dark and well worn. By contrast, Joanna's shabby dress was covered with a soiled apron, which draped past her knees. It possessed a dull white color that was spotted with permanently embedded red and brown stains. Our disguises were perfect, but would be of little benefit unless the situation changed.

The barkeep placed our half-and-halfs before us and said, "That'll be ten pence."

After paying, I moved in closer to Joanna and whispered, "Not a very promising lot, eh?"

"We must be patient, for most of those present are middle aged or older," she whispered back. "It is the younger patrons who will be familiar with others in their age group."

Just then a loud argument broke out at the dartboard, with angry words clearly being spoken. The barmaid quickly intervened and, with a wide smile, settled the dispute. She chatted briefly with the two before turning to the barkeep and shouting, "These blokes need another round of rum."

The pub returned to its usual hum of conversations, with new arrivals entering, but none were young and thus of little interest to us. Most of them appeared weary, with sour expressions, from being overworked and underpaid, as was the lot of those who toiled along London's busy docks.

"Perhaps we should chat with the barmaid who seems to know everyone," I suggested.

Joanna quickly shook her head. "Barmaids are the most talkative creatures on the face of the earth. One hint of suspicion would rapidly turn into a full-blown rumor."

"What, then?" I asked impatiently.

"We wait."

Another quarrel erupted at the dartboard, with words angry enough to indicate that a fight was in store. Despite his stoutness, the barkeep flew over the bar and placed himself between the two near combatants. He gave them a stern warning that in the event of another outburst they would be shown the door and not allowed to return. Peace returned to the pub.

A new arrival, in his early thirties and wearing a thick, woolen pea coat came up beside us and, with a cordial nod, took a place at the bar. Tall and well built, he stood erect and had the appearance of someone with military experience.

"Bit of a chill out tonight," he said, rubbing his palms against one another. "And it may well bring a sprinkle of snow."

"I've seen enough snow to last two lifetimes," Joanna complained mildly.

"Haven't we all?" he agreed. "But strangely enough, whilst at sea we never saw so much as when on land."

"So I have heard," said Joanna, measuring the man's posture and the pea coat he was wearing. "You have the look of a seaman in His Majesty's navy."

"I had the honor for five years and enjoyed every moment of it, but a terrible gale put an end to that."

"A gale, you say?"

"Aye," he replied in navy speak. "A bloody storm in the North Sea, the likes of which none aboard had ever seen, tossed our ship about like a toy in bathtub water. I was thrown so hard against the steel railing that I shattered both my hip and arm, forcing me to leave the service, much to my regret."

"Did the fractures not heal?" I asked.

"The healing was incomplete, so they had no choice but to discharge me," he said unhappily. "And now I work on a trawler in the Channel, with my fighting days behind me."

The former sailor turned as a thin, attractive woman with a fair complexion and long, blond hair, approached. "Ah, here is my lovely lass."

They shared kisses on the cheek and a warm embrace before he ordered three halfpennies worth of rum for both of them, then came back to us, saying in a most affable fashion, "This here is Dolly and I'm Nick."

"Pleased to meet you," said Joanna. "I'm Annie and this is my mate, Harry."

"Pleasure," the couple responded together.

"I was telling them about my misfortune at sea," Nick told his girlfriend.

"Did you mention that the ship you were on was sunk by a bloody German U-boat a month after your discharge?" Dolly asked.

"I did not," he said.

"With all hands lost," she added.

"I saw no need to speak of it."

"Well, you should in your prayers, and maybe thank God for fracturing your bones so you would live."

"I should have been on that ship," he said wistfully.

"No, you should not have," Dolly insisted and swallowed her rum in a single gulp. "Now let us refill our glasses to wash away those terrible memories and say no more of it."

"Aye, aye, captain," Nick said, managing a smile for the woman he obviously adored.

Dolly waved to the barkeep for refills, then looked to my wife. "Sometimes we women have to take control of things, you see."

"Well done," Joanna said.

We heard a loud bang against the door to the kitchen as a server backed out carrying a large, food-laden tray above his head. "Make way! Make way!" he said cheerfully.

"The shepherd's pies go to the table by the window, Hugh," the barmaid called out.

Joanna's eyes, as well as mine, abruptly went to the server as he passed by. It was Hugh Marlowe wearing a stained apron that was far too short for his tall frame. He gracefully weaved his way through the gathering in the center of the pub and did a flawless ballet move before reaching a side table where he deposited a steaming dish of food. He then backed away and, with an obviously choreographed bow, said, "Your supper is served, sir."

It was a masterful performance and those at the table chuckled and applauded the well-done act. One of the diners handed the young server a gratuity and, with it, came a request. "Give us that line about the king begging for a horse, if you will."

Hugh Marlowe picked up a long knife and held it aloft, like a man preparing to do battle. The actor pranced about, fending off one imaginary enemy after another. "A horse! A horse! My kingdom for a horse," he bellowed out, with every word reaching the farthest corner of the pub.

Once again the applause came, louder this time, as the young actor gave a final bow and retreated to the kitchen. The mood in the pub lightened, with even the combatants at the dartboard smiling widely.

Joanna saw the perfect opening and immediately captured it. "Why, that bloke should be on the stage," she said, with an appreciative nod.

"He already is, dearie," Dolly responded. "He is a real actor who has worked at theaters on St. Martin's Lane."

"Go on!" Joanna said in disbelief.

"Oh, yes," Dolly affirmed. "Not big roles, mind you, but those sure to draw one's attention."

"Have you actually seen him on the stage?"

"I wish I had, but those tickets are far too pricey for me," she replied. "But Georgie, who owns the pub, saw his acting once and said he was bloody good."

"So he works here part time to put bread on the table," Joanna inquired casually.

"That he does," Dolly answered. "He serves and does a bit of cleanup, and for those tasks Georgie gives Hugh a room upstairs above the pub."

"And no doubt allows him access to food in the kitchen as well."

Dolly lowered her voice and, with a mischievous smile, said, "But in private, Hugh has mentioned that the shepherd's pie here is the worst he has ever tasted."

The smile left her face as a shrill whistle sounded outside. The entire pub abruptly went silent. No one moved, not even a centimeter, as we all waited for the dreaded warning to come. Once more the whistle sounded, but now it was followed by the voice of a constable passing by on a bicycle. "Take cover! Take cover!"

"All to the underground!" the barmaid shouted, dropping her tray and dashing for the door.

Every living soul in the pub made a rapid exit into the dark night, for twilight had long passed and the lamp posts turned off so as not to attract the approaching German bombers. We moved quickly along the footpaths, now shoulder to shoulder with the fleeing residents of Canary Wharf. Traffic had come to a stop on the avenue, whilst motorists abandoned their vehicles and hurried with us to safety. Yet there was no panic and the evacuation of the nearby buildings was carried out much like a practiced drill. It was a fine example of the British stiff upper lip.

Fortunately, the underground was only two blocks away, and the ever-increasing crowd reached its destination just as they heard the thunder of exploding bombs in the distance. We stepped onto the moving staircase and descended slowly into the dimly lit underground station. The benches were quickly occupied, and most people seated themselves on the cold, tiled floor where they waited anxiously. It was impossible to hear the drone of the approaching bombers from our position, so we had to depend on the noise of the explosions themselves to determine how close the bombers were to us.

We were fortunate enough to find a seat on the floor which allowed us to rest our backs against the tiled wall. Joanna nudged me gently with an elbow and gestured with her head to the people huddled together on our left. There, amongst them, was Hugh Marlowe and the barmaid who were engaged in an easily overhead conversation. We turned our faces away, but kept our ears pricked.

"So, is your mum any better?" she asked.

"I am afraid not, for she is dwindling away before my very eyes," Marlowe replied.

"How sad."

"Sadder yet, for there is little that can be done for her."

"But your journeys to Slough must cheer her up."

"It brightens her day, but I am told it disappears once I depart."

"You are a good lad for making the trip as often as you do."

"I only wish I could do more to see that she is cared for."

"Is there not a home or similar facility where she could be looked after?"

"There is one, but it is far beyond my means."

A deafening explosion rocked the underground station with such force that tiles fell off the walls and the lights suddenly dimmed further. The air was fitted with audible gasps, mainly from women, whilst the men tried to steel their nerves, all realizing that the initial wave of bombing was often followed by another, and this was particularly so for favored targets, such as the docks of London.

But good luck or perhaps the hand of the Almighty was with us that night, for there was a prolonged period of silence which was broken only once by an explosion in the far distance. The huddled mass slowly got to their feet and began to chat with one another, obviously relieved that the danger had passed. We kept our heads down and our backs to Hugh Marlowe and the barmaid whilst waiting for them to depart, and only spoke when we saw them ascending on the moving staircase.

"I think we can safely say that greed was not the driving force behind Hugh Marlowe's participation in the blackmail," I said in a quiet whisper.

"It was need that drove him, for that can be far more powerful than greed," Joanna noted, and said nothing further as we sensed the rumble of an approaching train.

8

THE SALACIOUS PHOTOGRAPH

As our taxi approached Sir William's estate, I continued to ask myself a question which had no apparent answer. It was an obvious question and an important one, yet it strangely did not seem to concern Joanna. With this in mind, I whispered to my wife, "Why did the blackmailer send a third photograph so quickly and demand another five thousand pounds?"

"Because his appetite has been whetted," Joanna whispered back. "You will recall that the word *another* was used in the third ransom, which indicates that Sir William has acquiesced to the blackmailer's second demand."

"I find it difficult to think that a man of such high caliber would react so recklessly," I said.

"Given enough duress, even the strongest of men will break," she responded. "And a broken man can be forced to reveal military secrets which must be kept concealed at all costs. The knowledge contained in such documents would be of incalculable value."

A chill ran down my spine at the mere mention of this treasonous act. "Surely, you are not speaking of information gained by Sir William from his seat in the War Cabinet."

"But I am, for its eventual disclosure to the blackmailer falls within the realm of possibility."

We were met at the entrance of the limestone mansion by a butler wearing a finely tailored black suit and escorted through a marbled vestibule that had frescoes painted on the ceiling. He opened a mahogany door which led into an expansive library decorated with hanging tapestries and works of art which immediately caught the visitor's eye. Prominently displayed was a colorful seascape by J. M. W. Turner, who was by far the most notable English artist of the past century. His paintings were eagerly sought after and commanded the highest price at auction. We heard the door close softly behind us.

Sir William and his wife, whom he introduced as Lady Charlotte, stood beside a highly polished Victorian desk, atop which was placed a small bust of King George V's easily recognizable face.

"My wife insisted on being present, for she feels we are about to face a monumental scandal from which we may never recover," he said.

"She may be correct, but we have recently come across clues which might help untangle your dilemma," Joanna stated, injecting a limited ray of hope.

"I would very much like to know of these clues," Lady Charlotte requested.

"It is best they remain hidden, for any disclosure of their existence would work to our disadvantage, much as your prompt payment of the second ransom has done."

"I do not see how the payment causes additional problems," Lady Charlotte argued.

"I am of the opinion that your blackmailer will now speed up the pace of his demands, which gives us less time until he bleeds all of your assets dry."

"I should have thought of that," she admitted.

"But I should share part of the blame," Sir William interceded. "Although I initially resisted, I agreed with my wife to pay the ransom, together with a note begging for this nightmare to end. It was a foolish move on my part."

"Foolish indeed," Joanna asserted. "But perhaps there is something to be learned from your payment."

"Such as?"

"Such as details, Sir William," my wife continued on. "I can assure you there is no perfect crime. Only bumbling investigators who overlook telling clues. The evidence is there, waiting to be uncovered."

"I fail to see how my payment can provide an important clue."

"It is his method, not yours, Sir William, which will help us unravel this mystery," Joanna explained. "I need to know every move you were instructed to make. You are to include even the smallest detail on how, when, and where the money was to be delivered."

"It was the same on both occasions," the elder statesman narrated in an even voice. "I received a late-night phone call at my residence and was instructed to follow every letter of the blackmailer's directions, which would be given at noon the next day. Any deviation would result in the public being made aware of the distasteful photograph."

"I take it he was aware that your granddaughter's father remained away at sea."

"Obviously."

"And what of Anne's mother?"

"She is confined to a tuberculosis sanitorium in Berkshire."

"Pray continue."

"First, the ransom was to be paid in hundred-pound notes placed in a single stack, which was to be secured in a large, manila envelope. The currency was to be used, but not overly so. It was to be delivered at midnight to different locations, but always in the Canary Wharf district."

Joanna and I exchanged knowing glances, for that was the location of the pub where Hugh Marlowe worked and lived. He could lurk on the back streets and alleys at night without arousing suspicion.

"On both occasions, I alone was to drive a black motor vehicle to a narrow street at the rear of a closed warehouse. But the addresses themselves changed."

"Yet both were on West Indies Avenue," my wife interjected.

Sir William's brow went up, obviously taken aback by Joanna's knowledge. "How could you possibly know this?"

"It is my business to know things others don't," she said, deftly avoiding the source of the information. "How was the money to be deposited?"

"I was told to drive to the alleyway at the rear of the warehouse and remain there until I received a signal, which consisted of a waving torch. The money was to be placed beside a large, metal bin that was protected by an overhanging roof. Once done, I was to drive away."

"You earlier mentioned that the first two demands were delivered by late night phone calls."

"Correct."

"And yet, now he wishes to contact you at noon."

"That, too, is correct," Sir William stated. "Is that of significance?"

"We shall see," said Joanna, but I suspect she had the same concern that was passing through my mind. Perhaps the blackmailer was having the estate surveilled to determine if any suspicious newcomers were arriving at the time for the scheduled phone call. "Allow me to view the blackmailer's message which was again written on the back of the photograph."

Sir William reached for the photograph which lay beside the bust of King George V, and passed it to Joanna. I glanced over my wife's shoulder at the scribbled message. It read:

Another 5000 pounds, with directions at noon tomorrow

She used her magnifying glass to study the writing, but did so only briefly before turning the snapshot over face up. Lady Charlotte averted her eyes, clearly disquieted by the image and unwilling to view it yet again. The snapshot showed Anne Atwood and Hugh Marlowe seated on a straw mat as before, but on this occasion their embrace was more intimate. He was positioned behind her, with both of his arms wrapped around her narrow waist. His head was nestled upon her shoulder, and was so near her cheek that strands of her hair crossed his forehead. And she was smiling.

"Most disturbing," Joanna said, and viewed the photograph at length with her magnifying glass. Up and down she went, then side to side, examining every aspect of the picture, as if searching for another revealing clue. After inspecting the image one final time, she returned the snapshot to Sir William. "I am afraid there will be more disreputable photographs to come."

"Oh dear," Lady Charlotte gasped.

"Can't you bring this nightmare to a stop?" Sir William asked desperately.

"I can make no promises," said Joanna, and paused to glance at her watch. "We have ten minutes before the phone call, and we must be prepared to take advantage of any mistake on his part. The longer your conversation with the blackmailer, the more likely he is to have a slip-up. I shall be at your side, with my ear close to the receiver, which will allow me to overhear his message. My participation must remain entirely silent, and to this end I shall need pen and paper to jot down instructions to you."

"Why not employ hand signals?"

"Because they alone will not suffice," said Joanna, and glanced once more at the photograph now resting on the desk. "Has Anne been shown the latest snapshot?"

"We dare not," Lady Charlotte replied. "For her behavior has taken a terrible toll on the child. She stays in her room most of the day and her lively chatter, which we once so enjoyed, has disappeared. It would appear that depression has set in, as one might expect with this never-ending turmoil."

"Has her absence been noted by your neighbors?" my wife asked.

"I am afraid so."

"Who in particular?"

"Mostly by Lady Ellsworth, a dear, sweet woman, who unfortunately is confined to a wheelchair with rheumatism, but does spend time in her garden. She inquired because Anne always found a moment to stop by and chat with her, which the dear lady truly enjoyed. I believe she misses Anne's visits."

"I am certain she does," Joanna said, before tapping a finger against her chin, as if trying to recall a thought. "As I think back, Anne mentioned another neighbor whose name was Halderman. Has he inquired as well?"

"Not a word, but we rarely see him, for he is a bit of a recluse. He is no doubt nouveau riche, with expensive choices, but little taste." She turned to her husband before continuing. "I believe that was your description of him as well."

Sir William nodded his response. "But he did, however, invite us to a fine charity gala for a children's hospital which was nicely attended, but our stay was brief."

"But long enough for one to see that the furnishings were somewhat gaudy and lacking in style. Would you not agree, William?"

"Except for his collection of antique pipes, which was most impressive. As a dedicated smoker myself, I appreciated the excellent display and the manner in which the pipes were presented. I must say some were unusual, to say the least."

The telephone rang loudly. Sir William quickly pointed to a desk drawer.

Joanna rushed to open the drawer and removed pen and paper, then moved alongside Sir William to a position which allowed her to share the receiver with him. "Now," she commanded on the third ring.

"Yes?" he said into the receiver.

"This is Sir William."

After a long pause, he stated, "I understand. Please talk slowly so I can write down your instructions."

"Five thousand pounds to the same address at which the first delivery was made." A short pause followed, during which time Sir William cleared his throat in an effort to prolong the conversation. "Yes. Ten-ten West Indies Avenue. I have that."

"Midnight tomorrow, then."

Joanna rapidly shook her head and wrote down directions on a slip of paper. *Too soon! Need time to gather 5000 pounds.*

Sir William relayed the message and added, "I must inform you that all my accounts have been severely drained. Surely you must realize that a loan must be arranged for such a sizeable sum."

"I will try my very best, but this cannot be hurriedly done," Sir William said, and gestured to Joanna for help by pointing to his timepiece.

My wife furrowed her brow as she considered the request, then opened her palms and spread them wide apart.

The elder statesman quickly interpreted the silent message. "I require more time, sir. You are asking me to do the impossible on such short notice."

There was yet another long pause before the conversation resumed. "I must insist you allow me some delay," he said, with a facial expression that pleaded for more assistance.

Joanna hastily glanced around the expensively decorated library, with her eyes going from one painting to the next. It required only seconds for her to jot down the word *auction* and motion to the exquisite seascape by Turner that hung on a nearby wall.

"I have an idea," Sir William spoke rapidly into the receiver. "I possess a superb Turner I would be willing to auction off. Please permit me time to contact Sotheby's and arrange for an auction in the immediate future."

"A week, I should think, would be required for a formal bidding."

Another pause came and went.

"No, no," he objected. "A rushed auction will not allow me to fetch the highest bid."

"Thank you, sir. Thank you. I shall await your next call," Sir William said and, breathing a sigh of relief, placed the receiver back into its cradle.

"The bloody scoundrel," he growled at the phone.

"That he is," Joanna concurred. "But I must say your performance was in every way convincing."

"Should I contact Sotheby's?"

"Yes, but do not give them a definite date. Say only that you are giving thought to auctioning off a Turner seascape and should very much like to know what the initial asking price would be."

"What is the purpose of such a call, then?"

"If our blackmailer is as clever as I believe him to be, he will contact Sotheby's and inquire if they have a seascape by Turner available. On receiving a *maybe in the near future* response from the auction house, he will be satisfied that you have put the proper wheels in motion."

"But I will eventually have to sell the Turner," Sir William said regretfully. "That will be a sad day, for it has been passed down through the generations."

"I shall do my best to see that the painting stays where it belongs," said Joanna, then turned to Lady Charlotte. "I have one last request. Please give me the exact locations of nearby neighbors."

"Lady Ellsworth resides to our east," she replied and gestured in that direction. "Mr. Halderman's estate is located to the west. You will know his place by an overbearing iron gate which has the initials EH in its center."

"Very good," Joanna said, returning to the elder statesman. "Regardless of the hour, you must inform me immediately if there are further calls from the blackmailer."

"I shall," Sir William promised.

"And with your permission, I should like to take the photograph for further analysis."

Sir William nodded at the request, but added a condition. "You must destroy it once your study is completed."

"Of course," my wife pledged.

We departed without further discussion and strolled slowly to our waiting taxi. The butler followed us with his eyes until he closed the door to the mansion behind him. Even then, we spoke in low voices.

"What about the photograph so captured your attention, other than its highly suggestive nature?" I asked.

"Two items have disappeared," Joanna replied.

I reached for the photograph in her hand and studied it carefully. "The white pipe is no longer present, which indicates he was instructed to conceal it."

"That would be most unlikely, for a strange voice from outside the private room would have greatly upset Anne. It would have told her that they were being watched by a secret observer."

"How then?"

"I suspect this snapshot was taken during a second encounter, and on this occasion the pipe was no longer present," said Joanna. "You will also notice that Anne is wearing a different dress, which indicates the couple had multiple engagements."

"So you believe there are more photographs to come."

"Beyond a doubt, as evidenced by the second missing item, which was the dazed expression Anne once had upon her face. It has now been replaced by a sensual parting of her lips. She appears to be thoroughly enjoying the moment, with the anticipation of more to come."

I was taken aback by Joanna's disclosure, but then again, the feminine eye is acutely attuned to changes in emotional feelings. "Are you suggesting the couple is involved in a scandalous affair?"

"That is a consideration."

"Which would indicate that Anne Atwood is not telling us all."

"That, too, is a consideration."

We entered the taxi and remained silent until we came to the main gate of Sir William's estate. But rather than turning left, which would have taken us back to West London, Joanna instructed the driver to proceed to the right.

"But, madam, that will drive us north to Golders Green," he objected.

"I am aware, but that area is of interest to me."

We rode on and passed the neatly manicured lawn of Sir William's estate. Despite the cold winter, brief episodes of spring had caused the trees and shrubbery to turn a glorious green. But the flowers remained bare. Up ahead was a large, sturdy, iron gate, and on passing it we saw the giant letters EH at its center. It was clearly the entrance to Eric Halderman's residence.

"Please decrease your speed," Joanna requested of the driver as she rolled down the rear window.

In rushed a blast of chilly air, along with the loud sound of a motorized lawnmower. The lawnmower was being guided by a gardener attired in heavy workman's garments, with a woolen cap that covered his ears. The noise from the passing machine was strong enough to vibrate the rear door of our taxi.

"You may now head back to Baker Street," Joanna called out to the driver.

"Very good, madam," he said, and slowly turned his vehicle around, which again brought us close to the din of the lawnmower.

My wife moved in near to me and whispered, "I heard that very sound earlier."

"From whence?" I whispered back.

"In the phone call Sir William had with the blackmailer. I noticed the sound in the background, but could not identify it with certainty. Nevertheless, I could not help but wonder if the noise originated from a nearby source. You will notice that no such sound comes from Lady Ellsworth's estate, which we are now passing."

"So it is Eric Halderman, after all."

"He is the merciless scoundrel behind everything."

"But how do we prove it?"

"By baiting a trap he cannot resist."

9

THE SHOOTING

At six thirty the following morning my father entered our bedroom and awakened us with obvious urgency. This behavior was most unusual, for he rarely intruded into our bedroom and never at such an early hour.

"What is it, Father?" I asked.

"A prime suspect has been shot," he replied.

"Eric Halderman?" I inquired, wiping the sleep from my eyes.

He shook his head in response. "It is Hugh Marlowe and he has been gravely wounded."

"Is it a head wound?" Joanna queried, instantly awake and alert.

"I am afraid so," my father reported, as he departed. "Now, you must dress quickly whilst I have Miss Hudson brew up a steaming pot of Earl Grey."

As she changed into a pale blue dress with a lace collar, Joanna worried aloud, "I fear we may have brought about Hugh Marlowe's demise."

"How so?" asked I, slipping into my trousers.

"By not keeping our moves close enough to our vests," she replied. "Perhaps our surveillance of the actor was not as clandestine as we had hoped."

"But why kill him?"

"Because I suspect he was the most vulnerable."

"Do you believe Eric Halderman was behind it?"

"Who else?"

We entered the parlor where my father sat reading the last from a stack of newspapers. He took no notice of our entrance whilst concentrating on an inner page, indicating the article that described the shooting was lengthy and hopefully filled with details.

Finally, my father looked up and placed the newspaper aside. "The *Daily Telegraph* serves our purpose best, for it talks of Scotland Yard's involvement which no doubt includes the presence of Inspector Lestrade, who at times can be a most valuable ally."

"Any involvement with Lestrade in the blackmailing scandal would have to be done under the cloak of extreme secrecy," I said.

"But even then it would be risky," Joanna cautioned. "For it would have to include the commissioner and perhaps other superiors at Scotland Yard, thus leaving us open to unwanted disclosures, which would result in disaster for Sir William and his entire family."

"Yet we may have no choice," my father chimed in.

"If that be the case, then let it be our very last resort," Joanna said, and reached for the *Daily Telegraph*, whilst I chose the *Guardian*.

We carefully studied each and every article written of Hugh Marlowe's misfortune, passing the morning newspapers between us until the last of the stack was read. The reports all shared a commonality, with many of the details virtually identical. Hugh Marlowe's best day had turned into his worst. The young actor had been awarded a role in a murder-mystery play which would soon open at a theater on St. Martin's Lane. He had persuaded the theater's late-night custodian to look away whilst Marlowe practiced his part on the actual stage upon which the play was to be performed. The actor was instructed not to touch any of the props or other articles which were to be used on opening night, and the items included a pistol that fired blanks. Apparently, Marlowe decided to employ the pistol whilst rehearsing, and it misfired, with the blank striking him in the head. On hearing the shot, the custodian rushed back into the theater and found the actor lying on the stage and bleeding profusely from the self-inflicted wound. Scotland Yard was notified and arrived prior to Marlowe being transported to St. Bartholomew's Hospital. The word *suicide* was never mentioned.

"What say you, Joanna?" I asked, placing down the newspaper.

"I say it was cleverly done," she responded.

"You seem to be of the opinion that the wound was not the result of a misfire," my father surmised.

"Let us establish a few basic facts before arriving at a conclusion," said Joanna. "As we all know, there are four major causes of death, these being natural, suicidal, homicidal, and accidental. Obviously, the actor's demise was not natural, and I believe it not to be suicidal, for the evidence states otherwise. Here was a happy man, who showed no signs of depression, and was now stepping up the ladder to a far better position in the acting profession. Just think of his prior existence in life. He was barely scraping by as a server in a pub and had to depend on the generosity of the owner for a room in which to sleep. Suddenly, he is on St. Martin's Lane, with both his status and income substantially elevated. This is not the picture of a man contemplating suicide."

"Moreover, he did not leave a note behind," my father added. "Such a farewell message is almost always present in suicides."

"Another excellent point, Watson," she concurred. "Which leads us to the homicidal and accidental causes of death. Should we favor one over the other?"

"Both are equally possible," I opined.

"The evidence says otherwise," my wife argued mildly. "Allow me to draw your attention to Marlowe's role in the play. He was to portray the caring brother who rushes to his sister's aid and takes a bullet meant for her. Several of the newspapers mentioned that this act of heroism was critical to the plot of the play. Now, I ask you, why would Marlowe require a pistol in his rehearsal? What purpose could it possibly serve?"

"Perhaps he was briefly assuming the role and station of the shooter," my father suggested. "He may have wished to portray the shooter with pistol in hand."

"And then looked down the barrel to determine if it was functioning properly?"

"Most unlikely, for he would have certainly aimed the weapon in the direction of the target."

"Next, we come to the most telling clue mentioned in all the reports," Joanna went on. "I am referring to the position of the pistol which lay beside the grievously wounded Marlowe."

"It was in his hand," I recalled.

"And in all of the suicidal and accidental shootings we have witnessed, pray tell where was the pistol located?"

"On the floor, by their side," my father answered at once. "The weapon was never in the victim's hand."

"Why not?"

"Because it was immediately dropped."

Joanna nodded her affirmation. "Even if the wound causes instant death, the weapon leaves the victim's hand, for all of their muscles relax one final time."

"I am surprised Inspector Lestrade did not realize the importance of the pistol's location."

"Do not underestimate him, for his skills are growing sharper and sharper," she warned. "He may be on the quiet whilst gathering more evidence to back up his suspicion."

"Is he that clever?"

"I believe so, and perhaps clever enough to know that he is in over his head," she said, with a mischievous smile. "We of course would offer our assistance if asked to do so."

"Is there a method to prompt Lestrade in that direction?" my father asked. "If so, we could gain the resources and influence of Scotland Yard without divulging our involvement in the blackmailing of Sir William."

"A capital idea, Watson!"

"But how do we go about subterfuge?"

"With guile," my wife replied, then absently tapped a finger against her lips, suggesting that such a plan was already in the making.

There was a brief rap on the door and Miss Hudson entered, carrying a complete tea setting. She sensed the importance of our silence and departed without pouring a cup or uttering a word. Once the door closed, we continued our discussion.

"A moment earlier you mentioned our surveillance on the actor may have been noticed, which led to Marlowe's demise," I recalled. "But surely our activities were well concealed."

"Do not be so certain of our concealment," Joanna rebutted, and walked over to the Persian slipper for her first cigarette of the day. After lighting it, she began her customary pacing of our parlor. "Think back to our visit to the fine tobacconist where Eric Halderman was a known client. Perhaps he stopped in for a new pipe and was told by a most accommodating clerk of our interest in a white pipe. He might even thank Halderman for referring us to Fielding and Marsh for our forthcoming purchase. Imagine how our blackmailer would have received that bit of information."

"Do you believe Halderman would be clever enough to connect your visit to the white pipe in the photograph?" my father asked.

"He would be a dunce not to," Joanna replied, drawing deeply on her Turkish cigarette whilst pacing. "Then there were our questions and chatter with the former royal seaman and his girlfriend at the pub in Canary Wharf."

"But those questions and comments were innocent enough," I opined. "I very much doubt they aroused any interest in the young couple."

"So it would seem, but perhaps a busybody overheard our conversation and mentioned it to Hugh Marlowe who later relayed the incident to Eric Halderman. Thus, Marlowe foolishly revealed himself to be the weak link in the blackmailer's chain and became disposable."

"But these are all assumptions," my father countered. "And as you know, dear Joanna, assumptions can lead one down the wrong road."

"You raise an excellent point, Watson, and that is why we must now travel a different path."

"To where?"

"Slough."

"And what do you hope to find there?"

"Hugh Marlowe's mother."

10

SLOUGH

I could not believe that Joanna would take advantage of a grieving mother, but she assured me she would be performing a service, for it was unlikely the poor woman had a telephone and thus would not as yet been notified of her son's grave condition. Rather than her receiving a brief, emotionless note, we would be delivering the dreadful news in a compassionate fashion, along with a bouquet of flowers. If important information came to light whilst performing our service, so much the better. It again reminded me that my dear wife was so like her famous father, in that both could remain entirely emotionless when investigating a case or seeking justice. They would simply not allow feelings to disrupt their finely tuned brains. Joanna had exhibited this remarkable ability in our very first adventure together.

As our train moved through the English countryside, I could not help but think how similar our original case was to the current case, in that in both instances murder was masquerading as suicide. Our initial foray as consulting detectives began seven years ago when an aristocratic family beseeched my father, the close colleague of the long-dead Sherlock Holmes, to investigate the apparent suicide of their eldest son. My father was less than eager to pursue this mundane matter until the family mentioned that the key witnesses were Joanna Blalock and her ten-year-old son, Johnny. Suddenly, my father became intensely interested, for he was the only person on the face of the earth who knew that Joanna Blalock was the concealed daughter of Sherlock Holmes. She was conceived during a one-night encounter between Holmes and Irene Adler, the famous opera star who once outwitted the Great Detective. But alas, the expectant mother developed the toxemia of pregnancy and died shortly after delivery, but only after naming the baby girl Joanna. Holmes refused to serve as father and raise the child, and thus Joanna was adopted by a loving couple, with the legal papers forever sealed.

Joanna enjoyed a wonderful childhood and, as she grew older, it became obvious she was remarkably attractive and bright, with a consuming interest in crime. She was eventually to become a nurse at St. Bartholomew's Hospital, where she excelled using her keen cognitive abilities and where she met and married Dr. John Blalock, a talented surgeon. They enjoyed a happy marriage that was made happier by the birth of a son, Johnny. But tragedy soon struck when her husband died of cholera, leaving Joanna no choice but to move into the mansion of her father-in-law, the elderly statesman, Lord Blalock. Since Joanna and her son were key witnesses, my father and I visited the Blalock mansion to interview them. I could still recall the exact words which were spoken following a formal introduction.

"We are here to investigate the death of Charles Harrelston," my father said.

"No, Dr. Watson," Joanna replied. "You are here to investigate the murder of Charles Harrelston."

And so became the start of the Daughter of Sherlock Holmes mysteries, which I was more than eager to chronicle. Nevertheless, even with this background, I remained uncomfortable with Joanna's approach to a soon-to-be-grieving mother. It seemed rather ruthless, I thought, as our train arrived at the station in Slough, which was shrouded in a midmorning mist. No street signs were in sight, so we meandered down a main thorough-fare that had little traffic and mostly empty shops, a few of which were permanently shuttered. At the first intersection we spotted a patrolling constable who gave us directions to Mrs. Marlowe's house, but made no mention nor showed any interest in her son, which told us that the news of the actor's tragic wound had not reached the small town twenty-five miles west of London.

The Marlowe home was hidden away on a back alley that was occupied entirely by a row of small, weathered houses, all with peeling paint. Even the thatched roofs were in poor repair as depicted by their clearly visible bare spots, having been worn away by time.

I rapped on the wooden door and back came a weak, feminine voice. "What do you want?"

"We have news of your son," Joanna replied.

"What's he up to?"

"I am afraid he has been hurt."

"Come in, come in, then," she said in a rush.

We entered a cramped parlor, with threadbare furnishings and a black stove which blocked the way into a tiny kitchen. Mrs. Marlowe seemed to be propped up on an overstuffed chair, with her swollen, edematous legs elevated onto a cardboard box.

"What news have you, then?" asked the woman, who appeared to be aged far beyond her years. She had snow-white hair, a deeply lined face, and pursed blue lips that were struggling for air. She was obviously suffering from congestive heart failure as evidenced by her shortness of breath and peripheral edema. The blueness of her lips indicated she was not receiving enough oxygen.

"We are the Watsons from the Actors' Guild, of which your son is a member," Joanna introduced us, whilst handing the woman a bouquet of daisies. "I am afraid your son has suffered a severe injury and we have been sent to notify you of it."

"What—what sort of injury?" she asked, leaning forward with deep concern.

"He was accidentally wounded on stage," Joanna replied. "A pistol was fired whilst a rehearsal was ongoing, and the round struck your son. He was rushed to St. Bartholomew's where he is receiving the very best of care."

"Will he recover?"

"We can only hope, but I must be truthful and tell you that the wound places his life in danger."

Mrs. Marlowe slowly shook her head in maternal anguish, as tears filled her eyes and dripped upon her cheeks. "He is such a good, good lad who looks after his mum and never lets me down. Why, only last week he stopped by to give me a twenty-pound gift. Twenty pounds, mind you!" She repeated the amount as if it were a great fortune, then paused to catch her breath, which required effort. Once more air was allowed in, she continued on. "And he told me there was more to come, with his new role on stage. Imagine that! My boy being a great actor in London."

"A most caring son," my wife noted.

"Most caring indeed, for he has been my sole support," Mrs. Marlowe went on. "Dear Hugh has always managed to help me along, although he earns barely enough as an actor to look after himself. But, with his new position and an income far more than ever expected, he can easily provide me with the necessities, and then some. Why, he even took out a life insurance policy for several hundred pounds in my favor should he have the misfortune of a terrible ending. What a kind lad he is." She reached into a cloth bag by her side and asked, "Would you like to see the policy itself?"

"Very much," Joanna encouraged and was handed a single sheet of thick, engraved paper. It showed a certificate from the Channel Insurance Company which indicated the insured on the policy was Mr. Hugh Marlowe and the beneficiary to be Mrs. Evelyn Marlowe. It was listed for two hundred pounds and issued eight days ago, well after the first blackmail payment.

"How thoughtful," said Joanna and gave the certificate back to Mrs. Marlowe, then waited whilst the woman folded it carefully and redeposited it into the safety of her cloth bag. "Now, with your worry and your son in the hospital, is there anyone who can assist you during this difficult time?"

"Oh, I can depend on my dear friend, Gladys, for she is like a sister to me."

"Does she help you clean and cook?"

"She does, and won't accept a farthing for it. What a sweetheart she is."

Joanna glanced around the parlor before focusing on an open door which led to a small bedroom. "Does she clean Hugh's room as well?"

"Doesn't have to, for my son always leaves his room neat as a pin."

"Now, if you will permit, I must ask you a very confidential question."

Evelyn Marlowe narrowed her eyes, as if expecting the worst. "Ask away, then."

"Do you trust your dear friend, Gladys?"

"With my very life."

"Is there any other relative you can turn to?"

"Nary a one," she said. "There is a long lost son who I have not seen in too many years to count. He never calls or visits and shows no interest in my well-being. Yet, according to my Hugh, his half-brother is quite well-to-do."

"Does he associate with Hugh?"

"Not to my knowledge. I think the nasty little bugger—he was always mean as a snake—wishes to forget his poor beginning and avoids any mention of his past."

"Perhaps we should notify the half-brother of Hugh's most unfortunate accident," Joanna urged.

"He would only give the news a cold shoulder."

"Nevertheless, he should be informed by the Actors' Guild, as a simple courtesy."

"Very well, then."

"May we have the name and address of the half-brother?" Joanna requested.

"I do not have that information," Mrs. Marlowe replied. "But Hugh told me the unpleasant bloke has changed his last name and now calls himself Halderman or something like that. It is a fancy moniker for someone who started out as a street urchin."

Joanna and I exchanged quick glances at the unexpected connection between the two blackmailers, but kept our faces expressionless. The clue explained so much, but left major questions unanswered. "A sad story," my wife concluded, breaking the momentary silence.

Mrs. Marlowe shrugged indifferently. "He is a bad memory to me and little else."

"Well, with all that in mind, you must place all of your trust in Gladys."

"Which I do without hesitation."

"Then listen carefully to what I am about to tell you," said Joanna, lowering her voice as if to stress the importance of the message she was about to divulge. "Am I correct in assuming that Hugh did not have a bank account?"

"He did not trust those bloodsuckers, nor do I," she replied, with an edge to her words.

"And I doubt very much that he would carry all his newfound money on his person, for the streets of Canary Wharf are not safe."

"It would be foolish for him to do so."

"Then, where would he safekeep the tidy sum he was now earning?"

"I don't know."

"There is only one person and one place Hugh would trust absolutely," my wife said and pointed directly at the woman, then at the floor.

The woman's eyes opened widely. "Of course! Of course! He would conceal that money here. As a lad he would always hide his toys and the few farthings he saved in secret places."

"In his room, then?"

"Yes! Yes! His hiding places were always in his bedroom," she replied excitedly.

84

"You should not breathe a word to anyone other than Gladys who must be sworn to secrecy," Joanna directed. "Once that is done, the two of you should search every nook and cranny of Hugh's room for the money."

Mrs. Marlowe nodded with avarice at the suggestion. "Gladys comes tomorrow to help me clean and that is when we shall begin."

"I must stress again, you are not to utter a word to anyone."

"Not a word," she vowed.

Joanna took my arm and, turning for the door, said, "We shall arrange for you to be notified of any change in your son's condition."

"Thank you for your visit and kind advice, dear lady."

We departed into a misty noon, with the sun only beginning to break through. The small town appeared much livelier than before, with motor vehicles and horse-drawn wagons now on the main thoroughfare. After crossing a busy intersection, we strolled along a narrow footpath that was crowded with shoppers who gave us subtle, curious glances. The noise surrounding us was loud enough to drown out our conversation, but we continued to keep our voices low to avoid being overheard.

"Why were you so certain Hugh Marlowe had a hidden cache of cash in his mother's dwelling?" I asked.

"You must consider the amount of money he had on hand," Joanna replied. "The blackmailer had already received a total of ten thousand pounds from Sir William, and I think it fair to assume that Hugh Marlowe was given at least ten percent for his participation. That sum would obviously incriminate him and thus assure his silence and allegiance. Now I ask you—where would he safeguard one thousand pounds? He could not open an account at a bank, for that large an amount would certainly arouse suspicion, particularly with his financial background. Nor could he carry it around Canary Wharf where street robberies are all too common. And most surely he could not hide it in his room at the pub, which in all likelihood does not have a locked door, and, if it did, the pub owner and others would have a key. So where would he hide such a tidy sum?"

"At his mother's house," I supplied the obvious answer.

"And he no doubt reverted to an old childhood habit and used the same hiding places he employed as a youngster."

"Which would be located in his bedroom."

"Quite so, for old habits are difficult to break, particularly when stress is applied."

I placed my arm around Joanna's narrow waist and, pulling her closer, kissed her, whilst reminding myself to never underestimate my dear wife and her intentions.

"What was the loving act for, may I ask?" she inquired.

"You knew where Hugh Marlowe's cache of money was hidden, and that was the purpose of our visit," I replied. "You wished to make certain his mother would be well provided for in the event of her son's death. It was a very noble act on your part."

"I have my moments," she said modestly.

"Would we have made the visit had you known of the recently issued life insurance policy?"

"Of course, for there would still be clues to be found, and the addition of two hundred pounds to the hidden cache makes for a very comfortable life during the poor woman's last days on earth."

"It is unfortunate that she will never be aware of your kindness."

Joanna shrugged unconcerned. "Did you know that in some religions anonymous gifts are considered the most treasured?"

"You don't say."

"I do say," she quipped. "And now let us put aside idle chatter and focus on the major clue that was uncovered. Which, of course, was the relationship between the two blackmailers."

"Brothers, mind you!" I said, shaking my head in astonishment. "I had no idea."

"Nor did I, but I did wonder why Halderman chose a young actor to be a participant in the blackmail."

"Who, he disposed of as soon as Hugh Marlowe became a vulnerability."

"There may have been another reason why Halderman had his brother dispatched."

"Pray tell, what?"

"Perhaps Hugh Marlowe became greedy and demanded a larger share of the ransom," she answered. "Here we have a blackmailer blackmailing another blackmailer, and Halderman is smart enough to know that the blackmailing never ends until the subject is penniless or dead."

"Good God!" I blurted out. "How can one brother kill another?"

"With no hesitation," Joanna said, as we approached the train station. "Consult your Bible and you will find that Cain killed Abel for far less."

11

NEW REVELATIONS

U pon returning to our rooms at Baker Street, we found my father smartly attired in a pressed tweed suit and preparing to depart. His knee was apparently well healed, for there was now a lively bounce to his step.

"About to take a stroll, Father?" I inquired.

"I am afraid my leisure time is over, for I have been summoned to St. Bart's because of my expertise on catastrophic head wounds."

The news was almost too good to be true. "Have you been asked to be a consultant on Hugh Marlowe?"

"I wish that were the case," he replied. "But rather, they want my insight into wartime head wounds, of which I am most familiar. With the war continuing to rage on the continent, more than a few of our lads have suffered such injuries and have been returned to England for treatment. A small ward has been set aside at St. Bart's for these soldiers."

"Ah, yes," I said, drawing their connection to my father, who had served as an army surgeon during the Second Afghan War. He had more experience with missile-induced head wounds than all the surgeons in London combined. "I recall the superb lecture you gave on that very subject at grand rounds some years back."

"I never thought that my military service would elicit so much attention," my father reminisced. "Nor did I ever believe that the article we published in *Lancet* would command such interest thirty years later."

"It was a notable contribution on the treatment of horrific head wounds, Father," I said.

"Let me hope it applies to those men who now lay in coma at St. Bartholomew's."

"Whatever the outcome," Joanna noted, "I am certain the families of those fallen soldiers will greatly appreciate your practiced hand."

"I fear there is little I can offer from a therapeutic standpoint."

"But even the smallest assistance may be of value."

"Let us pray that is the case, but in all likelihood those poor lads will remain in their hospital beds until death decides to move in."

"Did the surgeon at St. Bart's mention how many wounded were on the ward that was set aside for them?"

"Four, with several additional beds available for those surely to arrive later."

Joanna's eyes brightened as she considered the accommodations. "Is it possible that Hugh Marlowe, with his terrible head wound, now occupies one of those empty beds?"

"It is indeed likely, for such an arrangement would allow a single nurse to circulate amongst those patients so afflicted," my father responded. "There is a nursing shortage at St. Bart's, you see."

"With that in mind, Watson, it could prove quite helpful if you were to offer your services to the wounded actor as well," my wife suggested. "A careful study of the actor's wound could provide us with information of the utmost importance. In particular, I need to know its dimensions, and the exact location where the blank missile entered the skull. If there is an exit wound, all the better, for its site could tell us the angle from which the shot was fired. And finally, a detailed examination of the tissue surrounding the entrance wound could be most revealing. If possible, use a magnifying glass to determine whether any charring is present."

"I shall do my best," said my father. "But why all this sudden interest in Marlowe's head wound?"

"Because there are now pieces of this strange puzzle which do not fit together," she replied. "Allow me to present to you the most unexpected turn of events in the blackmailing of Sir William's family."

Joanna stepped over to the Persian slipper for a Turkish cigarette, which she lighted, and promptly began pacing. I noticed her stride was more rapid than usual, indicating her brain was shifting into a higher, more exciting gear. Point by point, she related our findings to Watson, who would serve as her sounding board, just as he had for Sherlock Holmes. She began with a description of Ms. Marlowe's humble home and her poor medical condition before emphasizing Hugh Marlowe's apparent rise to some fame and fortune, and his eagerness to share his newly acquired earnings with his dear mother. Then she went on to recount the life insurance policy issued to the actor eight days prior to his shooting, and the near-certain existence of hidden money in the Marlowe abode. She saved the best for last.

"And now, my dear Watson, you must hold on to your derby for the most astounding revelation," she said. "We were told by his mother that Hugh had a half-brother of a particularly nasty nature who had long ago divorced himself from any family connection and was now quite well-to-do. Would you care to submit a guess as to the name of this unpleasant half-brother?"

My father shrugged his response. "I haven't the faintest idea."

"Try Eric Halderman on for size."

My father's jaw dropped. "What?"

Joanna allowed for the astonishing divulgement to set in before continuing. "What a merry little family of blackmailers we have here. The half-brother brings in his young brother, for he knows of the actor's deep poverty and desire to support their mother, whom the lad loves dearly."

"But would such a clever scoundrel trust his half-brother?" he asked.

"I suspect it was not a matter of trust, but one of involvement," she replied. "The actor would dare not speak of his well-paid participation, for blackmailing—particularly of a high official—carries a most severe punishment. Young, handsome actors do not look forward to a long sentence in one of His Majesty's cruel prisons."

"Yes, yes," my father agreed, now connecting all the newly gathered clues. "But with Hugh Marlowe's suddenly increased income, why does he continue to work as a server in a pub and live in a single room above that establishment?"

"Perhaps he wished to conceal the criminal origin of his newfound wealth," Joanna surmised.

"But you stated earlier that Hugh Marlowe has now risen on the stage and, with his recently acquired position, he will have a comfortable income," my father argued. "That widely known information would explain his greatly increased income."

"What makes you so certain that Hugh Marlowe has this new, elevated role on stage?"

"Well, first off he bragged of such a promotion to his mother."

"An empty boast to explain his more than generous gifts to her."

"But his rise on the stage was duly noted in all the newspaper reports following his shooting," my father countered.

"Pray tell, what was the source of this information?" Joanna asked.

"I am not certain," he replied hesitantly.

"Nor am I, but I know better than to trust the accuracy of a newspaper article which was rushed into print," she cautioned. "Please remember that the shooting occurred late in the evening, yet this happening found its way into the following morning's newspapers."

"Are you suggesting the actor's rise to fame was fabricated?"

"More likely exaggerated, which is a curse newspapers have when a story must be hurried into print."

"But how does one separate the fact from fiction?"

"By obtaining a more reliable source," Joanna replied. "Namely, one who is acutely aware of all that occurs on the London stage."

"Such as?"

"A highly successful theatrical agent."

After extinguishing her cigarette, my wife reached for the telephone and dialed a number she knew by memory. A moment later she was speaking with Aaron Edelstone.

"And good afternoon to you, Mr. Edelstone," Joanna greeted the agent. "But I am afraid my call carries unpleasant news with it. One of our daughters has come down with a severe case of scarlet fever and our physician has prescribed a prolonged period of bed rest. I must of course cancel the planned birthday party until she is completely recovered."

"Yes, yes, it can be quite contagious, and we are taking every precaution to prevent its spread."

"Well, thank you for your concern," my wife continued on. "The two actors we were so impressed with will have to be notified."

She listened at length before stating, "I did read of the accidental shooting in the newspaper, but had no idea it was the same actor who auditioned for us. The article noted that the victim was a prominent actor which indicated to me he would not be seeking such a small part."

Again, she concentrated on the incoming response, nodding to herself as if agreeing with every word. "Quite minor, then. That would surely explain his need for additional work."

She nodded a final time and said, "We shall contact you on that happy day our daughter recovers completely."

Joanna replaced the receiver into its cradle and turned to us with a satisfied expression on her face. "As I suspected, the newspaper article was filled with inaccuracies and inconsistencies. First off, Hugh Marlowe was and continued to be an actor of little notice. His role on the St. Martin's Lane stage was brief and he was an understudy, no less. His pay was minimal, which accounts for his job seeking. Moreover, the shooting during the play was not a major scene in the play, but had been inserted to heighten the drama."

"Can we trust the word of a theatrical agent?" my father asked. "For they, too, are known for their exaggeration."

"In this instance I am confident we can believe his descriptions, for he is most familiar with the play, having seen it in its entirety. You see, he represents its starring actress and watched her rehearse every line."

"Which throws us into a bit of a conundrum," my father concluded.

"That it does, Watson, for now we cannot place any trust in the written word of the articles we so carefully read," she said, before admonishing herself. "I should have remembered my father's disdain for secondhand evidence. Unless it is personally verified, it has little value. With that in mind, Watson, you must somehow manage to observe every aspect of the actor's wound."

"I shall give it my best try, but in all likelihood the wound will be tightly bandaged, which will limit my examination."

"Duly noted, but the bandage may have separate blood stains indicating the presence of both an entrance and exit wound."

"And as you noted earlier, that will provide us with important infor-mation on the exact angle from which the shot was delivered," my father recalled. "In essence, it would tell us the position of the pistol, and be a major factor in determining if suicide was in play here."

"It will tell us more than that, Watson, for blank rounds are made of wadded paper which do not have nearly the penetrating power of a metal missile," Joanna elucidated. "An exit wound would indicate the round was made of metal, and thus would not have been fired by a stage prop."

"Is it possible that someone surreptitiously inserted a genuine bullet for the blank?" my father asked.

Joanna waved off the notion. "That is a remote possibility, for it is most unlikely that Hugh Marlowe would tell others of his plan to secretly visit the theater and use the pistol as a prop."

"You raise an excellent point," he agreed before sighing resignedly. "But we remain faced with the difficulty of performing a proper examination of the head wound, for such injuries bleed profusely and thus stain the entire bandage, making it impossible to determine if the bullet had an exit as well."

"It is a problem you must surmount," she implored. "A close examination of the wound would provide a wealth of data."

"Of course, if Scotland Yard were involved, it would be a simple matter for Lestrade to include our presence when the bandage was changed."

"Scotland Yard's involvement is a must at this juncture," Joanna said. "But, as we discussed earlier, it has to be accomplished with no mention of blackmail."

"And how does one go about arranging that?"

"With carefully constructed guile."

There was a soft rap on the door and Miss Hudson looked in. "Your taxi has arrived, Dr. Watson," she announced.

"Thank you, Miss Hudson," said my father, and reached for his derby.

"May I accompany you to St. Bart's, where a desk packed with work awaits me?" I requested.

"With pleasure," he replied.

"And with the two of you on your way, I can make a final, most important phone call," said my wife.

"To what end?" I asked.

"To encourage Lestrade to invite our participation."

"But he will demand a reason."

"And I will provide one," said Joanna, who, after lighting another Turkish cigarette, went back to pacing, for there were other pieces of this tangled puzzle which commanded her attention.

12

HUGH MARLOWE

On my arrival at St. Bart's, I was met by a desk overflowing with paper-work which had accumulated during my absence. Most of the neat stacks were reports to be read and signed, but there were also letters which required a response and phone calls to be returned. I was dealing with the final stack when my secretary knocked on the open door and hurried in.

"Dr. Watson, you father just called and needs your immediate presence in the surgery amphitheater," she said with urgency.

"Did he state a reason?"

"No, sir, but the tone of his voice suggested the sooner you arrive, the better."

"Thank you, Rose."

I dashed out of my office and into the corridor, then up the stairs, all whilst wondering why my immediate presence was needed. Surely, it involved Hugh Marlowe. But how so? Was there some life-saving procedure being performed which offered a modicum of hope? Or was the actor near death, and would his departure on the operating table provide us with the opportunity for a rapid examination of the deceased before the body was carried away? Or at least, would a seat close to the ongoing surgery afford us a clear view of Marlowe's head, which might tell us if there was both an entrance and exit wound?

I hurried into the amphitheater and located my father seated in the front row, which was an honor given to senior, retired physicians. The operating table itself was surrounded by masked surgeons and nurses, the most prominent of whom was Mr. Harry Askins, who was known for his expertise in skull injuries. The air smelled of ether.

"What has transpired, Father?" I asked, taking a seat beside him.

"On the surgery ward, the patient had a massive seizure, with his arms and legs flailing about," he said. "With all the violent movement, the bandages flew off and the wound began spurting blood. Firm pressure was applied, but to no avail, and thus he was rushed to the operating room."

"Were you able to observe the wound?"

My father shook his head in response. "I was three beds down, attending a young soldier with half his skull blown off by a mortar round. When I looked over, the actor's entire head was covered with blood, as was much of his bed."

"What of the actor's current condition?"

"Unsteady, but he is somehow managing to hold on."

"Then why the urgent call?"

"Because death is on the doorstep and he will be most fortunate to survive the operation," my father replied. "If he were to expire on the table, we could move quickly and take the opportunity to examine the head wound, and thus answer Joanna's questions."

"The orderlies have the ability to sense coming death and are on alert to rapidly transport the body to the morgue."

"Which is the second reason for my call to you," he went on. "Should there be his last breaths, it is of vital importance that you and not your young associate Dr. Quinn receive the body and perform the autopsy."

"He always seems more than eager to test his newly learned forensic skills," I remarked.

"In your absence, he would be more than happy to do so, and in the process no doubt destroy much-needed clues."

"Such as cracking open the skull and removing the brain to assess the full extent of the damage."

"Whilst paying little attention to the tissue around the entrance wound."

"I shall issue a directive which states that I, and only I, am to perform autopsies on patients with head injuries, suggesting it may be of some importance to the military."

We watched the surgeon step away from the operating table and strip off his gloves. "You may close, Dr. Maycoff," he said.

My father quickly rose and took my arm. "Let us depart before Askins sees us and inquires about our interest in the grievously wounded Hugh Marlowe."

We strolled down a wide corridor, passing colleagues who waved and nodded not only to me, but to my father, who had a long and distinguished career whilst on the clinical staff at St. Bart's. When we were well out of hearing distance, my father said in a low voice, "During my stay on the surgical ward, I gathered a few tidbits of interesting information."

"Such as?"

Ahead and walking toward us was an elderly, cane-assisted physician, with badly stooped posture. "Watson, how good to see you up and about," he said cordially.

"It is a pleasure to be up and about, and to see you again," my father returned the greeting.

Once we were clear of others who might overhear our conversation, I asked again, "Pray tell, what tidbits?"

"There is obvious expense when one occupies a bed at St. Bart's," my father replied. "I have learned that the government will cover the cost of the badly wounded soldiers. But I could not discover who will be paying for the impoverished actor."

"Surely, there has to be a guarantor."

"We should find out who that individual is."

"Not Eric Halderman, I would think."

"Do not be so certain, for the sister caring for the wounded lot told me that Marlowe has had a frequent visitor who is most concerned. Would you care to render a guess as to the identity of the visitor?"

"Eric Halderman," I replied at once.

"The very same."

"He is here no doubt to make certain his half-brother remains in a comatose state and thus unable to speak of their criminal adventure," I reasoned.

"Of course, and according to the sister he wishes to be notified immediately on his half-brother's demise," my father added. "Which will occur in the near future, for there is no hope the young actor will survive. I was told by the sister that infection has set in and the end is near."

We reached the elevator and pushed the button to signal our need. My father glanced over his shoulder to assure our further conversation could not be overheard.

"Another thought came to mind whilst I was examining a soldier with a similar head wound," he went on. "Our country is at war and in desperate need of fighting men. Is that not so?"

"Quite so."

"Then why has an apparently healthy, young man, such as Hugh Marlowe, not conscripted into the military?"

"There must have been a reason for his exclusion."

"Yes, but what?" my father asked as the elevator door opened.

13

GUILE

Whilst she was clearing our breakfast table, my father complimented Miss Hudson. "I must say, the bacon was again prepared to perfection, with each strip crisp and tasty."

"Thank you, Dr. Watson," she replied. "It was prepared with a recipe that has been passed down through the generations."

"With adequate amounts of butter, no doubt," Joanna surmised.

"And a touch of pepper which must be carefully applied," she noted and handed us the morning newspapers. "These two were promptly delivered, but the remainder were delayed by last night's heavy snowstorm."

"Very good," my father said, passing the *Guardian* to Joanna, whilst opening the *Daily Telegraph*. This was the usual order of reading, with me in line for the third newspaper whose arrival was yet to come. I watched my father quickly scan the front page, as he viewed the headlines to determine which ones interested him the most. "Ah," he said with satisfaction. "I see here the St. Martin's Lane shooting has again been brought to the front page."

"Are there any new revelations?" Joanna asked.

"We shall see," my father responded, now lifting the newspaper to read the lower half of a long column. His eyes narrowed at something which obviously drew his attention. "Well, well, it seems we have a reporter who has delved deeply into the supposedly accidental shooting."

"Supposedly?" she asked pointedly.

"His words, not mine," he replied and focused on another item in the article. "There is also mention of the recently issued insurance policy on the young actor's life, with his impoverished mother being the sole beneficiary."

"So, for once we seem to have a newspaper reporter who has the skills of an investigator," I remarked.

"Oh, and there is more," my father continued on. "I see a correction regarding the actor's role in the upcoming play. In contrast to what was published earlier, Mr. Marlowe had the position of understudy in a relatively minor role. All of which asks the question of whether the shooting was truly accidental."

"How interesting," Joanna commented. "For the very same words appeared in a similar article in the *Daily Telegraph*."

"Perhaps the two reporters collaborated in this now important investigation," I suggested.

"I would think that is the case," my father concurred. "Why, the reporter even tells of the poor actor's part-time position as a server in a Canary Wharf pub."

"That is true in the *Daily Telegraph* article as well," my wife noted.

"Surely such a collaborative effort has to be commended," said I.

"I would not be so quick to praise them," she warned.

"Why so?"

"Because of their professional nature," Joanna replied. "In your wildest imagination, could you envision two reporters from competing newspapers collaborating on such an interesting story? They would slit each other's throats over a finding which could break this story wide open and bring great acclaim. Furthermore, how in the world did two reporters of little note discover all these startling facts in less than twenty-four hours?"

"And with such remarkable accuracy, no less," my father mused aloud. "Somebody must have informed them."

"Yes, of course. But who?" she asked, as a most mischievous smile crossed her face. "Who could have been responsible?"

"You!" my father and I blurted out simultaneously.

"Why would I do such a thing?" she asked, still smiling at us.

"To entice Scotland Yard," my father answered at once, then shook his head gently. "Time and time again, my dear Joanna, you remind me of Holmes. He was also adept at drawing the former Lestrade's attention when needed."

"It was truly quite simple, with all the necessary pieces in place," she went on, deflecting the praise. "We have an interesting story about to fade from view, for the shooting has been deemed accidental in an already troubled world. Then, along comes an anonymous phone call to the editors of London's prominent newspapers. The facts given to them were easily verified, with phone calls to officials in Slough and visits to the pub in Canary Wharf. And suddenly they have a fascinating story which includes poverty, St. Martin's Lane, a recently issued life insurance policy, and a shooting which may not be accidental, but rather murderous or even suicidal."

"The public will devour it," I said, which was what the others were thinking. "They will read every line twice."

"And so will the insurance company, with the distinct possibility of suicide now being considered," Joanna assured us. "For there will be no payment to the beneficiary if the owner of the policy did himself in."

"Will they send their own investigators?"

"This case is far out of their league, so they will no doubt put pressure on Scotland Yard to do the heavy work for them."

"How can you be certain they will do that?"

"Because in my anonymous phone call to the insurance company, I suggested this would be the smart move and the one most likely to bring the matter to a rapid conclusion."

"Did they not demand to know your name?"

"At first, but then they became too occupied jotting down the tearful story of a struggling young actor who was trying desperately to support an impoverished mother, whom he loved dearly," Joanna replied. "And now, with these new revelations, intense pressure from the newspapers, the public, and the insurance company will force Scotland Yard to become involved, with Inspector Lestrade leading the investigation, for he is the best of the lot."

"Perhaps Lestrade will be tempted to solve the case on his own, and thus gather all the glory," I predicted. "We all know how much he loves the limelight."

"But he is no fool and will quickly realize that this tangled mystery is far beyond his depth," she said. "He is also aware that once the case is solved, it is he and Scotland Yard who will receive all the credit."

"With no mention of you," I grumbled.

"That is of little consequence," she responded, with a gesture of indifference. "For it keeps us in his good graces, and when we require his involvement, he is more than eager to join the fray."

"When do you believe Lestrade will call?"

"He will be sitting in our parlor before nightfall," Joanna foretold. "But prior to the inspector's arrival, there is additional information we must gather from an impeccable source."

"Which is?"

"Ned Bailey, who was once London's premier blackmailer," she said, reaching for her bonnet. "Do you care to join us, Watson?"

"I would be happy to do so, but my presence is needed at St. Bart's, where we are contemplating the construction of a plate to cover the skull defect in one of our patients on the soldier's ward."

"Is there hope for survival?"

"Perhaps, with a little good fortune."

"Would the same hold true for Hugh Marlowe?"

"I am afraid not, for the head wound is deep and infected, with death now waiting on his doorstep," my father replied.

"And here again Lestrade would play a pivotal role," Joanna added. "If Marlowe's shooting continues to be deemed accidental, there will be no requirement for autopsy, and that being the case, his caring half-brother would insist there was no need for a postmortem examination and that a proper funeral, with the body intact, be done as soon as possible."

"Is he that clever?"

"And then some."

14

NED BAILEY

During our ride to Lower Lambeth, Joanna told me the remarkable story of how she saved the life of a once notorious blackmailer. Ned Bailey was a master craftsman at this trade and was so skilled that Scotland Yard never came close to apprehending him until he was double-crossed by a partner in crime. When Bailey arrived at an agreed-upon site to pick up the ransom, he was surrounded by police and fled, but left behind his hat, which unfortunately had his name engraved on the inner band. He was convicted and sentenced to a five-year stay at Pentonville, one of His Majesty's harshest prisons. There, his diabetes worsened and, despite his daughter's plea for early release, he remained imprisoned. His daughter, Pamela, believed her father to have been framed and came to Joanna as a last resort. Ordinarily, my wife does not involve herself in such cases, but this one appealed to her because of Pamela's sincerity. In a matter of days, Joanna convincingly showed that the convicted man's hat, which was found at the crime scene, did not belong to him. She had the inner band of the hat tested for glucose and none was detected, which proved the hat did not belong to Bailey, for perspiration of diabetics is laden with glucose and should have accumulated in the inner band. The framed blackmailer, going blind and in failing health, was released to the care of his daughter.

Our taxi came to a stop in front of a new row house, which had freshly painted shutters and a colorful flower bed outside its window. The driver was given a five-pound note to await our return. It required only a single rap on the door before it opened and we were warmly greeted by a plump, attractive woman, who took Joanna's hand and brought it up to her cheek.

"Oh, Mrs. Watson, what a pleasure to see you again," Pamela said.

"It is my pleasure," Joanna responded. "I hope you do not mind that I have my husband with me."

"Not at all, for he, too, is welcome," Pamela said and escorted us into a nicely furnished parlor that was overheated by a glowing fireplace. Seated before the burning logs was a thin, frail man who was attired in a thick, woolen turtleneck sweater. He had a blank stare upon his face, which was often seen in the sightless.

"Dad, Mrs. Watson and her husband are here to see you," said Pamela.

"Jolly good!" Bailey replied, as a wide smile came to his face. "Welcome to both of you."

"It was kind of you to make time for us," Joanna said.

"Time is something I have an abundance of," Bailey remarked. "And I am delighted to share as much of it as you wish."

"Excellent," said Joanna. "For I have questions which relate to your former profession."

"So I thought, but just allow me to thank you once again for delivering me from hell and saving my life in the bargain."

"It was not difficult." Joanna played down the achievement.

"Not for the daughter of Sherlock Holmes," he said. "But now let us turn to the purpose of your visit, for I know your time is most valuable."

"I need information on Eric Halderman."

"A snake!" Bailey replied at once.

"How so?"

"He was the one who so cleverly framed me and sent me to that hell on earth called Pentonville."

"I require details."

"And you shall have them," he commented. "May I inquire as to your interest in Eric Halderman?"

"It is a most confidential matter, and I must insist that our conversation remains within the confines of this room."

"It shall," Bailey pledged. "And I trust you will excuse my daughter, Pamela, as she busies herself with a trip to the greengrocer."

"I shall be on my way, having already forgotten the mention of Eric Halderman," she vowed. "But I cannot resist the urge for Mrs. Watson to bring nothing but misery to that lowest form of life."

Joanna made no promises as Pamela bundled up in a topcoat and heavy scarf before departing the parlor. Only when the front door was firmly closed did my wife proceed with her inquiry. "So you knew him well."

"But not well enough, for I placed my trust in him and should have known better," he answered, with an edge to his voice. "I take it he is still practicing his trade."

"With some skill."

"He is a clever one, but evil down to his marrow."

"Pray tell how your paths crossed."

"It was his doing," Bailey replied. "At the very same time, we were both blackmailing the same target, a bloke named Harrington, who had some very strange sexual proclivities. We had photographs of the banker actually performing these acts and he was willing to pay dearly for them. Of course, this began some years ago long before my stay at Pentonville."

Joanna's brow went up, for this was the banker who committed suicide for his apparent mismanagement of Lady Wellesley's account at Lloyd's of London. My wife and I exchanged knowing glances, for here was the explanation for John Morton Harrington's criminal plundering of the stately woman's wealth. He was being blackmailed and trying desperately to save his good name. On being confronted by Scotland Yard as the individual being blackmailed, Harrington fabricated a story that involved the misdeeds of a family member he wished to protect and wanted the matter closed. But Scotland Yard remained suspicious and began to look into the source of Harrington's blackmail payments. He eventually realized the police were examining his banking position and thus was prevented from further draining Lady Wellesley's deposits. When he could no longer pay the ransom, he took his own life rather than face the consequences.

I watched Bailey carefully pack a pipe with tobacco and light it, all the while thinking he had once been a despicable blackmailer, but to my wife he was nothing more than a much needed source of information, who owed her a favor.

"So you and Halderman decided to become partners," Joanna said, breaking the silence.

"It seemed like a good idea at the time," Bailey replied. "With of course an even split of the ransom."

"Was there some argument you had with Halderman over this arrangement?" Joanna asked.

"Not at first," Bailey answered. "He thought it best we combine our photographs into a single collection and slowly dole them out, so as to prolong the payments. He actually invited me to his mansion to discuss such a plan."

"Tell me of the meeting, and here I will require details."

"At the appointed time of late afternoon, I traveled out to Hampstead Heath where he had a bloody big limestone mansion. Once there, I entered a grand library and was greeted by this small, thin man, with carefully groomed gray hair and thin lips that never smiled. Halderman arose from behind a king-sized desk to study the photographs I had brought with me, then opened the safe that held his."

"It must have been a quite sturdy safe to contain such valuable documents," Joanna surmised.

Bailey hesitated whilst thinking back. "It was not that large—maybe the size of a night table—but it was an unbreachable Chubb, with an outer combination lock and an inner one which could only be opened with a special key. There was a most unusual feature to the safe, in that it stood on four metal legs, each of which was bolted to the floor. I had never seen one like it and assumed it to be bespoke. I can assure you that the very best safecrackers in all England could not break into that safe. And if they tried, they would be met by a bloody big rottweiler who sat by it and eyed anyone who came close."

"A most dependable guard, then."

"Aye, but there was more. In addition to the monster dog, I was watched by a manservant, a brute of a man, who was tall and broad-shouldered, with hands the size of a ham. He had the coarse features of a Slav, with a stare that would cause the bravest of men to back off."

"One can only surmise there were more than a few priceless items in that safe."

"It appeared to be packed with papers and envelopes, none of which I could describe until he placed before me the photographs of the banker in a most telling activity. They were somewhat different from those I possessed, so we agreed to combine our efforts and slowly suck the banker dry, with the two of us alternating the pickups of the ransom. I considered it a worthwhile proposition."

"Am I correct in assuming you were wearing your customary derby at the meeting?" asked Joanna.

"I was and I handed it to the manservant as I entered the library. He examined it briefly before hanging it on a nearby rack, at which time he no doubt noticed my engraved name on the inner band." Bailey paused as a look of anger crossed his face. "And that was the very beginning of me being framed. With me out of the way and stuck in dreadful Pentonville, there was no need for Eric Halderman to divide the payments from the banker."

"You chose bad company to associate with."

"Which nearly cost me my life."

"With all the arrangements having been made, I take it your meeting ended."

"Quite abruptly, I must say, for it was near six, at which time Halderman always dined."

"That is rather early for supper, I would think."

"But that is his custom, for he told me the urge to sleep came promptly at seven, at which time he was comfortably under the covers."

"The man has a somewhat unusual body clock," I noted.

"That he does, for he awakens at midnight to begin his daily activities," Bailey added. "He revealed that schedule as if he was honored and privileged to have it."

"You have given us a most excellent description of Eric Halderman," said my wife.

"Is there anything more you need to know of him?"

"Only why neither you nor your daughter mentioned Eric Halderman's involvement to me or Scotland Yard whilst I was striving to gain your release from Pentonville?"

"I had no choice but to remain silent, for if I were to incriminate Halderman he would see to it that my dear Pamela would meet a most painful death," the former blackmailer replied. "Such a threat no longer concerns me now that the daughter of Sherlock Holmes is closing in on the devil."

"Let us say simply that I have him in my sights," Joanna said, then gave Halderman's schedule further consideration. "Are you certain he always awakens promptly at midnight, with only five hours of sleep?"

"So I was told."

"A strange habit," she said, and appeared to docket the unusual fact.

"Quite so indeed," Bailey agreed. "On that note, I departed and was joined by Bruno, the manservant. I had a taxi waiting at the front entrance, and Bruno requested a lift to the nearest underground station, where he would board a train to Whitechapel. Since my drive south would take us through that district, I offered him a ride to his location. As we drove away, I could see Halderman watching us from the large bay window in the library."

"Was that the only window in the library?" Joanna asked.

"There was a somewhat smaller one behind his desk, but I could not tell what it overlooked," he replied. "Is that of importance?"

"Only if it, too, offered a clear view of the frontage," she said. "With that in mind, I believe Halderman wanted you to see him watching your every move, which suggested he would do so in the future."

"The conniving bugger," Bailey spat out.

"Beyond any doubt." Joanna went on with the subtle questioning. "Tell me of your taxi ride to Whitechapel with Bruno."

"There is not much to tell," he said, without giving the matter thought. "He stated he was going to the Polish-English Club where he had friends and where polka music was played every Friday night."

"Was he a dancer?"

"He didn't say, but on departing the taxi he asked the driver if he could return to the Whitechapel address for a return fare to Hampstead Heath at ten-thirty sharp."

"Did the driver agree?"

"He did," Bailey said and had yet another recollection. "And now that I think back, there was one other unusual feature the manservant had. He continued to perspire excessively despite the cold weather. Over and over he had to mop the perspiration from his forehead, and even rubbed his palms against his trousers to remove their wetness. I could detect no odor, but then again he had the rear window down."

The front door opened and Bailey's daughter entered, carrying a basket of groceries.

"Am I too early?" she asked.

"Your timing is perfect," Joanna replied, rising to her feet. "I must tell you that your father was most helpful."

"I am so pleased he was, and as a reward, Father, I have brought with me the newest Braille papers for your reading pleasure."

"Jolly good!" Bailey blurted out, obviously delighted.

"We shall be on our way, then," said Joanna. "And thank you again for meeting with us."

"It was a pleasure being in your company once again," the blind man replied, his fingers already rapidly running over the Braille paper.

Pamela led us out to the footpath and spoke the warmest of words to my wife. "God bless you, Mrs. Watson, for your wonderful kindness."

We waved farewell and strolled away as the door closed behind us. Before we crossed the street to our waiting taxi, I could not help but remark, "Does it not bother you that you were responsible for having a guilty blackmailer released from prison?"

"None whatsoever," Joanna replied. "He was convicted on false evidence, and thus the verdict had to be withdrawn. If the Crown wished to retry him, they were free to do so. But they chose not to because of insufficient evidence, which proved to be a blessing on his part and on ours as well. My good deed paid a healthy dividend, you see."

"For it provided us with a much-needed source of information."

"That it did," she said, rubbing her hands together gleefully. "Now we know the location of the photographs of Anne Atwood, which Halderman no doubt checks on before retiring promptly at seven. He then awakens at midnight to set his evil doings in motion."

"And the more misery he inflicts, the deeper he sleeps."

"So it is with the evilest of men," Joanna concurred. "We also learned that Bruno, the manservant, departs on Friday nights at six sharp for a soiree at the Polish-English Club in Whitechapel and does not return until after ten. Thus, the library in Halderman's mansion is unattended every Friday evening."

"If you are considering a break-in, you must keep in mind the presence of a vicious rottweiler and a Chubb safe, with a double lock, which seems impenetrable," I cautioned. "How does one overcome those obstacles?"

"With the utmost of care," she replied as we entered the taxi.

"The hound could be put to sleep," I suggested in a quiet voice.

"True."

"But how does one open a Chubb safe with a double lock?"

"That may not be necessary," she said, resting her head back and closing her eyes, obviously giving the obstacle additional thought.

15

LESTRADE

It was near five that afternoon when Miss Hudson rapped on our door to announce the arrival of Inspector Lestrade. We rapidly cleared the parlor of all evidence related to the blackmailing of Sir William's family, making certain to conceal the scandalous photograph of Anne Atwood and the detailed sketch of Eric Halderman's library, with all of its contents clearly depicted.

As my father placed the sketch in a desk drawer, he commented, "It was quite remarkable how Ned Bailey recalled Halderman's library with such clarity. And even more remarkable how he knew of the blackmailer's peculiar sleeping habits."

"One might think that some time ago he was thinking of a break-in," Joanna surmised.

"But that monstrous dog and impenetrable safe no doubt stood in his way," I said.

"Formidable obstacles, but not impossible to overcome," she said.

My father asked, "Do you believe Bailey thought that you, too, were considering such a bold entrance?"

"He would have to be a dimwit not to."

Our conversation was interrupted by a brief rap on the door.

"How much should we reveal to Lestrade?" I asked quickly.

"As little as possible," my wife replied. "Allow the inspector to fill in all the blank spaces with a minimum of prompting."

I opened the door on a welcoming note. "How good to see you again, Inspector."

"And I, you," he said, and trudged into our parlor like a weary man at the end of a long day. The heavy bags under his eyes attested to my conclusion. "I am sorry to intrude on you so late in the afternoon."

"You are never considered an intrusion," Joanna said and motioned to an overstuffed chair by the blazing fireplace. "Pray have a seat and tell us of your visit, which I assume has some urgency."

"It does indeed, for the commissioner himself wishes your assistance in a most difficult case," Lestrade replied and reached in the pocket of his topcoat for a lengthy, coiled strip of leather that he placed on his lap. He then extracted a small cigar from his jacket, which he lit and sat back to enjoy its flavor. "You will excuse me if I take a moment, for it has been a very long day, with journeys to Slough and Canary Wharf, then a return trip to Slough before ending up in the office of the Channel Insurance Company who guard a policy as if it is the Holy Grail."

"The Holy Grail, you say?" Joanna queried.

"Ah, but I get ahead of myself," he said and took another satisfying draw on his cigar. "I am here in regards to the supposedly accidental shooting of an actor on a stage at St. Martin's Lane. You no doubt have read of the accident in various newspapers."

"That we have."

"Well then, what has been reported and what happened do not always coincide, so allow me to give you the facts which I myself have verified," Lestrade went on. "I shall begin at the very beginning, for I was called to the scene shortly after the shooting. On my arrival, I found the young actor lying on the stage, with a gunshot wound to the side of his head."

"Could you give us the precise location?" Joanna requested.

With an index finger the inspector pointed to an area well behind the right temple. "There was a fair amount of blood around it, but it was undoubtedly the entrance wound."

"Was there an exit wound?"

"None that I noticed, but then again he was lying in a pool of blood. In any event, the pistol which fired the shot was beside him, with its barrel free of any warmth. There were no other rounds in the weapon. The stage was empty of any additional props except for this strip of leather." He held the coil up for our inspection. "It is curious that the stage manager could not recognize it as a prop, so we were of the opinion that the young actor had brought the strip of leather to his rehearsal."

"For what purpose?" my wife asked.

Lestrade shrugged unconcerned. "That remains unknown."

Joanna gave the matter further consideration. "Where exactly was the coil found?"

"Near the tightly drawn curtain."

"I should like to examine the coil."

"Of course," the inspector said and passed it over to my wife.

Joanna unwound the coil and held it out for all to see. It was well over two feet in length, no more than half an inch in width, and made of sturdy, unshined leather. My wife paid particular attention to its very ends before she used her magnifying glass to carefully inspect the strip in its entirety. "May I keep this for further examination?"

"You may," Lestrade acquiesced, but could not control his curiosity. "Did you discover anything of interest?"

"Nothing of certainty," she replied, but the sparkle in her eyes said otherwise. "Please continue with your description of the shooting."

"I found the nighttime custodian badly shaken, but able to tell me what had transpired prior to the accident. He had allowed the young actor entrance because such requests are not uncommon in those appearing on the stage for the first time. He occupied himself with other duties in the depth of the theater when, in a matter of minutes, he heard a shot ring out. In a full sprint, he dashed up to the stage and came upon the badly wounded actor. He then promptly summoned Scotland Yard."

"Was he quite certain no others were in the theater at that late hour?"

"Quite so, and he emphasized that all doors remained locked, which would have prevented any surreptitious entrances."

"Did you test the rear doors behind the stage itself?"

Lestrade nodded his response. "They were locked and secured."

"Please be good enough to describe the locks that you encountered."

"They were sturdy Chubbs which had been installed on all doors some time ago because of several break-ins."

"Rather expensive locks for a theater, one would think."

"Not when you consider the repeated loss of costumes and stage equipment, which needed to be replaced at a cost of over a thousand pounds."

"And only the custodian has the keys?"

"Only he."

Joanna pondered the situation at length. "Might the custodian have dozed off during the quiet time and failed to secure a side door?"

"Possibly, but his face showed no signs of recent slumber."

"Those signs quickly vanish in the face of a deadly shooting," my wife noted and, after lighting a cigarette, began her customary pacing, with her head down and a trail of white smoke following her. Back and forth she went before returning to Lestrade. "You mentioned multiple journeys to Slough and one to Canary Wharf. May we know the purpose?"

"I was verifying the accounts given in the recent newspaper articles," he replied. "The wounded actor's mother was indeed impoverished, and poor as a church mouse according to the local authorities. The young actor earned a minimum wage as an understudy, but looked after his mum as best he could. He supplemented his income by working as a server in a Canary Wharf pub, but his earning there was a meager pittance. Yet he still came by enough money to purchase a life insurance policy which named his mother as sole beneficiary to the sum of several hundred pounds."

"A lesser insurance policy may have been more within his reach," my father interjected.

"True enough, Dr. Watson, but his premium was doubled because of his heart condition."

"What sort of heart condition?"

"It was vaguely stated in the policy, which the insurance company held close to their vests," Lestrade replied. "But they allowed me to view it when threatened with a court order."

"But with the distinct possibility of suicide, which would preclude any payment, I should think the insurance company would be happy to open their files."

"So one would think, but utter secrecy on such matters seems to be their standard," he said. "For this reason, I took a return journey to Slough in order to track down the doctor who had examined the actor for his insurance policy. According to the examiner, a loud heart murmur was heard, although the patient showed no evidence of cardiac distress. So, to sum it up, we have a young actor who may or may not have shot himself accidentally. There are a variety of parties who wish this matter settled once and for all, and thus the commissioner would very much like you to assist us in bringing this case to a rapid resolution."

"We should be happy to do so," Joanna volunteered, but not too eagerly.

"The commissioner will be pleased to hear of your participation," said Lestrade. "I am to place the resources of Scotland Yard at your disposal. Where would you like to begin?"

"With the custodian at the theater," she replied. "Ten o'clock tomorrow morning would be most suitable."

"I shall make the arrangements," Lestrade said and, with a tip of his derby, prepared to depart.

"I have one further question," Joanna called out, as the inspector reached for the door. "Was the strip of leather coiled when it was discovered?"

"No, madam," he replied. "It appeared to be laid out. Is that of importance?"

"Perhaps," she said evasively and bid Lestrade a pleasant evening.

Once the inspector was well gone, Joanna flicked her cigarette into the fireplace and promptly lit another one. "Lestrade has a keen eye and his power of observation is coming along, but, for reasons beyond me, he refuses to concentrate on the most important piece of evidence in hand."

"Which is?" I asked.

"The coil of leather," she replied, as she began pacing again. "Do you not see its significance?"

When there was no answer forthcoming, she continued on. "The strip of leather is not a prop; it is out of place and does not belong. It served no purpose for the young actor, and thus it is reasonable to conclude he did not bring it to the stage."

"Then who did?"

"The man who fired the shot, of course."

"But where is the proof?" my father asked at once.

"Within the leather strip, if we are fortunate."

"And how will you uncover this evidence?"

"With a carefully applied reagent," she replied. "But first, let us set the scene for this murder. Here we have a young actor who now has yet another small role at a major theater on St. Martin's Lane. For him, it is the dream of a lifetime. However, his new position was that of an understudy, which might well pay him less than his earlier role; he may thus be depending on his share of the ransom to comfortably support his impoverished mother and himself for the foreseeable future. That is not the picture of an individual contemplating suicide. Also, note the position of the head wound which is located *well behind* the temple."

"A most awkward position," I said.

"Indeed," Joanna agreed, then extended her index finger and aimed it at the site Lestrade described. "So awkward, he would have considerable difficulty squeezing the trigger. Thus, it appears most unlikely that this was the wound of an attempted suicide, and even more unlikely this deadly wound was inflicted by a misfire. For his brief role, there was absolutely no need for the actor to bring the weapon up to the rear of the forehead. With this in mind, we can exclude suicidal and accidental causes, which leaves us with natural and homicidal explanations. Which do you choose?"

"Homicidal," my father replied at once, "but then again you have no evidence to back up that contention."

"Patience, my dear Watson, for there is more to come. It is clear how Hugh Marlowe gained entrance to the theater late at night. But what of the murderer? How did he secretly enter the theater, with all of its doors locked? And even if he found a way in, how did he silently tiptoe across the stage and catch Marlowe unaware? Remember, the theater was empty and quiet, yet you ask me to believe the murderer crept across the stage and surprised Marlowe, then overpowered him, took the weapon, and fired a blank round into the young actor's head."

"It is possible if the murderer was strong and stealthy," my father argued. "He may have actually practiced a silent approach."

"That is possible, though unlikely," said Joanna. "But assuming that scenario is correct, you will have to inform me how the murderer knew Marlowe would be rehearsing on the stage that evening."

It was a critical point, which both my father and I had overlooked. There was only one answer and I provided it. "He either told someone or perhaps invited that individual to his upcoming rehearsal."

"Which tells us the attempted murder of Hugh Marlowe was planned."

"By his half-brother Eric Halderman, no doubt."

"Of course."

"Do you believe he hired a professional assassin?"

"There was no need," Joanna responded. "His manservant Bruno performed the service for him."

"Based on what evidence, may I ask?" my father inquired.

"The strip of leather," she replied, and fetched the evidence for my father. "Give it your close eye, Watson."

My father carefully examined the strip of leather end to end, then repeated his inspection under a bright light. He completed the study using a high-powered magnifying glass before passing the strip back to my wife.

"I could only see a few scratches which I deemed to be of little significance," he said.

"Your observation is spot-on, but I am afraid your conclusion is off the mark," Joanna apprised. "Did you not see a bit of white matter in the deepest scratch?"

"I did, but I considered it debris."

"It was indeed, but a particular type of debris," she said, and laid the strip out on the workbench. With care, she used a metal pick to loosen the white matter and deposit it on the black surface of our workbench. "You may wish to reexamine a key piece of evidence."

My father applied his reading glasses and, with the aid of a magnifying glass, studied the debris once again. It only required a moment for his eyes to suddenly widen. "Is this the chip from a fingernail?"

"The very same," she said. "And that portion of a fingernail belonged to Hugh Marlowe."

My father and I exchanged puzzled expressions, for neither of us could connect the leather strip with its embedded nail chip to Marlowe. How in the world did the chip end up there?

Joanna gave us additional time to find an answer, but when none was forthcoming, she provided one for us. "Marlowe was being strangled by the leather strip and tried desperately to pull it from his throat, and in the process he lost a portion of a fingernail."

"But he did not die, for dead men do not bleed," my father countered.

"He was not meant to die at that moment," my wife explained. "He was incapacitated by a lack of oxygen and in all likelihood slumped to the floor in a semiconscious state. And that was when Bruno, the manservant, fired the blank into Marlowe's head to simulate a suicide."

"You are assuming it was Bruno because of his close and faithful service to Halderman, are you not?"

"I am assuming nothing, for there is evidence which indicates the manservant's involvement," she said. "Allow me to draw your attention to both ends of the leather strip. Then tell me of their feel."

My father touched the ends with a fingertip before applying more pressure. "They are quite damp," he described.

"Indeed so, and the dampness has persisted despite the strip laying in a cabinet for days at Scotland Yard," Joanna went on. "In all likelihood, the leather was wetted because it was being tightly held by an individual with hyperhidrosis."

"Hyperhidrosis, you say?" my father questioned at once, although he was well aware of the disorder in which individuals perspire profusely for no apparent reason. "How are you aware the manservant carries this diagnosis?"

"Because of Ned Bailey's description of Bruno whilst they shared a taxi ride," I answered, and recounted the blackmailer's depiction of the manservant perspiring so heavily that he had to repeatedly mop his forehead and dry his palms despite the cold weather. Even with the obvious connection, I added a precautionary note. "But damp leather does not necessarily indicate hyperhidrosis."

"Nor does a nail clipping in the leather strip prove strangulation," my father noted.

"These doubts will be answered when my husband performs the autopsy on Hugh Marlowe, for I believe it will reveal bruise marks on the anterior surface of Marlowe's neck and, most likely, a fractured hyoid bone which is inevitably present in strangulation victims."

"Then we should hold our conclusions until the autopsy is performed."

"Not necessarily," Joanna insisted. "You would agree that deep bruising occurs when a rough leather strip is used to throttle a victim who is struggling mightily."

"It is present in every case I have examined," I said.

"Then let us see if Hugh Marlowe was good enough to leave a spot of blood behind."

She hurried to a cabinet of reagents and removed a bottle of guaiacum which can detect a minuscule trace of blood. Once applied to a given surface, it will turn a deep blue color if blood is present. Joanna deposited a few drops of the reagent near the deep scratch marks. In a matter of seconds, a deep blue color appeared. "The pieces of the puzzle come together," she declared.

"Indeed, they do," my father said, nodding his concurrence. "But earlier we assumed Marlowe may well have invited a visitor to the rehearsal," he thought on. "Pray tell why would he invite Halderman's manservant?"

"That is to be determined."

"Does any reason come to mind?"

"I can only guess, but that would serve no purpose."

"That being the case, I doubt there is more to be learned from the days-old crime scene, which by now has been scrubbed clean," said my father. "Should we cancel our meeting with the theater custodian?"

"Absolutely not," Joanna asserted. "I need to question him further."

"To what end?"

"To learn why he is not telling the whole truth."

16

THE DUKE OF YORK'S THEATER

At ten sharp the following morning, Joanna ascended the stairs to the stage at the Duke of York's Theater, with my father and I only steps behind. Lestrade and the custodian stood off to the side of the dimly lit stage in an otherwise darkened auditorium. My wife insisted on these conditions which simulated those present the night of the shooting.

With a nod of greeting to the inspector, Joanna began examining the stage, foot by foot, paying particular attention to the shadow at the base of the drawn curtain where the leather strip had been discovered. It answered the question she had asked at breakfast: Why did Bruno, the manservant, leave the leather strip behind? More than likely, he dropped it in the poorly lighted area after incapacitating Hugh Marlowe and could not find it in his hasty exit after the shooting. Next, she moved to the spot where the red stain could not be completely scrubbed away. Although my wife did not show it, this finding was of concern, for it revealed the entire area had been washed clean and thus may have removed other clues left by the murderer. After a final glance beyond the drawn curtain, Joanna went over to Lestrade and the custodian, who was well past his middle years, with thinning gray hair and long, unkempt sideburns. He was obviously anxious at being questioned yet again by Scotland Yard, and particularly so for now they were accompanied by the daughter of Sherlock Holmes.

"I understand your name is Graham," she began.

"Yes, ma'am," the custodian replied, averting his eyes in a submissive manner. He shuffled his feet involuntarily as his nervousness increased.

"Thank you, Graham, for showing up so promptly," she said in a comforting voice.

"Yes, ma'am."

"Now I realize you were quite upset the night of the shooting."

"Never saw anything so bloody frightening in my whole life."

"As would be true for most, and having Scotland Yard here must have added to your anxiety."

"That it did, for I could not sleep even a wink."

"Which is understandable after viewing such a horrific sight."

"Yes, ma'am," he replied, continuing to shuffle his feet.

"And whilst under such a strain, you might have unintentionally omitted things you saw earlier," Joanna said in a non-accusatory tone.

"I told the inspector all I remembered."

"I am certain you did, and you are to be complimented for doing so."

Graham nodded rapidly and took a deep breath, much like a man would if he had just dodged a bullet.

"But I do wish you would answer one additional question for us," Joanna went on. "In particular, why did you leave the rear door unlocked?"

"Wha—what?" the custodian stuttered, caught completely off guard. "I did no such—"

"Come, come, Graham," my wife interrupted. "We have evidence to that effect, so you had better stay straight with us or you will be charged with obstruction of justice, which brings with it most unpleasant consequences."

The custodian tried desperately to regain his composure, but to little avail. "Am I in danger of losing my position?"

"Your position is and will remain safe," Joanna guaranteed. "Nevertheless, we require a full and accurate accounting of what truly happened that fateful night. Leave out no detail and the contents of our conversation will remain on this stage."

The custodian took another deep breath, as if preparing himself for a recital. "I had no idea it would come to this."

"Get on with it," Lestrade growled impatiently.

"Start at the very beginning, and speak slowly as your recollections return," Joanna soothed. "Do take your time."

"It was an innocent enough request," Graham recounted. "The young actor was expecting a guest to arrive shortly to review his rehearsal. I was to have a door unlocked for her. He offered me a guinea for my service, but I refused. He would have none of that and stuffed a pound note into my shirt pocket."

Joanna quickly interrupted once again. "You stated that the arriving visitor was a *her*. Are you certain?"

"Quite so, ma'am. He distinctly said *her*."

"There was no doubt in your mind that the invited guest was a woman, then."

"None whatsoever," he affirmed before continuing. "I left the rear door unlocked for her and thought no more of it until I heard the shot ring out."

"Exactly how much time elapsed between you unlocking the door and the sound of the gunshot?"

The custodian gave the question momentary thought, then replied, "No more than fifteen minutes."

"Did you actually time the period?"

"No, ma'am," he said honestly. "My timepiece is broken and I have not yet had it repaired."

"So how do you arrive at fifteen minutes passing before the gun was fired?"

"After leaving the stage, I went to the substage area to make certain all the machines operating the lifts were in fine order and to oil those which required lubrication. This work takes me more than fifteen minutes, and I was nearly finished when I heard the gunshot."

"Very good," my wife said, pleased with the accuracy of the timing, "Pray continue."

"I rushed up to the stage itself and found the wounded actor, with his head all bloodied," he recalled, as a brief wince crossed his face. "It was then I heard the sound of a horse-drawn carriage. I ran for the rear door and discovered it wide open. Quickly I looked out, hoping to find someone to come to the young actor's assistance. But all I saw was the carriage at the end of the alleyway."

"Could you make out the driver of the carriage?"

"No, ma'am, for the lighting in the alleyway was poor, but I reckoned it was the man I heard walking across the stage prior to the shooting."

"A man, you say?"

"Yes, ma'am. From my place on the substage, I clearly heard the footsteps of a man."

"Could it have been the woman he was expecting?"

"That could not be, for the footsteps were loud and heavy and most certainly belonged to a large man," he replied.

Like Joanna, my father and I rapidly assimilated the new and startling information. The woman Hugh Marlowe was expecting was no doubt Anne Atwood who was at that moment confined to Sir William's estate. Was that purely conjecture? I asked myself inwardly. No, came the quick answer. The waiting horse-drawn carriage strongly suggested that, following the rehearsal, the couple had planned to take yet another fairy tale–like carriage ride through the streets of West London.

The custodian interpreted our silence as being one of disbelief. His eyes danced back and forth amongst his interrogators before he pleaded his case. "I will swear on everything holy that I am telling the truth."

"I believe you are," Joanna said. "And your answers have been most helpful. But I do have just a few more questions about the footsteps you heard whilst in the substage. In particular, can you always distinguish between a man's and a woman's footsteps?"

"Oh, yes, for I have spent many years in the substage during a performance, and can easily tell the difference," he replied. "Men have a heavy, thumping sound, whilst women have a light, softer step."

"Now, think back to the man's obvious footsteps," my wife requested, and gave the custodian several moments to do so. "Were his footsteps rushed, like he was in a sprint?"

"Oh, no, ma'am, they were slow and even, much as if he was on a casual stroll."

"Did you hear any sounds of a struggle?"

"No, ma'am."

"Or of a heavy object falling?"

He shook his head in response. "It was quiet before I heard the gunshot. If there had been a fight, I would have heard it."

"Very good," Joanna said, with a dismissive gesture. "You may return to your duties."

Lestrade waited for the custodian to disappear in the darkness of the auditorium before turning to Joanna. "Pray tell, Mrs. Watson, how could you possibly have known the rear door was left unlocked? I should remind you that when I arrived at the scene of the shooting, the rear door was securely locked."

"It was locked because the custodian relocked it prior to your arrival," my wife elucidated.

"But you only became aware of that sequence after the custodian revealed the entire story to you," Lestrade agreed. "You could not have known the door was left unlocked beforehand."

"Oh, but I could, from the clues you yourself discovered earlier," she said. "You were clever enough to know this death was not a suicide, which is the reason you came to our rooms at Baker Street yesterday afternoon. The clues which you uncovered all pointed to murder. Here we have a young actor on the rise who is now in a play in St. Martin's Lane, and who is smart enough to know that there is no payment on a life insurance policy when the death is caused by suicide. That is not the picture of a man who takes his own life."

"But payment is made if one hires an assassin to do the killing," he interjected.

"That is a possibility, but an unlikely one," Joanna rebutted. "But why do the deed on a stage? He lived in Canary Wharf, which is a rough neighborhood where a robbery with a deadly blow to the skull would have sufficed."

"And that scenario would have been quite plausible," Lestrade agreed.

"Whatever the case, it was clear an intruder had done the killing, and had entered the theater through a rear door, which was secured by a sturdy Chubb lock. Now, according to the custodian, only fifteen minutes passed between his departure from the stage and the sound of gunfire. This time sequence fits well with the report you gave us yesterday, in which only minutes transpired during the custodian's absence from the stage. All of which tells us the intruder had fifteen minutes at the most to pick a notoriously stubborn Chubb lock. And that would be impossible, for even the most skilled lockpicks in all London require an hour or more to open a Chubb. Thus, the intruder could only gain entrance through an already unlocked door. Now, who would that be?"

The inspector slowly nodded as all the subtle clues came together. "It was the man whose heavy footsteps were heard on the stage above and who escaped in the fleeing carriage."

"Which all adds up to a planned murder," my wife concluded.

"But why? Why attempt to murder a struggling actor who is only beginning to get his footing?"

"I am afraid that will require further investigation."

"Perhaps his half-brother will have some insight which could prove helpful," Lestrade suggested.

"A half-brother, you say?" Joanna asked innocently.

"He has a half-brother of considerable means who is most concerned," the inspector said. "He is taking the situation rather badly and, according to the sister, is a frequent bedside visitor."

"He would be worthy of questioning," said my wife. "That would be particularly so if he was close to his brother."

"I have scheduled an interview with him at St. Bart's today, if you would care to join us."

"I would indeed," Joanna replied with subtle eagerness.

"Two o'clock at bedside, then," Lestrade said, with a tip of his derby, but turned back for a final question. "Despite your promise, I believe the custodian should be charged for withholding evidence. Do you not agree?"

Joanna waved away the notion. "That serves no purpose, for it is Hugh Marlowe who must shoulder the entire blame, as this was all his doing. And besides, inspector, we have bigger fish to fry here."

"Undoubtedly so," he said and, again tipping his derby, departed.

We waited until Lestrade had left the auditorium, but even then spoke in low voices.

"What do you make of it?" Joanna asked quietly.

"It was all planned from start to finish, including a meeting on the stage, followed by a horse-drawn carriage ride," I replied. "It was a repeat performance of their first encounter."

"You must dig deeper," my wife prompted.

"To what level?"

"The level of Eric Halderman's involvement," she went on. "And of course he had to acquiesce to the use of the horse-drawn carriage that fateful night, with the driver no doubt his manservant Bruno. But here is where the divide between the two brothers occurs. Marlowe believed the setting was a perfect romantic interlude, whilst to Halderman it provided an ideal way to dispose of his troublesome half-brother. After all, Marlowe had served his purpose and there were still more photographs in hand. Even more importantly, Marlowe's devoted love for Anne Atwood had become apparent and could disrupt the blackmailing."

"So there was mutual passion between the actor and the former debutante," I concluded.

"That is yet another measure the female eye is quite skilled at detecting."

"But under no circumstances would Sir William's family permit their precious Anne to marry a struggling actor."

"Try to convince Anne Atwood of that and you will find your words fall on deaf ears."

"How then will she react to Marlowe's impending death?"

"Badly, I am afraid, which brings us to our upcoming visit with Eric Halderman at St. Bart's," Joanna cautioned. "We must play our hand very carefully here. He is a clever devil and it is imperative we conceal any connection to Sir William's family. Watson can provide assistance in that regard."

"How so?" my father asked.

"I have heard you speak of the metal plates which are being made to cover the hideous wounds of war," she replied. "I wish for you to give us a demonstration in Halderman's presence."

"Easily done," my father said. "The plates are fashioned from metal and used to hide the horrific facial wounds. Some are actually painted to closely resemble the color of complexion."

"What of a skull plate?"

"We have those as well, each of which can be fitted and worn as a cap."

"Have one ready to be employed on Marlowe should he survive."

"But there is little hope for his survival."

"Yet just the possibility will send shivers up and down Halderman's spine, for should Marlowe regain consciousness he will surely turn on his half-brother," said Joanna, and smiled mischievously. "You must remember that the cleverest of devils dread the thought of capture."

"But if Harry Askins, the surgeon, is present, he will tell of the brother's dire prognosis."

"Then you must counter with the famous words of a battlefield surgeon of yesteryear who stated, 'I treat, God cures.' Even Askins would not contradict that faint hope."

"Which would certainly spoil Eric Halderman's afternoon," I predicted.

"And might well lead him to more desperate measures."

"Would that include yet another attempt on his brother's life?"

"I suspect that would be at the top of Halderman's list."

17

ST. BARTHOLOMEW'S

We gathered at bedside to watch my father demonstrate how the medical profession had come to the aid of soldiers whose features had been disfigured by the wounds of war. In his hand he held a facial mask which was constructed to bear a striking resemblance to the patient's lower face prior to the severe injury. The soldier's chin and bottom lip had been destroyed by an exploding shell, but when my father applied the mask to the lad's face, a miraculous transformation occurred. His appearance was restored in every way. And this remarkable achievement was the work of Anna Coleman Ladd, the wife of a physician, who took it upon herself to construct the masks of mercy.

"Mrs. Ladd was an artist of some note and found the plight of such injured men most distressful," my father explained. "Those poor soldiers would struggle in their return to public view with their tragic appearances or broken faces, as they at times are called. This devoted lady came to their rescue by making plaster casts of their faces and, after correcting for the damage, she shaped masks of copper which were painted with hard enamel to match a human complexion. These devices could be attached to the patient's face by rubber bands and give him a presentable appearance."

"But my brother has no need for such a device," said Eric Halderman, who was nearby at his brother's bedside. The blackmailer was attired in an expensive cashmere topcoat, and appeared to be even smaller than Ned Bailey had depicted. He was of narrow frame, with a height that barely reached five feet. His thin lips seemed pasted together and only parted when he spoke. "As you well know, Hugh's face was unharmed."

"But his skull has a large defect which must be covered," my father said, and opened a box which contained a copper cap that would fit nicely over the missing bone. "We can try it on for size if you'd like."

"Hardly worth the effort, I would think," the surgeon Harry Askins chimed in, as he completed an examination on a patient in an adjacent bed. "His chances of survival are virtually nil."

"But we should be prepared in the event he does," my father countered. "On rare occasions, the fallen continue to live despite the severity of the head wound. I always recall the words of a battlefield surgeon who stated, 'I treat, God cures.'"

"Well put, Dr. Watson, well put indeed," Askins agreed, acknowledging my father's experience with the wounds of war.

"And if he were to survive, perhaps he could tell us what truly happened the night of the shooting," Lestrade entered the conversation.

"Was it not accidental?" Halderman asked at once.

"We have questions in that regard, sir," the inspector answered. "For there is evidence which suggests otherwise."

"Oh goodness!" Halderman feigned distress at the unexpected news. "May I know what brings you to that conclusion?"

"There were several such findings," Lestrade replied. "First was the location of the gunshot wound. It was located behind the temple which would be a most unusual position for a misfire. And then there was the weapon being found in the young actor's hand. That should not have been."

"Why so?"

"I should allow Mrs. Watson to provide you with the particulars, for she is an expert in these matters, and thus the reason why both Scotland Yard and the insurance company have requested her assistance."

"It was a straightforward observation," Joanna informed. "In misfirings or in an attempted suicide, the weapon is never found in the victim's hand. Once the shot is delivered, the muscles relax and the pistol is dropped away from the body. When all the evidence is put together, it seems most likely that the shooting was intentional and done by another."

Halderman's bow went up in surprise. "Why would anyone do such a thing?"

"We were hoping you might help us answer that very question," said Joanna. "Do you know of any person who would wish harm to your brother?"

"Absolutely not," Halderman replied firmly. "He is a good lad and is admired by friends both on and off the stage."

"I am told he had no wife."

"True."

"A girlfriend, then?"

"Not to my knowledge."

"You mentioned friends on the stage," my wife inquired. "Did you have the opportunity to meet any of them?"

"Not to my recollection," he replied, with a shrug of indifference. "My business is most time-consuming and I have little interest in the theater. But Hugh did speak of the warmth he felt for his colleagues."

Halderman was a very accomplished liar, I thought, trying not to stare at the merciless devil. He knew how to choose his words and avoid any reference which might associate him with his brother's shooting.

"Did he ever express fear that his life might be in danger?" Joanna asked.

"Never, and had he I would have surely brought it to the attention of Scotland Yard."

Suddenly, Hugh Marlowe's comatose body began to move, with abrupt spasms in his right arm. Then his right leg followed suit.

"Stand back, sister!" my father ordered a bedside nurse, addressing her with the term often applied to nurses in England. "These movements may well be the start of a generalized seizure."

Which proved to be the case, but it only lasted for a half-minute or so. Quiet returned as the patient drifted back into a lifeless form.

"That is the second seizure he has had today," the sister remarked, as she approached the bedside to see if her assistance was needed. "The first one lasted longer and was more violent. Let us remain alert in the event he again utters a word or two."

"Did he actually speak?" my father asked at once.

"Only a garbled utterance which was difficult to decipher."

"Very good," my father said. "Perhaps his level of consciousness is improving which would be a very good sign."

"But at times, Dr. Watson, the candle brightens just before it is finally extinguished," Askins noted.

"I have seen that as well," my father concurred.

I noticed that Eric Halderman was now leaning forward to catch every word spoken by the doctors. The sudden however brief improvement should have brought joy to the half-brother's face, but it did not. Instead, his expression was of deep concern.

Another seizure began, but on this occasion, it only involved the right arm, which beat violently against the sheet. Then his right leg began to twitch, and we could only hope this was not the opening stage of status epilepticus, a prolonged type of seizure that can lead to death.

But the spasms abruptly diminished and, as if on command, Hugh Marlowe blurted out three distinct words. "No more pay!"

Gradually, the movements stopped altogether and the patient lapsed back into a comatose state. We waited in the stillness in the event more seizures and words were in store, but none were forthcoming.

"Should we administer barbiturates?" the sister asked, breaking the silence.

"Let us put that on hold for now," my father advised. "It will not be required if there are no further seizures."

I refocused my attention on Eric Halderman, whose expression was one of obvious worry. And for good reason. If his half-brother was to regain consciousness, Halderman's blackmailing days would come to an abrupt end.

"What is this business about *no more pay*?" Lestrade asked, scratching at the back of his head.

"I have no idea," his half-brother said, and quickly tried to come up with a covering explanation. "Perhaps he was referring to his pay from the play he was participating in. For now, that would no longer exist."

Lestrade nodded his agreement. "His future income from the theater was somewhat better than his meager income as a part-time server in a Canary Wharf pub."

"After all is said and done, could my brother be showing signs of a recovery?" Halderman asked.

"As I stated earlier, his chances are small," Askins replied candidly. "And if he were to survive, there would be significant brain damage, with considerable loss of function."

"So sad."

"Indeed."

"Well then, I must be on my way to a previous engagement," said Halderman, glancing quickly at his gold wristwatch. "I do wish to thank all of you for your help in this most distressing matter."

"We shall do our best to bring your brother's case to a final resolution," Lestrade assured.

"I am certain you shall," he said and, with an appreciative nod, departed.

Whilst Askins stayed behind to change the dressing on another patient's head wound, we accompanied Lestrade to the front entrance of St. Bartholomew's where a motor vehicle awaited the inspector.

"Nothing very productive there, eh?" he asked.

"Nothing which would change the course of our investigation," Joanna replied evasively.

"I am unconvinced that Mr. Marlowe did not make enemies in his professional life, for actors can at times turn quite nasty and vengeful. With this in mind, I plan to interview the cast of the play and others involved. You may join me if you wish."

"I prefer to take a different route where the pickings may be more fruitful," my wife gently refused the invitation.

"Would the company of Scotland Yard be of assistance to this different avenue?"

"I think not," she replied. "You are no doubt aware, Lestrade, that handsome, young actors often have multiple girlfriends, and I plan to seek such women out, for lovers tend to share secrets, good and bad. That being the case, the girlfriend would be more likely to reveal those secrets to another, understanding female."

"You raise a good point," he said and reached for the rear door of the waiting motor vehicle. "Please inform us of any new findings."

"I shall," Joanna assented. "But there is one last matter you may wish to attend to in regards to Hugh Marlowe."

"Pray tell what?"

"It might be wise to place one of your detectives near bedside in the event the news spreads that Marlowe is now speaking a few words," Joanna advised. "If such information reaches the wrong ears, the young actor's life could be in further danger."

Lestrade's eyes narrowed at the suggestion. "Are you inferring someone may try to do him in?"

"They tried before and may try again."

"I shall see to it that Mr. Marlowe is watched over," he said, with an affirmative nod.

As the inspector's motor vehicle drove away into heavy traffic, I said, "That was a clever device to put Lestrade off our trail, for Marlowe had no hidden lovers behind the scenes."

"Ah, but he did, and her name is Anne Atwood who we must question again," Joanna reminded. "And there remains blank spaces that only she can provide the answers to."

"What a tangled mess Hugh Marlowe has weaved," my father noted. "He finds himself madly in love with the woman whose family he is blackmailing into bankruptcy."

"And he desperately wanted out of his dilemma," she added. "That is why he cried out in his subconscious state, 'No more pay.' He was demanding that his brother stop the blackmailing."

"Which tells me why Halderman had his manservant Bruno fire a shot into Marlowe's head," my father concluded. "What a clever, diabolical human being."

"He is both clever and diabolical, but he has made a fatal mistake."

"Which is?"

"Depending entirely on Bruno, who will turn out to be the weak link in the blackmailing chain."

18

THE BAKER STREET IRREGULARS

Once we were settled in our parlor, Joanna's first order of business was to call for a messenger to deliver a note to the Baker Street Irregulars, as they were far too poor to possess a telephone. There was a most interesting history behind the Irregulars which dated back to the days of Sherlock Holmes. The Great Detective had gathered up a gang of street urchins whom he employed to aid his causes. They consisted originally of a dozen or so members, who could go anywhere, see everything, and overhear anyone without being noticed. When put to the task, they had a remarkable success record. For their efforts, each was paid a shilling a day, with a guinea to whoever found the most prized clue. Since Holmes's death, most of the guttersnipes had become ill or drifted away, but their leader, Wiggins, remained and took in new recruits to replace those who had departed. At present, the entire gang had dwindled down to three which included Wiggins, Little Alfie, and Sarah the Gypsy. They resided in Whitechapel and knew every block of the crime-ridden district, which explained why my wife was calling on them yet again. Bruno, Halderman's manservant, visited Whitechapel on a regular schedule.

Outside, the onset of evening brought with it a deep chill, as evidenced by the ice crystals forming on our window. The newly lit logs in our fireplace were beginning to blaze and bring needed warmth to our parlor.

Joanna stirred the fire with a metal stoker and watched the sparks fly into the air. "A most interesting day, would you not agree?" she asked.

"Are you referring to Marlowe or his half-brother?" my father queried.

"Both, but let us begin with Eric Halderman," she replied. "What do you make of him, Watson?"

"I don't particularly care for his looks, but, then again, that may be so because I know the evil which lay behind them," he responded.

"At times the cover tells us a good deal about the book," she agreed mildly. "His narrow face and predatory eyes are reminiscent of a badger, which can be quite fierce and dangerous when threatened."

"A finely attired badger," I noted.

"Indeed so," said Joanna. "You no doubt took stock of his bespoke cashmere topcoat."

"I did."

"Did you not also notice his handsomely crafted shoes, which had a leather strap atop, indicating they were made by Church's in Northampton?"

"I must admit that I overlooked his expensive shoes."

"Most expensive," my father emphasized. "Which are far beyond the reach of most."

"As was his gold Cartier-Tonneau wristwatch," my wife went on. "He is obviously intent on displaying his wealth for all to see, which of course is a feature of the nouveau riche."

"And beneath those trappings is the evilest of men, one so evil he attempted to kill his own brother," my father said. "Do you truly believe he will try yet again?"

"Oh yes," Joanna affirmed. "For here is a most cruel man who carefully knots and centers his silk tie, who has his graying hair meticulously trimmed, and whose trousers are precisely tailored so they reach his shoes without a break.

He obviously crosses all of his t's and dots all of his i's. I can assure you he will not leave a loose thread hanging, and that loose thread is Hugh Marlowe."

"That may not be required if nature runs its course, for Marlowe's chances of survival are beyond hope."

"But Halderman will now be unsure after hearing his half-brother cry out 'no more pay,'" my wife said. "Like most men of new wealth, he will do anything to hold onto it, and in fact already has."

"Cain and Abel," I thought aloud.

"The very same."

"And the longer Marlowe remains alive, the greater the pressure mounts on Halderman," my father said.

"And there will be even more pressure placed on Eric Halderman when he learns Scotland Yard is searching for the name of a hidden girlfriend," Joanna told us, with a mischievous grin.

"But how will he become aware of the search for such a girlfriend?" I asked at once.

"Oh, Lestrade will inform him."

My father and I exchanged quizzical looks before I asked the question which came to both of our minds. "Why would he do so?"

"Because you have a cunning wife," she replied. "Allow me to show you the appetizing pieces I carefully placed before the inspector. First, I mentioned that I would be investigating the possibility of a hidden lover whilst he planned to search for possible enemies Marlowe may have had in the acting profession. Now, which of the two avenues would you consider to be the most promising?"

"The search for a hidden lover is the obvious answer," I replied.

"Of course, and Lestrade, who is turning into a solid investigator, would think likewise and interrogate the cast about such an arrangement."

"I will wager a guinea he comes up empty," I ventured.

"And you would lose that guinea, dear heart," she continued on. "Surely, the cast in the play would have noticed an aristocratic, young lady who visited backstage on a number of occasions and always seemed close to Hugh Marlowe. Feelings of love are difficult to conceal to even the practiced eye. They saw it. They noted it. In all likelihood, they talked of it."

"Would they know her name?"

"I would think not, for Marlowe would not introduce her to the others in an attempt to hide their closeness and mutual affection," she replied. "Nevertheless, the cast would no doubt remember the charming young lady. Lestrade, now breathlessly on the trail of a nameless lover, will proceed with vigor, for he will recall the woman who was scheduled to meet with Marlowe the night of his planned rehearsal. He will then seek out the next best source of information, who is Marlowe's half-brother. Keep in mind that Lestrade believes they are warm, caring brothers who might share details of the affair. He does not know they are estranged."

"Ho! Ho!" my father bellowed out, with some glee. "Can you imagine Halderman's reaction when he learns that the persistent Lestrade is on the hunt for Anne Atwood?"

"Yes, I can, although the search will be unsuccessful," Joanna said, pleased with my father's response. "But that is beside the point, for now the pressure will be enormous on Halderman. He will foresee everything unraveling before his very eyes."

"And perhaps a lengthy stay at Pentonville will cross his mind as well," I interjected.

"That will not concern him at the moment," my wife said. "You must remember there are only three bona fide witnesses to the entire blackmailing scheme—Halderman, Bruno, and Marlowe. The first two will not talk, and the third will shortly disappear from this world."

"Then why go through with this charade?"

"To force Halderman to act," she replied. "At this juncture, he must either give up the game, which is most unlikely, or make a final, exorbitant demand from Sir William with a promise to turn over all of the scandalous photographs."

"At least the latter will end the nightmare, which Sir William has endured with such strength and dignity," I said hopefully.

"But only if he is dealing with an honorable man, which he is not," Joanna forewarned. "Halderman will make the promise and collect the ransom, but hold the most scandalous photographs in abeyance for use at a later date."

"But she will be married by then," I countered.

"Which will make the photographs even more valuable, for now he can blackmail two families. He will make demands on Sir William as well as on the wealthy family of the groom."

"Then we will have gained nothing."

"To the contrary, we will be gaining valuable time which I need to bring this scoundrel to his well-deserved justice. You will recall from our earlier conversation that Halderman is a most careful man, and careful men do not act in haste."

My father brought his extended fingers together and formed a steeple upon which he rested his chin. His expression indicated a bothersome thought had come to mind. "I fear for Anne Atwood's life. Sooner or later, she will realize that the man she loves is part and parcel of a blackmailing scheme. She will thus be tempted to go to the police, will she not?"

Joanna waved off his worry. "Why would she come forward and expose the entire family to shame and ridicule, yet gain nothing from it?"

"Still, Halderman might consider her a threat to his future and do away with her—accidentally of course."

"No, no, Watson, that would never happen," said Joanna assuredly. "Keep in mind that the photographs are only of great value to Halderman with Anne Atwood alive. With her death, there would be no upcoming marriage and no scandal, and Eric Halderman would be the poorer for it."

There was a brief rap on the door and Miss Hudson looked in. "The Irregulars are here, Mrs. Watson. Shall I show them in?"

"Please do, Miss Hudson, and be good enough to delay supper, for our meeting will take some time."

As the door closed, we rapidly removed from sight all evidence related to the ongoing blackmail. My wife rearranged the chairs so that the Irregulars would stand by the fireplace directly in front of us, then she reached for her purse in anticipation of the payment which would be forthcoming shortly.

"We should not mention Eric Halderman by name, for our young workers will be making inquiries in the far corners of Whitechapel, where secrets never stay hidden," Joanna instructed. "It would be a great disservice to our investigation were Halderman to learn someone was probing into the whereabouts of his manservant."

"In Whitechapel, no less."

"Whose secrets can be bought and sold for three halfpenny worth of rum."

With a loud rap on the door, the Baker Street Irregulars entered, all three bundled up in multiple layers of clothing against the cold. They were led to the warmth of the fireplace by Wiggins, who had not changed since our last encounter. Tall and thin in his late twenties, he had hollow cheeks and dark eyes that continually danced around at his surroundings.

"We came at our quickest," Wiggins said in a deep Cockney accent. "That will be two shillings for the ride over, if you please, ma'am."

Joanna handed over several coins, then stepped back to inspect the trio. Their inexpensive garments were well worn and in places threadbare and stained, which was the usual attire of the street urchins who plied their trade with such skill. They carried with them the odor of burning coal.

"There is a visitor to Whitechapel whom I wish you to follow," she began.

"Easily done," said Wiggins.

"You will start at an establishment which is known as the Polish-England Club."

"I know the Polanski well, ma'am."

"Then be good enough to inform me of its specifics, down to the smallest detail."

"It is a dance hall which is a favorite of immigrants from Middle Europe," he replied in a casual tone. "They drink heavily and dance to the bloody polka all night long."

"Tell me of the structure itself."

Wiggins paused for a moment to gather his thoughts. "It is a two-story, brick building, with a large dance floor on the first level, where there is also a bar which serves the cheapest of drinks. One night they offered up spoiled beer which nearly caused a riot."

"And what of the second floor?"

"That is where the gambling takes place."

"What sort?"

"Cards, dice, and darts."

"And the stakes?"

Wiggins shrugged in response. "I never indulged, ma'am, but I am told there is a strict house limit."

"I see," said my wife, seemingly uninterested in the information, but I knew the importance of her inquiry. Were Bruno a heavy gambler, he might well have overwhelming debt. Such men can be bought. "The man I am interested in arrives at the Polanski every Friday promptly at seven. He goes by the name of Bruno."

"He is someone you do not wish to cross," Wiggins said in a voice so serious it drew the attention of Little Alfie and Sarah the Gypsy. "You do so at your own peril."

"Do you know him?"

"I know of him, and even by Whitechapel standards he is a dangerous man, with an explosive temper. People step aside in his presence, according to my good friend Bennie."

"Who is Bennie, may I ask?" Joanna inquired. "And how does he come to be so well informed of Bruno?"

"Bennie has been my best friend since childhood," the leader of the Irregulars replied. "He was born with a bad leg, he was, and requires a cane, but his hands are skilled and he plays the accordion so well that he leads the band at the Polanski. It is there where he has witnessed Bruno's behavior. The mean bloke dances to every bloody polka with the same bird, and if you happen to knock into them, you had best run for your life. The man is nasty down to his marrow."

"Do you have qualms about following him?"

"No, ma'am," Wiggins said without concern. "But I shall keep my distance."

My father interjected, "Would there be real danger if he became aware of you?"

"Some," Wiggins admitted. "But I have friends in Whitechapel who know how to deal with the likes of Bruno."

"All well and good," said Joanna. "However, do make your presence and inquiries most discreet, for the information you gather must be held in strict confidence if it is to be of value."

"Worry not, ma'am, for there will be two individuals following him at different intervals. Little Alfie and Sarah the Gypsy will be changing places and garments in a fashion which ensures our presence goes unnoticed."

"But only you will be allowed into the Polanski because of age," my wife cautioned. "Your two mates will be considered too young."

"I can arrange for them to have small jobs near the bar, such as emptying trash bins and the like," he replied. "Of course, a bribe will be required, which must be included in our fees."

"So noted," Joanna agreed. "Now, here is the information you must gather. According to a reliable source, Bruno arrives at the Polanski only Friday evening at seven sharp."

"Your source is off the mark," Wiggins interrupted. "He is about White-chapel on a more frequent basis."

"But I am told he often starts at the Polanski."

"That is most likely true."

146

"Then I wish to know what activities he participates in whilst there. If he dances so often, does he ever change partners? If he associates with a single woman exclusively, who is she and what is their connection? If he gambles, at which table and how excessively? And when he departs from the establishment, to where does he travel, how long does he stay, and at what time does he make a final exit?"

Wiggins carefully considered the assigned tasks at length. "He is an outsider, so he probably arrives and departs by the Underground."

"I am told he arrives from Hampstead Heath via the Tube at seven and departs late in the evening," Joanna verified.

"Before midnight then, for that is when the Underground closes."

"It must be precisely determined if and when he returns to Hampstead Heath," my wife insisted. "That is of the utmost importance."

Wiggins scratched at the back of his head. "That will take some doing, ma'am, for there will not be many in the station at closing time, and Bruno will be aware of those around him. That will be particularly so if the likes of street urchins follow him into the station and into the tube itself."

"I can see to that," Little Alfie volunteered, who despite his youthful appearance was easily the smartest of the lot. At fifteen years of age, he seemed younger, with his unkempt brown hair and short stature. "We shall have Sarah the Gypsy on his tail at the very last, whilst I await Bruno's arrival at the Underground station. Dressed in my best topcoat, I shall have tickets for all the lines which pass through. Whichever tube he takes, I will follow and note the station of his departure."

"Very good," Joanna said, pleased with the plan. "But do not follow him when he departs. Wait until the next stop, which I believe is Golders Green, before returning."

My wife turned to Sarah the Gypsy, a dark-complected teenager who was beginning to bloom into womanhood. "Will you be feigning a limp whilst keeping an eye on Bruno?"

"That depends on the length of his travels," Sarah replied. "If he goes a short distance, an obvious limp will work well, for he will see me only once. But during a longer stroll, he may notice me and my ailment several times and become aware of my presence. If that be the case, it is best I change into different topcoats and hats and walk in a normal fashion."

"That should do."

Wiggins stepped forward with a request. "I wonder, ma'am, if we might be given an advance, for there will be bribes to be made, clothes to be bought, and multiple Tube tickets to be purchased."

"Will a fiver cover all of your activities?"

"Nicely."

My wife handed him a five-pound note and said, "Be on your way, then."

Once we heard their footsteps hurrying down the staircase, I remarked, "Ned Bailey was off on the number of weekly visits Bruno makes to Whitechapel. I have to wonder if there were other inconsistencies."

"Perhaps," Joanna said, unconcerned. "For, as we noted before, second-hand information should never be depended upon until verified. Nonetheless, Bruno may have in fact recently increased the frequency of his visits. With that in mind, why would he do so?"

"Has he become addicted to gambling?" my father suggested.

"Possibly, but here is a man of considerable income, for he is no doubt well paid for his service and silence by Halderman," she rebutted. "Furthermore, an individual with a solid addiction would not be interested in games of such low stakes."

"But you cannot rule out that possibility," he said.

"True, but we will have that question answered soon enough by Wiggins. If Bruno spends most of his time dancing the polka and rarely goes to the second level, we can safely say that he is not addicted to games of chance."

"And it cannot be alcohol addiction, for a man of his means would not visit a bar which is known to serve spoiled beer," I reasoned. "Yet, with all these factors in mind, I tend to believe that Ned Bailey gave us incorrect information on Bruno."

"I am of a different opinion," Joanna said. "Think back to Bailey's fastidious memory on his past ventures and on the smallest details of Halderman's library. Here is a man whose mind is tuned into accuracy."

"I am afraid I must side with Joanna on this matter," my father joined in. "When an individual gives you the exact time and day of an event, it tells of a steadfast recollection."

"Seven sharp every Friday," my wife recalled and, after lighting a Turkish cigarette, began pacing across the lengthy floor of our parlor. Back and forth she went, puffing on her cigarette and leaving a trail of pale white smoke behind. Her pace increased as she continued to mutter to herself, considering one possibility after another without reaching a conclusion. She was about to light another cigarette from the one she was smoking when she abruptly stopped.

"It's the dancing!"

"What about his dancing?" I asked at once.

"It is his dancing partner," she replied, nodding convincingly to herself. "Recall that Wiggins informed us of Bruno dancing every polka with the same woman who he is no doubt attached to. She is the reason he has increased his visits to Whitechapel and why he becomes so combative when the pair is bumped into on the dance floor."

"He feels he must protect her, as one does with his dear heart," my father added. "It is also a way to impress her with his masculinity."

"Spot on, Watson, and no doubt the Baker Street Irregulars will confirm our deductions."

"I take it their confirmation is of some importance."

"Indeed it is, for I do believe we have just happened upon the crucial link I have been searching for."

"The crucial link to what, may I ask?"

"Halderman's downfall."

19

A SUDDEN DEATH

Near noon the following day, I entered the pathology laboratory and found Dr. Jonathan Quinn, my young associate, studying slides under a Zeiss microscope. Back and forth he moved the slide, as if attempting to document a suspicious finding. He waved with one hand, whilst using the other to adjust the magnification of the microscope.

"I will be with you in just a moment, sir," he said.

His utterance of the word *sir* caused me to feel my age, as it always did. But then again, I was a good fifteen years older than the rosy-cheeked pathologist and the director of the pathology department at St. Bartholomew's, whilst he was the youngest member, only months out of his residency training. Thus, I merited the title of *sir*, and he would have it no other way.

"What so captures your interest?" I asked.

"The debris within the brain tissue of Mr. Hugh Marlowe," he replied.

"Be good enough to describe the debris."

"It consists of scattered black particles of varying shapes and sizes," Quinn depicted. "They surely do not belong in brain tissue."

I tried not to show my intense interest in the finding, for matters relating to Marlowe's head wound were under criminal investigation and clues therein were not to be casually discussed, even amongst the pathology staff. Nevertheless, the black particles could answer the question Joanna had repeatedly asked: How close was the pistol to Mr. Marlowe's head when the shot was fired?

"I take it the specimen of the patient's brain was removed whilst the surgeon was attempting to stem the bleeding," I said.

"So the surgical report states," Quinn affirmed. "They found the bleeder beneath the dura and clamped it off. In the process, a bit of macerated brain had to be dissected away."

One could only imagine the difficulty the operating surgeon had faced. Mr. Harry Askins had to venture underneath the dura, a thick band of connective tissue which encapsulates the entire brain, then dig even deeper to locate the ruptured blood vessel. Quinn was now closely examining the brain tissue, which by necessity, had to be removed.

"Were the black particles in every section that you examined?" I inquired.

"They were, sir, although obviously more dense in some areas," Quinn replied, pushing himself away from the microscope. "But their source remains undetermined. Would you care to have a look, sir?"

I seated myself and, peering into the microscope, studied the brain tissue which came clearly into view. Several areas were macerated, others were intact, but all contained the mysterious black particles. Although minuscule, they were obviously foreign objects which had been introduced into the tightly guarded brain. But what were they? And had they been inserted into the brain by a gunshot or by the surgeon?

"Could it simply be dirt?" Quinn queried.

"Possibly, but pray tell how did it get entrance into the brain?"

"Perhaps soil, then?"

"I would think that unlikely, for the particles vary far too much in shape and size," I responded. "And we can exclude bacteria by those same criteria."

"Could it be they were carried in by the bullet itself?" the young pathologist surmised. "Might the round have been covered in filth before being fired?"

"A very good thought," I agreed. "But how would one go about proving it?"

"That would be most difficult."

"Then for now, simply describe the black particles in your report and state that their origin remains to be determined," I directed. "But it might be helpful for you to consult the literature for articles on foreign particles in brain tissue and compile a list of those that might apply to the case before us."

"A splendid idea, sir," he said enthusiastically. "Would it not be grand to get to the bottom of this quandary and perhaps write a paper for submission to *Lancet*?"

"I am certain they would find it of interest," I concurred, particularly when they learn the black particles may represent a telling clue in the commission of a brotherly murder.

The swinging doors to the pathology laboratory burst open and my secretary Rose hurried in, pausing a moment to catch her breath.

"Detective Sergeant Stone just called from the surgery ward," she said in a rush. "Your presence is needed at once."

I dashed out into the corridor with a single thought racing through my mind. Something had obviously gone awry with Hugh Marlowe. I rapidly ran through the possibilities as I ascended the stairs to the second floor. Either the young actor had died mysteriously or someone had attempted to end Marlowe's life prematurely. If it was an attempt, who and how?

Upon entering the surgery ward, my questions were partially answered. Movable curtains now sealed off the bed of Hugh Marlowe, with the entrance into the bedside surrounded by Detective Sergeant Stone, the sister, and Eric Halderman. There was no sound coming from within.

Detective Stone stepped forward and announced, "Mr. Marlowe has passed on. Death was confirmed by an intern at ten past ten. I was instructed to inform you immediately."

"Was there any motion prior to his death?" I asked.

The sister answered in a neutral voice, "His right arm began to flail against the sheet, but that lasted for only seconds before his respirations ceased. I could detect no pulse and called the intern on the ward."

"Who was nearest the patient at the time of the seizure?"

"Mr. Halderman and I were at bedside, with the detective standing guard in the passageway," she replied.

"Were there any visitors prior to the seizure?"

"None other than Mr. Halderman."

I began to move in for a closer study of the uncovered corpse, but Stone quickly blocked my entrance, saying, "Sorry, sir, but, on orders from Inspector Lestrade, no one is allowed in until Mrs. Watson arrives."

"I take it she has been notified."

"Yes, sir. A car has been dispatched to Baker Street," Stone replied. "She should be here shortly."

"Very good," I said and returned to the sister. "Were any medications given to Mr. Marlowe this morning?"

"None, sir."

"No injections, then?"

"No, sir, for none were ordered."

"But intravenous fluids were being administered, were they not?"

"A single bottle of saline had been in place since early morning," she responded. "It was near empty and being replaced when Mr. Halderman arrived."

"Did you note the time?"

The sister opened the patient's chart to a middle page. "The new bottle of saline was started at nine fifty, which was twenty minutes before Mr. Marlowe breathed his last."

"Dreadful business, this," Eric Halderman remarked. "One knows death is coming, but one is never truly prepared for it."

Oh, you knew it was close at hand, I thought morbidly, but kept my expression even. Halderman was certain of it from the moment he ordered a shot to be fired into his brother's head. "Death in the family is always sad," I managed to say.

"The IV saline is no longer running," the sister observed. "Should I remove the bottle?"

"Please leave it in place," I directed, wondering if it might have been meddled with. But that was highly unlikely, with the sister close by and watching every move. Yet all that would be required was a single distraction for the sister to look away and a poison to be administered. And Halderman was clever enough to do it or have it done. My basic instincts told me that this evil man was involved, but proving it was another matter.

The group outside the movable curtains turned as my wife's footsteps approached. At her side was another detective, which was certain to make Halderman feel even more uncomfortable, for here was the presence of Scotland Yard in force.

"Good morning, Mrs. Watson," Stone greeted her cordially, as he had worked with us on several cases in the past. With his strawberry blond hair and fair complexion, he seemed too young to be a detective sergeant, but the set of his square jaw and his penetrating dark eyes indicated he was a man not to be trifled with.

"And to you, Sergeant Stone," Joanna returned the greeting, and immediately peered in behind the curtain. She carefully surveyed the area, with her eyes moving from bedding to corpse to the hanging bottle of intravenous fluids. "I require a summary of events," she requested, but her gaze remained on the corpse.

I gestured to the sister who gave a concise synopsis of all the happenings which transpired prior to Marlowe's death. She emphasized there had been no unexpected visitors or intrusions during the entire morning.

"No one had touched the patient, then?" Joanna inquired.

"Only myself to test for pulse and blood pressure," the sister answered, then quickly added, "Oh, Mr. Halderman patted his brother's shoulder to wish him well. He often does that on his arrival to bedside."

"As would be expected," my wife said, but her eyes went briefly to Halderman's ungloved hands. Without further words, she led the way into the death chamber, with me a step behind. Sergeant Stone, the ever-resourceful detective, positioned himself so that neither Halderman nor the sister could view our examination or overhear our quiet voices.

"A convenient death, eh?" Joanna asked softly.

"Quite so," I agreed.

"Did you notice Halderman's ungloved hands?"

"I did."

"And what of the large, gold ring, with an oversized opal in its center?"

My mind immediately went back to an espionage case we had solved months ago. "The German agent," I replied in a whisper, recalling a deadly ring worn by the spy in the event of his capture. There was cyanide contained within its hollowed out stone, which could be injected by a small needle that appeared by pressing on a given area of the ring. "And Halderman patted his brother on the shoulder."

"No doubt he did so several times," said Joanna, and examined the corpse's bare shoulders with a magnifying glass. "There are no injection sites, but then again tiny needles leave unnoticeable puncture marks."

"But even if cyanide was injected into the skin, we have no method to detect it."

"Not in the skin, but perhaps in Marlowe's saliva."

"What!" I raised my voice in surprise. "I have never heard of such a test."

"Nor had I until I read a letter to the editor in a recent science journal," she informed me. "It is still in its developmental stage, but the results seem most promising. Apparently, after cyanide is administered, a breakdown product of the poison shows up in saliva. If one then applies iron nitrate to the specimen, it turns red in the presence of this cyanide product. How reliable the test is remains to be seen. But let us give it a try by obtaining a bit of Marlowe's saliva."

I rapidly reached for a cotton swab and wiped it about in the corpse's mouth, then wrapped it in gauze. "I shall have our pharmacologist perform the original test and repeat it on the salivary specimen."

"Good show," Joanna approved and moved to the corpse's head and neck. She no doubt gave thought to removing the bloodied bandage from Marlowe's head to inspect the wound made by the gunshot, but decided against it. Caked blood and other debris would have to be washed away for a proper examination and that could not be done under the circumstances. It would have to await the autopsy table. My wife decided to begin with the neck where she found obvious bruise marks around the laryngeal area. Several of the bruises were so deep they drew blood.

"The cardinal sign of strangulation," Joanna said, and returned to the corpse's head where she pulled down the lower eyelids to expose the conjunctiva. Upon them were multiple petechiae, which were red spots representing tiny blood vessels that had been ruptured by the marked increase in venous pressure within the eye. They were yet another hallmark of strangulation. "Can you imagine being throttled by a brute the size of Bruno?"

"It would have been impossible to escape," I replied.

"But I'll wager he tried," she said and closely examined the fingernails on the corpse's right hand. The ones on the index and third fingers were badly chipped and beneath them was a cluster of black material. Using a metal pick, my wife removed the dark debris and inspected it with her magnifying glass. "I see what appears to be pieces of dark leather, which were no doubt clawed away by Marlowe."

"A last gasp effort to survive."

"But to no avail," Joanna noted. "And perhaps the worst of it was he knew he was being murdered by his own brother."

"But without definitive proof."

"Oh, he had proof," she said. "Recall that the night custodian heard slow, loud footsteps crossing the stage just prior to the sound of a gunshot. That was Bruno who had come to tell Marlowe that the horse-drawn carriage was waiting. Then the thug must have secluded himself and waited until the young actor's back was turned before attacking. Once the strangulation device was applied, Marlowe knew he was a dead man and that his brother had sent the murderer."

I gestured with my head to the entrance between the curtains. "That man's cruelty knows no end."

We heard rapid footsteps arriving and Stone say, "The Watsons are here, sir."

Joanna quickly brought a finger to her lips, indicating it was best for now that we not discuss our findings with Lestrade, particularly with the presence of Halderman who might be within earshot.

The inspector entered and, with a hurried tip of his derby, went directly to the corpse for a cursory inspection. "An expected outcome," he concluded.

"So it would seem," Joanna said. "But it might be wise to wait for a complete autopsy to be performed, for it could disclose any hidden causes."

"Then we shall leave that in the good hands of your husband," Lestrade agreed.

"I trust there will not be great disfigurement with the autopsy," Halderman requested, now standing at the foot of the bed. "It will be hard enough on my mother as is."

"We shall keep that in mind," I said, trying not to glare at the bold-faced liar.

"I would hope his face and head would remain intact, so that he is recognizable."

"We shall do our best."

"Could you give me a time when all of the autopsy studies will be completed?"

"Within two days."

"I will plan the funeral arrangements accordingly."

"Do let us know the funeral home," Lestrade interjected. "For his girlfriend may be in attendance and we will wish to have a word with her."

Halderman's brow went up involuntarily. "Girlfriend? He had no girl-friend to my knowledge."

"Nor to mine until I spoke with his fellow cast members," Lestrade said. "On several occasions they recalled a rather charming woman coming backstage to congratulate Marlowe for his performance. They seemed quite close and actually left the theater together at least once, although they tried to conceal their departure. So we appear to have a secret lover."

"By chance, did they know her name?" Joanna asked, feigning real interest.

"They did not, but I shall shortly be off to Canary Wharf where the actor resided and worked," Lestrade replied. "Perhaps his friends will be able to give us more information on the hidden girlfriend."

Halderman asked hurriedly, "Do you believe this girlfriend was somehow involved in my brother's accident?"

"That is what we hope to find out," the inspector said before turning to Joanna. "Would you care to accompany me to Canary Wharf? I must admit you have the keen ability to draw information from barmaids and workers of that sort."

"I would very much like to join you, but I think my time will be better spent at my husband's side whilst he performs the autopsy," she declined gracefully. "As you well know, there are questions regarding the unfortunate death of Hugh Marlowe."

"Indeed there are," Lestrade concurred. "I trust you will notify me at once if any new findings are uncovered."

"We shall."

"Then let us proceed," I said. "Sister, please be good enough to summon an orderly and have the body transported to pathology in preparation of an autopsy. You may have this area scrubbed clean unless the inspector wishes to investigate further."

"We are done here," Lestrade responded and led the way out, followed by his two detectives.

Whilst my wife and I were departing, we heard Halderman asking the sister about the whereabouts of his brother's belongings and how he should go about fetching them. Joanna waited until we were well away from the death scene before taking my arm and guiding me to the side.

"Did you not find it strange that Halderman is interested in his brother's belongings?" she asked in a near whisper. "Here he is so richly attired in a cashmere topcoat and Church shoes, and he wishes to pick up a bag of bloodied, malodorous garments and carry them away."

"He is certainly not moved by sentimental reasons," I said quietly.

"Of course not," Joanna agreed. "In all likelihood, he fears the presence of any item which is somehow attached to the blackmailing."

"But what?"

"We shall find out soon enough," she said and pointed to the telephone at the sister's station. "Please call your office and have Rose pick up all of Marlowe's belongings at once. If she meets any resistance, she is to tell them that all of his items must remain in the department of pathology until the autopsy is completed."

I quickly made the phone call and sent the ever-efficient Rose on her mission. My secretary was a long-time employee at St. Bart's and knew every department like the back of her hand. She also had the subtle ability to persuade other secretaries and managers to do her bidding.

As we walked on, Joanna brought to mind another of Halderman's unusual requests. "And there was the matter of not disfiguring Marlowe at autopsy, for fear it would upset Halderman's dear mother whom he had not seen nor spoken to in decades."

"He obviously wishes us not to dissect into his brother's head and skull," I replied.

"Which indicates he knows little of autopsies, for the area of disease or damage always draws the most interest," she continued on. "But for some reason he prefers we not pay careful attention to the head and skull, which happens to be the area of the fatal gunshot wound."

"He wants something to remain hidden."

"And to remain hidden, it has to be overlooked."

Down the stairs we went and into the main corridor which was brimming with hospital personnel as the lunch hour approached. We made our way amongst rolling wheelchairs and gurneys before turning into a narrower corridor where there was far less foot traffic. We picked up our pace, for we were eager to examine Marlowe's belongings. But I slowed as we approached the laboratory section of the hospital.

"Let us make a brief stop," I said.

"For what purpose?" asked my wife.

"To have Marlowe's saliva tested for cyanide, using the methods you described," I replied and guided her into a well-lighted research laboratory, where a friend and colleague, Dr. Harold Markham, was busily shaking a conical flask.

"Ah, Watson," the director of pharmacology greeted us warmly and placed down the flask. "To what do I owe this honor?"

"Your expertise," I replied.

"What little I have is at your disposal."

"Excellent, then," I said and gestured to Joanna. "I believe you recall meeting my wife some time ago."

"Oh, indeed I do, for one does not easily forget the famous Joanna Watson," he said and gave her a welcoming bow. "Am I about to be involved in one of your mysteries?"

"Perhaps," she replied evasively. "We will know more once you complete a most unusual test."

"I am at your service," he offered. "Pray tell what test?"

"One that detects the presence of cyanide in saliva."

The pharmacologist's brow went up in surprise. "How in the world do you two know of this recent advance?"

"That is my wife's doing," I admitted. "I should leave the details to her."

"Let me assure you I have no experience with the test and only read of it in a science journal," she told him. "It involves the use of iron nitrate as an indicator."

"Yes, yes," Markham responded enthusiastically. "I, too, read the article you mentioned, but have not yet scrutinized the technique."

"Well then, you are about to."

"Tell me more."

"We have a saliva specimen from a corpse who may have died as a result of cyanide poisoning," she described. "We should like you to test it using a strip of iron nitrate."

"I would be delighted to do so," said he, accepting the cotton swab from me. "Of course I will have to test a number of control samples to make certain the results on your specimen are accurate."

"When can we expect to hear from you?"

"A day perhaps, two at the most."

"Keep us informed."

"Oh, rest assured I will."

We departed with a wave and hurried down to my office where Rose awaited us, with a wrinkled nose. She gestured to a side table that held a large cloth bag which reeked with the odor of stale blood and decaying human tissue.

"I did not attempt to deodorize it for fear of disturbing clues you might be interested in," Rose said.

"Well done," I praised. "And for your excellent service, you deserve an early lunch."

"And a breath of fresh air," she said with a smile and reached for her bonnet.

Holding the malodorous bag at arm's length, I carried it into my private office and deposited it on a stone slab which was usually reserved for skeletal parts. I stepped back and allowed my wife to search through the items, for she was particularly skilled at finding items concealed in garments. In one memorable instance, I recall her discovering hundred-pound notes in the lining of a corset belonging to the mistress of a world-class thief.

"Let us begin with the shoes," she said, carefully inspecting the inner soles and heels for secret compartments which were not present. Marlowe's socks were also unremarkable except for several holes about the toe level.

Joanna spent little time with the shirt that was heavily stained with blood and showed no tears or loss of buttons which would have indicated a struggle. The belt and its trousers were more productive. A side pocket contained five shillings, whilst a rear one held a shoddy leather wallet. Within the wallet was a single, wrinkled pound note and a number of cards. My wife sorted through them until she came to a recent photograph.

"Well, well," she said, holding it up for me to see. It was a lovely picture of Anne Atwood who was dressed in a formal gown. Joanna turned it over which gave us a clear view of the inscription written on the back. It read, "Forever yours, Anne."

"There can be no doubt they were lovers," I stated the obvious.

"There never was any doubt," Joanna said. "And now we must re-question Anne Atwood."

"To what end?"

"To learn why she is so desperately hiding the truth."

20

THE AUTOPSY

Even in death Hugh Marlowe was a most handsome man. He had a narrow, unlined face, with perfectly contoured lips and high-set cheekbones that partially concealed his dark brown eyes. His mouth was closed, which was an unusual feature of the dead. But his face was where the attractive features ended, for his chest had been split wide open and its contents removed. I was surprised to find that his heart was not enlarged nor dilated, which was commonly seen in those suffering from a chronic cardiac disorder.

"His heart is normal sized," I commented to my wife. "With a history of a loud cardiac murmur, I would have expected to see some obvious sign of dysfunction."

"Could the murmur have originated from a source other than his heart?" Joanna asked.

"It's possible, for an arterio-venous malformation in the chest can produce a similar sound," I replied. "But let us dig a little deeper."

With a sharp scalpel, I sliced through the thick outer muscle of the ventricles and discovered the reason for the murmur. There was an obvious defect in the wall which separated the right from the left ventricle. "He had an interventricular septal defect which caused the murmur. The opening itself was relatively small, so it made a loud noise, but did not result in dysfunction."

Joanna nodded as she viewed the abnormality. "It was a fortunate murmur, for it prohibited his recruitment into the military."

"He might have been better off on the Western Front, and out of reach of his half-brother," I said, and moved up to the corpse's neck. Under the bright, overhead light, the bruises about the laryngeal area were even deeper than anticipated. The skin was rubbed raw down to the dermis, with caked blood filling the gouges. I made a vertical incision into the area and exposed a badly fractured hyoid bone. I stepped aside so Joanna could have a look.

She leaned forward and examined the bone with her magnifying glass. "It is truly a crushing fracture which is typical of strangulation."

"So crushing that the bone fragments completely obstructed Marlowe's airway," I added. "Death was about to occur."

"But Bruno couldn't allow that to happen, for the death had to appear accidental."

I moved away from the neck and up to the head, which was now free of debris, with the dressing removed and the wound area cleaned of caked blood. The wound itself had been enlarged by the surgeon whilst he searched for the source of the bleeding, but the defect in the skull remained relatively small, as is the case in most entrance wounds caused by a bullet of lesser caliber. Now, with all the blood and debris washed away, one could see the obviously charred skin around the wound, which was clear evidence the pistol had been held close to Marlowe's head.

Joanna carefully washed the area with saline before using her magnifying glass to examine the wound. "The burn mark from exploding gunpowder is almost impossible to erase. It is literally engraved in the surrounding skin."

"And in the nearby brain tissue as well," I noted. "The surgical specimen submitted by the operating surgeon showed clusters of black particles embedded in the cerebral cortex."

"And thus, our young actor was strangled and shot at close range," my wife concluded. "You should clearly state these factual findings in your autopsy report, and see to it that a copy of the report reaches Inspector Lestrade, who will no doubt make Eric Halderman aware of it."

"With all the evidence at hand, I am not certain it would be worthwhile to saw open the skull," I said. "It would surely cause obvious disfigurement, which would only add to the misery of Hugh Marlowe's mother."

"It does give one pause," Joanna agreed hesitantly. "For it would be a living nightmare to have a grieving mother see a disfigured son one last time."

We stood silent and briefly pondered the decision, for we both knew that overlooked clues were invariably the most important. An autopsy which ignores a complete search of the damaged organ responsible for death is an incomplete autopsy by any measure. The skull had to be opened.

We nodded to one another, having both reached the correct conclusion. The entire brain had to be removed and the track of the bullet, with the damage it caused clearly delineated. I would instruct our senior technician to do his very best in reconstructing Hugh Marlowe's head and face.

"I shall give our orderly Benson a call and have him bring along his saw," I said, breaking the silence.

Joanna donned a pair of rubber gloves to again examine the wound, for Benson would surely saw through it whilst opening the skull. "Probably a small caliber weapon, then?"

"Most likely," I concurred.

"Which would account for the absence of an exit wound."

"I read Harry Askins's admitting note and he made no mention of an exit wound on his examination."

"Let us make certain, for Askins's attention would have been focused on the frontal wound," she said and lifted the corpse's head to expose the occipital area. There was no blood and no wound to be seen. She then reached for a metal comb and ran it through the hair about the occiput, but encountered no obstruction. As a last measure, she combed through the thick, dark hair atop the corpse's head and came to an abrupt stop.

"Hello!" Joanna called out.

"What have you found?" I asked at once.

"An elevated swelling which should not be there." She used her fingers to accurately locate the elevation then took scissors to the area and snipped away several locks of hair. Once again she employed her magnifying glass and repeatedly studied the area.

"Is there an obstacle of some sort?"

"Just a swelling," she replied and gave the matter lengthy thought before suddenly reacting. "A scalpel, please."

I handed her a clean blade and gazed over her shoulder whilst she made an incision into the small lump. No blood clot was forthcoming as I expected, but then she pressed on the edges of the incision and a distorted bullet came to the surface.

"The exit wound!" Joanna proclaimed. "And the metal bullet which made it."

"But it was supposedly a blank which was fired, and blanks are composed of wadded up paper," I noted.

My wife smiled humorlessly at the obvious conclusion. "But Bruno was instructed to insert a real cartridge into the weapon, and thus make certain the gunshot would be a mortal one."

"Eric Halderman was not leaving anything to chance," I said.

"And he realized that an autopsy of the brain may uncover a metal bullet and not a blank, which would uncover a murder rather than an accidental misfire." Joanna extracted the misshapen round and deposited it in a nearby pan, then stripped off her gloves. "Now we know beyond a doubt the reason why Halderman tried to persuade us not to open the skull. It had nothing to do with the mother's feelings, and everything to do with concealing his brother's murder."

"We now have two solid pieces of evidence which will back up the contention in any court of law," I said.

"Lestrade should be notified immediately," my wife recommended, whilst washing her hands in a close-by basin. "He will of course be obliged to inform the half-brother."

"Upon receiving the news, Halderman will surely feel the noose tightening around his neck."

"Not to the extent you think, for he will find comfort in the fact that only the word of his trusted henchman Bruno can send him to the gallows," Joanna reminded. "And were Bruno to confess, he, too, would be marched up those final steps to a waiting hangman."

"But you stated earlier that Bruno was the weak link in this diabolical scheme."

"He remains so," Joanna said and left it at that.

21

THERMODYNAMICS

After a long day we returned to Baker Street and were met on the first floor by a worried Miss Hudson. "I am afraid Dr. Watson's knee is acting up again, yet he insists on attending the special meeting tonight."

"Is it that bothersome?" I asked, for my father's gait was quite normal when I departed following breakfast.

"He is limping about badly and refuses to acknowledge his limitations," she informed us. "Each step seems to bring a grimace and, even with a cane, he is a bit unsteady."

"I shall have a word with him."

"At the very least, you may wish to accompany him to the meeting in the event he needs assistance."

"What meeting so requires his presence?" Joanna asked.

"It is a gala at the University of London honoring a close friend and former colleague of my father's who is a most distinguished scientist," I replied.

"In what field, may I ask?"

"Thermodynamics."

"That subject is beyond my grasp."

168

"It is for most people, for it delves into a substance we can feel but cannot see," I said. "It is called heat."

"I must confess I do not find such a topic of interest."

"You will when you learn that the scientist we are referring to is Sir Anthony Armstrong-Jones, who is a consultant to safe manufacturers around the world. As a matter of fact, he is so valued by the Chubb group that they have given him a permanent position."

"Why so?"

"Because of his knowledge in fireproofing," I replied. "According to my father, Sir Anthony is a foremost expert in making safes and vaults fireproof."

"Do you know the particulars?" Joanna asked, her interest suddenly piqued.

I shook my head in response. "This is far out of my depth, but my father has some insight into the mechanisms involved."

"Then let us inquire whilst you examine his ailing knee."

As we ascended the stairs to our parlor, I told my wife of my limited knowledge of Sir Anthony Armstrong-Jones. He occupied the chair of thermodynamics at the University of London and, for his remarkable achievements, he was being awarded the Marcus Medal, which was the highest honor that could be bestowed upon a scientist at the university. My father, being a longtime friend and former classmate of Sir Anthony's, was invited to a seat on the dais during the medal ceremony. Joanna waved away the personal information and was only interested in the awardee's skill at making safes secure from fire. Like her father before her, my wife's curiosity and need to acquire knowledge only applied to crime. Apparently, the intricacies of fireproofing a safe somehow appealed to her.

We entered the nicely warmed parlor and found my father seated by the fireplace, with his right leg extended and resting on a cushioned ottoman. He waved to us as he read our worried expressions. "I see you have been speaking with Miss Hudson."

"She is concerned for your well-being," I said.

"Overly concerned, I would think," he replied and flexed his knee without discomfort to prove his point.

"Yet she observed your rather noticeable limp."

"That is because I was performing a trial run on the stairs," said my father. "You see, I must mount a short flight of steps to reach the dais where I have been given an honorary seat."

Using his cane, he pushed himself up from an overstuffed chair and strolled about the parlor, showing little discomfort, although he did favor his right leg somewhat. "I shall be fine at the gala," he assured.

"With Joanna and I at your side," I interjected. "For my dear wife seems interested in Sir Anthony's work on Chubb safes."

"On making them fireproof?"

"More or less," Joanna replied. "For adequate fireproofing, one must insert a suitable retardant between the layers of metal. I have often wondered if that weakens the steel structure of the safe."

"I am certain Anthony can supply you with the answer," my father said. "Following the ceremony, I will see to it you meet my good friend of too many years to count."

"Excellent," she approved. "Now, be good enough to give us some information about the Marcus Medal Sir Anthony is about to receive."

"It is an award of the highest honor, which is conferred to only the most distinguished of scientists," he described. "How high, you might ask? I will only say that several of its recipients have gone on to receive the Nobel Prize."

"Quite impressive."

"And justly deserved, for Anthony's work on thermodynamics touches virtually every aspect of our lives," my father noted, whilst gesturing to various objects about our parlor. "The warmth from our fireplace, the lights from our lamps, and even the bricks in our walls require heat to be produced."

"All of which we take for granted."

"Thanks in large measure to the laws of thermodynamics," he said before glancing at his timepiece. "We should depart, for our taxi is scheduled to arrive shortly."

My father's limp became more noticeable as we descended the stairs, but he managed to hide his discomfort from our view. I should not have been surprised, for here was a man who never complained of his chronic shoulder pain which was inflicted by a jezail bullet during the Second Afghan War. Unbeknownst to most, a similar jezail bullet had found its mark in my father's left leg, but it damaged muscle and left bone untouched.

On our ride to the University of London, we occupied an oversized taxi with a large rear compartment which allowed my father to stretch out his ailing knee. There was a glass partition between the driver and his passengers, and thus our conversation could not be overheard. Still, we spoke in low voices as we told my father of our striking findings at autopsy. With the clear evidence of the young actor's murder, he, too, believed that Halderman would feel the mounting pressure and make a final demand for a large sum to bring the blackmailing to an end. But he was also of the opinion that it would be a false promise, for once the pursuit of Scotland Yard for the murderer faded, as it surely would, Halderman would return to blackmailing Sir William's family. To the evil half-brother it would be a bottomless treasure trove. When informed of Joanna's belief that Bruno was the weak link to be exploited, my father urged caution, for here was a vicious murderer who had an unbreakable allegiance to Halderman.

An unexpected downpour began on our arrival at the university, but fortunately the entrance into the building was protected by a canvas roof. A doorman dressed in a beefeater uniform ushered us into a large auditorium that was filled to near capacity. After helping my father to his chair on the dais, I returned to our seats which were favorably placed at tenth row center. To the front of us was a gathering of dignitaries that included the Lord Mayor of London as well as a group of richly attired benefactors.

My eyes must have widened when I saw a familiar face amongst them. I nudged Joanna gently with my elbow.

"Without staring, glance over to the left at the very front and tell me who you see," I said quietly.

Joanna focused her vision on Eric Halderman then looked away. "Mr. Halderman wears a variety of coats, does he not?"

"But why the interest in thermodynamics?"

"I doubt that is the purpose of his attendance," she replied. "Like most nouveau riche, I suspect he searches for ways to associate with the upper class in an effort to fit in. Recall the charity event he sponsored at his mansion, to which he invited Sir William and Lady Charlotte."

On closer inspection, I could see that Joanna's depiction of Halderman was correct, for around his neck was a blue ribbon that held a gold medallion. He was obviously a benefactor. "Should we attempt to avoid him?"

"No need to bother," my wife said. "If our presence throws him off-balance, so be it."

"What if he comes over to say hello?"

"We should be cordial and express our condolences on the passing of his brother."

The audience quieted as the ceremony began, with the dean of the university giving the introductory remarks. He emphasized how prestigious the Marcus Medal was and went on to name several of its famous past recipients. With the medal came a five-thousand-pound prize which Sir Anthony generously donated to the scholarship endowment fund for underprivileged students. The announcement of the gift was met with a standing ovation. Then came the long list of achievements by the recipient and the presentation of the medal, which brought on another, prolonged standing ovation.

Finally, Sir Anthony rose to the podium and began his gratitude to the university for its many years of support. As was the case with most scientists, he gave little attention to his attire and appearance. He was a small, thin man, with long, gray hair that had obviously avoided the barber's chair. The scientist was dressed in a tan corduroy suit with a sweater beneath it, partially hiding the tie he wore. But his voice and tone were that of an individual familiar with large audiences. In a clear, articulate manner he introduced the topic of thermodynamics so it was understandable to all. He emphasized that heat was the major source of energy which powered our entire society. Without it, factories could not produce, motor vehicles could not run, homes could not be heated, and life forms could not exist. But then he spoke of war and how engines converted petrol to heat which allowed ships to sail and planes to fly. Modern warfare was totally dependent on heat, and heat by itself could kill. As an example, he described the British tank, a heavily armored vehicle, which could deliver powerful shells, but in itself could become a death trap. If an enemy should penetrate the armor and set fire to the fuel line, the blaze within the tank would result in a temperature of two thousand degrees and incinerate everything it reached. The soldiers inside would be cremated.

Joanna leaned forward in her seat, intent on catching every word, as Sir Anthony told of the desperate need to fireproof the interior of the armored vehicles, for without such protection there was no hope of the crew surviving. For this reason, newer, more resistant forms of fireproofing were urgently needed.

Sir Anthony concluded his presentation on a more optimistic note, speaking at length about the universe's greatest source of energy, which was the sun. He predicted that the day would come in the not-too-distant future when we will learn how to harvest the heat from the sun, which will provide untold amounts of energy for all time. The ending promise of hope brought forth a final, sustained standing ovation.

Following the presentation ceremony, we gathered in a spacious reception room for celebratory drinks. Whilst sipping from glasses of chilled champagne, we watched my father mingle amongst old classmates, obviously enjoying himself. Although using his cane, he showed no evidence of a limp, but we were nonetheless pleased to have accompanied him in the event he required assistance.

Out of the corner of my eye, I saw a most unexpected visitor approaching. "Halderman is coming our way," I whispered to my wife, whose expression remained unchanged.

"Well, hello," Halderman greeted us, with a smile. "Are you also members of the Marcus Society?"

"Actually not," Joanna replied. "We are here in the company of the senior Dr. Watson, who is a former classmate and longtime friend of Professor Armstrong-Jones."

"Nevertheless, you are most welcome to our gathering to honor the distinguished professor."

"It is our pleasure to be in attendance," she said. "And allow me to take this moment to offer our condolences on the passing of your brother."

"Thank you for your kind thoughts," he responded. "As one might expect, it has been quite a shock to our family, particularly our dear mother."

"I can only begin to imagine," she sympathized.

Another beribboned guest waved cordially to Halderman, who returned the greeting. "Please excuse me whilst I say hello to an old friend."

"Of course."

Eric Halderman nodded genially upon his departure, but he appeared to gaze across the room for a brief moment before meeting with his acquaintance. I paid little attention to Halderman's apparent sighting, but Joanna surreptitiously followed his line of vision.

"Did you notice the subtle message he sent?" she asked.

"To whom?"

"Bruno, his manservant," my wife replied, then instructed, "You should smile and feign a chuckle before glancing over to the group stationed by the bar."

I went through the motions and stole a quick peek at the giant of a man who stood out amongst the security details which were present to protect the attending dignitaries. Bruno was huge, simply put, with a frame so broad it stretched the confines of his coat. His features were distinctly Slavic, with a wide forehead, high cheekbones, and lips which were pasted together and seemed incapable of smiling. He appeared to be returning my interest, so I looked away.

"Do you believe the message Halderman sent was to point us out?" I asked.

"Undoubtedly," she replied.

"Then he must be onto us."

"He would be a fool not to be," Joanna said and waited for a strolling couple to pass before continuing. "Halderman is most clever and has been aware of our involvement for quite some time."

"But I thought our moves were well concealed."

"Not to the eye and mind of a master criminal," she elucidated. "Put yourself in his stead as I go through the steps. First was our intense interest in the death of a young, unknown actor. This is not the sort of investigation which appeals to the daughter of Sherlock Holmes. Next, he may well have learned of our visit to the tobacconist where we made inquiries regarding a white opium-smoking pipe. The clerk at the shop would happily tell Halderman of the happening and thank him for referring the couple to Fielding and Marsh. Then there was our visit to Slough."

"Are you suggesting he had us followed?" I asked.

"More likely, he sent a spy to determine if we had paid a visit to Hugh Marlowe's mother and, if so, for what purpose. When told that a pair from the Actors' Guild came to inform the mother of her son's accident, Halderman would know the reason given was false, for the guild would never send such representatives for any actor, least of all for one of such lower standing. And the most convincing evidence of our involvement was our call to Sir William's estate."

"But surely Sir William and Lady Charlotte did not speak a word of our visit."

"But their servants no doubt did," Joanna went on. "Our presence was recognized by them the moment we stepped into that limestone mansion, and such domestics tend to talk and gossip with those of similar position at nearby estates. You see, they consider it an honor to have individuals of high status visit their households and are eager to spread the word as quickly as possible. Putting it all together, our involvement was obvious to Halderman."

"So the adversaries are clearly in the open on both sides," I concluded.

"And will continue to be as we watch one another's moves, waiting for a mistake to be made."

"Much like a game of chess, it would seem."

"With Halderman unfortunately holding the more powerful pieces."

At the moment and strictly by chance, I gazed about the large reception area until my eyes came to rest upon a small group of men gathered around another man in a wheelchair, all engaged in a friendly conversation. One of those standing was Sir William Radcliffe, who was adorned with a ribboned medallion.

I gently nudged my wife and said in a whisper, "Look to your left at those about the wheelchair."

Joanna stole a rapid glance before coming back to me. "Sir William will be wise enough to ignore us."

"And if he isn't?" I asked. "Remember, he is desperate for any news which advances his cause."

"Then we shall appear to be awed by his presence and delighted to be recognized."

I drew my handkerchief and pretended to stifle a sneeze whilst continuing to gaze at the men conversing around the wheelchair. To my surprise I saw Eric Halderman approach the group and exchange an amicable nod with Sir William, after which they spoke briefly. The audacity, I thought, watching Halderman smile at the man he was secretly blackmailing. It was quite similar to a predator cozying up to its prey, for all to see. Then I recalled that the more vicious predators enjoyed playing with their prey before killing it. "The man's conceit knows no boundaries."

Joanna had the same view of the gathering and remarked, "But his conceit is outdone by his cleverness, which makes him doubly dangerous."

She gave the man a moment's more thought, as if docketing a fact which might later prove to be useful. But her concentration was broken when my father came into view. She smiled and waved at the second most important man in her life. "Watson seems to be in such good spirits."

"Reliving pleasant memories invigorates him," I said.

My father was served a fresh glass of champagne whilst strolling over to rejoin us. Along the way he paused to shake hands with old acquaintances as he continued to enjoy the evening. There was now a bounce to his gait.

"Well, well," he said. "I noticed that you briefly had the pleasure of Eric Halderman's company."

"I believe he stopped by to show us his benefactor's medallion," Joanna opined.

"Oh yes, his type is always eager to enlighten others of their newly acquired status."

"He also took the opportunity to point us out to his ever-attentive body-guard who was standing by the bar."

"No need to let a good opportunity go to waste," said my father, as a brief scowl came and went from his face.

"I take it membership in the Marcus Society is not exclusive."

"All that is required is a letter of recommendation from a member, together with a pledge of a hundred pounds yearly," my father replied. "The money, however, goes to good causes, such as scholarships for the less fortunate students."

"And of course prospective members need not account for the source of their wealth."

"Were that a stipulation, I suspect half the membership would have been denied entry," my father said, and turned to welcome the approaching Sir Anthony Armstrong-Jones.

"Ah, Tony," he greeted his friend with a firm handshake. "Allow me to introduce my famous daughter-in-law Joanna, and her well-known chronicler, John, who also happens to be my son."

Sir Anthony gave us a courteous bow, saying, "It is my honor to meet you both."

"The honor is ours, Sir Anthony," replied Joanna. "I must tell you how much I enjoyed your splendid talk, which was most informative."

"May I inquire which portion you found so informative?" he asked, as his mind seemingly shifted back into science.

"The use of heat in warfare," she responded. "I am in particular concerned for our soldiers who are trapped within burning tanks."

"As we all are, madam."

"Can you not have those vehicles fireproofed?"

"We are attempting to do this, with the use of gypsum and asbestos, which is packed between the plates of armored steel."

"Will that not weaken the armor?"

"It actually strengthens it, for a material like gypsum forms a thick, hard layer by itself which does not melt," he described. "Our early studies reveal that such a layer offers some protection against a searing blast of heat."

"How much protection, may I ask?"

"Similar to that seen in safes," Sir Anthony replied. "It will allow for a temperature of three hundred and fifty degrees to be maintained within the safe whilst it is subjected to a room temperature of eighteen hundred degrees."

"But at that level of heat, humans cannot survive."

"We are quite aware of that, so we must do better."

Joanna gave the matter further consideration before asking, "Once the burning heat enters, can it somehow be dispersed?"

"No, madam, for it is in an enclosed space, and thus what goes in, stays in."

"A very difficult problem, then."

"Most difficult, madam."

Joanna pondered the dilemma, with her brow now furrowed in thought. To the dismay of individuals close by, she reached for a Turkish cigarette in her purse and, after lighting it, inhaled at length as the furrow in her forehead deepened. Rather than pace as was her usual custom, she stepped in place until an answer came.

"The two fire retardants you employ are gypsum and asbestos, correct?"

"That is correct."

"And I believe it true that the two have entirely different chemical positions, with gypsum being a sulfate whilst asbestos is a silicate."

Sir Anthony's eyes widened, as he was clearly taken aback by my wife's knowledge of chemistry. "That is so."

"Then they may well resist fire by different mechanisms," she went on. "Might it not be worthwhile to combine the two together and determine if the mixture is more powerful than the individual components?"

Sir Anthony nodded rapidly. "It might indeed."

"I am certain you will put it to the test, but I shall as well."

"How do you propose to perform your test?"

"I shall construct a model which allows me to determine the fire retardant ability of each such material singularly and in combination."

"Such models are not easily put together."

"They are if one employs an expert welder."

My father interjected. "I would advise you, Tony, not to doubt her ingenuity when it comes to solving problems."

"So I have read about," said he. "Do construct your model and inform me of the results."

The static from a loud speaker sudden filled the air, followed by the dean inviting all to raise their glasses for a final toast to Sir Anthony Armstrong-Jones.

We bid the distinguished scientist a pleasant good evening and slipped out the front entrance, for my father's knee was beginning to ache. As we approached a waiting taxi, I asked, "Should my father and I assist you in conducting your experiment?"

"Miss Hudson will provide all the assistance I require," Joanna said and, discarding her cigarette, left us wondering what role our gentle housekeeper would play in a most important experiment.

22

BRUNO

Just after breakfast the following morning, the Baker Street Irregulars arrived at our doorstep, which informed us that in all likelihood their mission had been accomplished. Whilst Miss Hudson was clearing the breakfast dishes, she inquired, "Shall I show the Irregulars up now, Mrs. Watson?"

"Please do," my wife replied. "And during your busy morning, I trust you will find time to contact your friend, the welder."

"I did so at daybreak, and Emmett will be happy to meet with you at your convenience."

"Five o'clock, then."

"Five, it will be," our landlady confirmed. "I sent him off with the list of materials you require, as well as the drawing of the construct you wish made."

"Did you mention that the blowtorch must be portable?"

"I emphasized it," said Miss Hudson, and departed with a full tray of empty dishes.

"Do you plan to set up the model in our parlor?" I asked.

Joanna nodded her response. "The experiment will be carried out in our fireplace, with you and your father in attendance if you wish. And with Watson's knee permitting, of course."

"I can assure you it will permit," my father said determinedly.

We heard footsteps ascending the stairs and quickly arranged the chairs so that the Irregulars would be facing us. "And remember not to utter the name Halderman in their presence," Joanna instructed.

"But you stated earlier that Halderman was already onto us," I said.

"But not to what lay in store for him, all of which revolves around his manservant Bruno."

After a brief rap on the door, the Baker Street Irregulars paraded in and marched directly to the warmth of our fireplace. They were attired in street clothes which did not have the appearance of having been slept in.

"Did you encounter any difficulties?" my wife asked.

"Not even a hint," Wiggins replied.

"Then begin, starting with your initial sighting."

"Bruno arrived at the Polanski on Tuesday evening at seven sharp," Wiggins narrated. "I was standing at the bar chatting up a barmaid so I had a good view of him. Lord! He's a big one, with a height that measures well over six feet and a weight that no doubt exceeds fifteen stone. You would have to be a fool to go against the likes of him. I should mention that his attire was a cut above the others and that he moved with the agility of an alley cat."

"Despite his size, I take it he was a good dancer."

"Quite good, ma'am."

"Did he step immediately onto the dance floor?"

"He waited off to the side for his partner."

"What made you aware he was waiting for someone?"

"Because not a minute passed before she showed up," he replied. "According to my friend Bennie, she must arrive promptly, for otherwise he becomes upset."

"Did Bennie mention the frequency of Bruno's visits?" Joanna asked.

"Every Tuesday and Friday, and always at seven sharp."

"Is he met by the same woman?"

"Always," Wiggins replied. "Shall I give you the particulars on her?"

"Hold that for now," she said. "I require more information on Bruno once he entered. Did he remain in the dance area or take the stairs to the second floor?"

"He stays on the dance floor and, according to Bennie, never gambles."

"Does he drink?"

"Never whilst I was stationed at the bar for the first hour, nor whilst Little Alfie was emptying the trash bins or mopping the floor."

"Did Little Alfie keep an eye on Bruno for the remainder of the evening?"

"He did, ma'am."

"And how did he avoid being seen?"

Little Alfie stepped forward. "I spent most of my time hidden behind the bar amongst the trash bins or in a side room where the kegs and cases are stored. Whilst in the room, it was easy enough to crack the door and peek out every few minutes. I can assure you, ma'am, he never left the dance floor."

"Did he partake in every dance?" Joanna asked.

"He never missed a single polka by Bennie's count," Wiggins rejoined the conversation. "The only time he stopped was when the band took a brief rest."

"Did he ever depart from the building?"

"Never during my watch," he replied.

"Nor during mine," Little Alfie added.

"Did he ever buy a drink for his partner?" Joanna inquired.

The two Irregulars shook their heads simultaneously.

"Was Bruno involved in any fisticuffs?"

"No way!" Wiggins replied at once. "People know to stay well clear of that one."

"So, on and on they danced without interruption."

"Never stopped, ma'am."

"What time did the couple cease to dance and depart from the Polanski?"

"Ten sharp," Sarah the Gypsy answered. "They only had to walk a half block before they arrived at Dolly's place."

"Ah, now we come to the woman," my wife said, with obvious interest. "Tell me what you know of her and their relationship."

"That took a bit of doing, ma'am, for she is the type who keeps to herself," Wiggins noted before providing the details. "Dolly Malone is her name, and she resides in rooms above a bakery where she works. Her shift goes from six to six except on Sunday when she puts in half a day. According to nosy neighbors, she shares a bed with the owner of the bakery on weekends, except Friday nights when she's with Bruno, and for that service is allowed to stay in her rooms rent-free."

"I take it the owner of the bakery and Bruno never crossed paths," said my wife.

"If they did, it would happen only once."

Joanna came back to Sarah the Gypsy. "After the couple arrived at Dolly's rooms, how long did Bruno stay? I require the precise time."

"For exactly forty-five minutes," the girl replied. "I can tell you of their activities in bed if you'd like, ma'am."

"How did you come by this viewing?"

"I climbed the fire escape of a nearby building, quiet as a church mouse, mind you, and had a look into the bedroom," she reported. "I saw nothing abnormal in their vigorous activities, which seemed to last for most of the forty-five minutes. On his departure he went directly to the Underground station."

"You followed well behind Bruno, no doubt."

"Well back and on the opposite side of the street, ma'am."

"When he entered the station, I was waiting for him, with tickets to the outgoing lines in hand," Little Alfie picked up the story. "I traveled to Hampstead Heath with him where he departed, then continued on to Golders Green before beginning my return."

"Are you certain he was unaware of your presence?"

"Quite certain, ma'am, for he paid scant attention to me and my shoe-polishing box."

"Shoe-polishing box, you say?"

"Yes, ma'am. Shoe polishers often take the late-night tubes to the other districts, where they polish the shoes of guests at the better hotels."

"You no doubt omitted the polishing box when you were following him earlier."

"Of course," Little Alfie said matter-of-factly. "I was eating a bloody big sandwich so he could not see my face."

How clever the Irregulars were, I thought, but then again to survive as an urchin on the mean streets of Whitechapel one had to be very clever indeed. I could not help but wonder what was to become of Little Alfie and Sarah the Gypsy once they matured. The pair would probably follow in Wiggins's footsteps, for there was no other avenues open to them.

"Will there be anything else, ma'am?" Wiggins asked.

"Only that you are to make no future inquiries regarding Bruno."

"We shall be on the mum, ma'am."

"Then be on your way."

Once the Irregulars departed, with the door firmly closed behind them, my father asked the question which was on my mind as well. "Why all this interest in Bruno? It's unlikely that he can be bought."

"Perhaps he can be bribed with a large sum of money that Sir William could provide," I proposed.

"Too risky," Joanna said at once. "I believe he is firmly committed to Halderman and any offer to bribe him would surely reach Halderman's ears. Should that occur, all would be lost."

"Is there a chance he could be turned through Dolly?" my father asked.

"That, too, is unlikely, for he appears to have little attachment to that woman who he treats in a most casual fashion," Joanna said. "But I am afraid that both of you are missing his most pronounced feature."

"Which is?"

"Bruno is a creature of habit," she replied. "He follows a most strict schedule in Whitechapel, performing the same acts over and over at precisely the same time."

"No doubt at Eric Halderman's insistence," I said.

"And that, dear heart, is the second most important point."

The telephone near my wife rang loudly.

"An early morning phone call is an ominous sound," she said and picked up the receiver. "Yes?"

Joanna listened intently, as if measuring each word, before answering. "Do not respond. We shall be there shortly."

"Bad news?" I asked patiently.

"Expected bad news," Joanna replied. "That was Sir William. There has been another ransom demand for an even more exorbitant amount."

23

THE EXORBITANT DEMAND

As we walked up the pebbled path to Sir William's limestone mansion, I could see fleeting faces in the windows watching our approach. It reminded me of Joanna's admonition that servants of esteemed estates enjoyed gossiping to others about the goings-on in their households. Our visit was thus quite likely to reach the ears of Eric Halderman and I wondered if that, too, was a part of my wife's plan. My thoughts were interrupted by thunder and lightning in the distance, announcing the impending storm. The dreary change in weather was no doubt certain to further dampen the mood of the family within the gilded manor.

We were met at the entrance by a dark-suited butler who escorted us through a richly decorated vestibule and into a spacious library where an obviously distressed couple awaited us. With a formal bow, the butler departed, closing the door so quietly it made no sound. But the silence was soon broken by Lady Charlotte's gentle sobs as she dabbed at the tears on her cheeks. She turned her head away in an effort to hide her anguish.

"Will this nightmare never end?" Sir William cried out in desperation, his aristocratic face now haggard and showing the signs of sleeplessness.

"He must have learned the value of a Turner seascape and has now increased his demand to ten thousand pounds." The elder statesman shook his head angrily. "This madness must stop."

"I will see to it," Joanna assured.

"How will you go about doing so?"

"With patience, for to act in haste will only prolong your torment," she replied. "But I will require your full cooperation, no matter how unseemly, to bring this unpleasant experience to a successful resolution."

"Pray tell, what do you ask of us?"

"Let us begin with the most recent demand," my wife commenced. "How was it delivered?"

"By letter," he replied. "We found the envelope in our post box this morning."

"Surely it was not delivered by post."

"No, Mrs. Watson, it was not. The photograph was contained within an unmarked envelope."

"I should like to see both the envelope and photograph."

"The photograph is most distasteful," Sir William cautioned and, upon handing them to my wife, asked, "Would it be worthwhile to have Scotland Yard search for fingerprints?"

"It will not serve your interest to involve Scotland Yard, for public disclosure would soon follow," she replied. "Moreover, I am afraid that would be a lost cause, in that I dusted the second snapshot for prints and none were found."

"Meticulous devil, isn't he?"

"Quite so," Joanna replied and moved her attention to the photograph, which caused a brief but discernible wince to cross her face.

I quickly glanced over my wife's shoulder to ascertain what about the print had caused such an unusual response from her. The exhibition on the photograph had gone far beyond inappropriate and now approached being tawdry. Anne Atwood and Hugh Marlowe were seen to be in a tight embrace, whilst indulging in a most passionate kiss. Her arms were wrapped around his neck, his hands on her bare shoulders. Other than the figures, the room was dimly lighted, making it impossible to discern its location.

"Most disturbing," I said and immediately regretted having done so, for my words brought forth a pitiful sob from Lady Charlotte, accompanied by more tears.

Joanna ignored the emotional outburst and turned the photograph over to read the written instructions. It read:

> 10,000 pounds to be delivered at last address on Canary Wharf
> a week from Tuesday night or more damaging photographs will
> be released.

My wife studied the snapshot back and front at length, making me wonder if there were important clues to be found. But my eyes remained fixed on the damning picture of the couple in a most amorous pose. Since the photographs were being released with an ever-increasing degree of sensuality, I could not help but imagine what the remaining ones would show. All concerned could only hope they did not reveal various stages of disrobing, for the damage such photographs could do to Sir William's family and reputation would be far beyond repair.

"How should we respond?" the elder statesman asked in a quiet voice.

"At this point, Sir William, you must allow me to act in your stead as a negotiator," Joanna proposed.

"Would you do so in written messages?" he asked.

"That will not work to our advantage, for it will consume more time and only prolong the blackmailing."

"How then?"

"The negotiations will have to be carried out face to face," she said. "Only then can a final payment be agreed upon."

Sir William's brow went up. "Do you know the blackmailer?"

"I know of someone who does, in that they belong to the same clan," Joanna answered evasively. "He has spoken to me regarding this matter, but he must remain anonymous in order to act as interlocutor."

"Should the powerful hand of Scotland Yard be brought to bear upon this anonymous source?" he asked. "In a most clandestine manner of course."

"That would only stir the pot and cause the source to withdraw," she warned. "If pressured, he would simply say that he is aware of the blackmailing from a third-person perspective."

"It seems we have no other course, then," he said. "How will you proceed?"

"With caution," my wife replied.

Sir William pondered the situation at length before asking, "Is it possible this despicable blackmailer somehow knew we would resort to negotiations? Is that the reason why he has given us over a week to deliver the ransom? That is longer than his prior demands."

Joanna shook her head in response. "He is not showing you any consideration, Sir William. The reason for the extension is that he realizes it would be difficult to gather ten thousand pounds on such short notice."

"He is coldhearted to the marrow."

"Most blackmailers are," she said. "And now we come to my second request, which I know you will resist, but which I assure you is most important."

"At this point, madam, nothing remains out of the question."

"I must interrogate your granddaughter once again, and of course in your absence."

Sir William gave my wife a sharp look. "Interrogate seems like a rather harsh term."

"Anne is involved far more than she admits, and there are details she is aware of which could prove to be quite helpful."

"Surely you are not insinuating that she is an active participant in the blackmailing."

"Not in a criminal sense, but she is obviously a blameless player."

"But she has suffered so much, with my poor dear now suffering with bouts of nausea so severe she can barely hold down breakfast," Lady Charlotte interjected. "Is there a real need to put her through more?"

"There is, madam. Otherwise I would not insist upon it."

"So be it then," Sir William directed. "Would you prefer to interview Anne in the library, with no one else present?"

"I think the garden would be more suitable," Joanna said. "But prior to our meeting, I require several questions to be answered. First and foremost, has your granddaughter seen the most recent photograph?"

"She has not," he replied firmly. "I saw no need to expose her to further embarrassment and humiliation."

"That is entirely understandable," said my wife. "Nevertheless, I shall have to bring it to her attention, in most discreet terms, of course."

"I will trust your judgment, but I implore you to be as gentle as possible."

"You have my word," she promised. "And now to my second question. Does Anne know of the young actor's accidental shooting?"

"I am afraid she does," Sir William sighed. "It was widely reported in the newspapers which Anne reads on occasion."

"Has she been made aware of his death?"

The information caught the elder statesman by surprise. "We were unaware of his passing, and Anne would have no way of knowing."

"Then let us proceed with the questioning," said Joanna. "My husband and I will find our way to the garden where we will await the presence of your granddaughter."

We walked out of the mansion and retraced the steps which brought us in, all the while feeling we were being watched but not seeing their eyes. Once on the pebbled path we turned about to the side of the great house and strolled on until we reached an expansive, neatly manicured garden.

A gardener pushing a wheelbarrow bowed respectfully to us, and promptly disappeared into a thicket of tall shrubbery. Overhead, the sky was darkening and I could only hope Joanna had enough time to interview Anne before the storm arrived.

"The misery is certainly taking its toll on Sir William and Lady Charlotte," I remarked quietly. "They seem to be floundering a bit."

"Every individual has their breaking point when enough pressure is applied," my wife noted.

"The last photograph, with its salacious content, would drive them close to that point," I said. "The snapshot was so sensual and suggestive that one has to believe even more such pictures are yet to come."

"That is the method of the best blackmailers," Joanna agreed. "They administer their stranglehold and gradually increase the force, so that the victim eventually breaks and submits to any demand which is made."

"Do you truly believe you can put a stop to the madness?"

"We shall find out soon enough."

Anne Atwood came down the path with a slow, hesitant gait characteristic of an individual about to face the unknown. Tall and attractive, with aristocratic features, she had long, brown hair which was carefully coiffured so it hung loosely about her shoulders. Unlike her grandparents, her face showed no evidence of distress, but rather a healthy glow.

"Thank you for agreeing to see us," Joanna began.

"My grandfather instructed me to do so, in the hope I could be of some assistance," said Anne in an even voice.

"That may well be the case," my wife encouraged. "Now I know our conversation will be difficult for you, but I must insist on your absolute honesty."

"I shall do my best."

"I am certain you will," said Joanna and gestured to a nearby bench. "Would you care to sit?"

"I prefer to stand."

"Then let us proceed to your deep involvement with Hugh Marlowe."

"We were friendly acquaintances."

"You were much more," Joanna challenged. "We know how deeply you cared for him and how he returned that care in great measure."

"I think you exaggerate, madam," Anne said in denial.

"I do not, for I have seen the most recent photograph, which shows the two of you in a most tender and passionate embrace."

Anne's face briefly lost its composure, but she quickly gathered herself. Without denying the affair, she asked, "Is he on the road to recovery?"

"I am afraid not," said my wife. "I bring with me the most dreadful news that Hugh Marlowe has passed away."

"Oh, no!" Anne cried out, stunned by her lover's death. "Oh, no! Please tell me it is not true."

"But it is true, for the wound he suffered was a mortal one."

Anne trembled with grief as tears flowed down her cheeks and onto the silk scarf she was wearing. "Oh, no! Oh, no!" she repeated over and over.

Joanna guided her over to a wooden bench and sat with her until the tears stopped. With effort, Anne took several deep breaths and managed to collect herself.

"Did he ever regain consciousness?" the young woman asked, sniffing back the remaining tears.

"He did not, for his head wound was far too severe," Joanna reported. "But I must tell you that there is more evidence to indicate the gunshot was not accidental."

Anne's eyes suddenly widened. "Are you saying he was shot intentionally?"

"So it would appear."

"But by whom?"

"That is what we must determine, and hopefully you can assist us in finding the individual responsible."

"Tell me how I can be of help," she said, with determination showing through the grief on her face.

"Describe in detail how you came to meet Hugh Marlowe."

"It all began when I went backstage to—"

"No, no," Joanna interrupted. "One does not simply walk backstage. Such an entrance has to be arranged."

"It was, by Mr. Eric Halderman, who is Hugh's half-brother."

All of the pieces of the puzzle suddenly came together. Eric Halderman was behind everything from the very beginning. He set up the initial meeting, obviously believing the young, attractive debutante would fall deeply in love with the handsome young actor. The affair would be the essential element in the scheme to blackmail.

"How did you come to know Mr. Halderman?" my wife was asking.

"It was by chance," Anne replied. "I was in the garden playing with my spaniel when the hound abruptly dashed over to the grove of trees which separates our estate from that belonging to Mr. Halderman. The dog was attracted to the Halderman's rottweiler who was having a seizure. Whenever the rottweiler detects the scent of a nearby hound, it often precipitates a seizure, for which Mr. Halderman apologized, in that he heard my dog barking earlier and should have kept his dog inside. In any event, whilst the animal recovered, we had a very pleasant conversation about the theater, for which I hold a great interest. I have actively participated at several lesser-known venues."

"As an actress, then?"

"I try my best and enjoy it immensely, much to the displeasure of my grandmother," she said, her mood brightening somewhat as the conversation moved away from the tragic death of Hugh Marlowe. "But my father approves and that is what matters most to me."

"I take it you told Mr. Halderman of your acting aspirations."

"I did indeed, and he suggested a meeting with his brother which might pave a way for me into a possible role," she replied, then blushed at the contradiction of what she had said previously. "I misspoke earlier when I told you my visit backstage was to congratulate the actors. It was arranged so I could meet Hugh."

"That was very thoughtful of him," Joanna commented, keeping all but a hint of sarcasm out of her voice. "Were you aware that Mr. Halderman provided the horse-drawn carriage for your most enjoyable ride through London with Hugh Marlowe?"

"Oh, yes," Anne replied. "It was so considerate of him."

"Most considerate," Joanna said, concealing the disgust we both felt for this jackal. "Being a dog fancier myself, I wonder if the rottweiler did, in fact, recover from its seizure."

"It eventually did, but remained unsteady on its feet," Anne recalled. "But before they departed, Mr. Halderman gave the hound a dose of anti-seizure medication."

"Was that the last time you saw your neighbor?"

"It was the last and only time, for Mr. Halderman is known to be a recluse."

"So I have heard," my wife said, rising to her feet. "Well then, you have been most helpful, and I do regret being the bearer of such sad news."

"You were very kind to do so," Anne said.

"Before we depart, there is one final matter to discuss," Joanna said. "It involves a rather delicate situation."

Anne was instantly on guard. "Regarding Hugh?"

"It is regarding you and your pregnancy which is becoming more obvious and which you will in short order be no longer able to hide."

Anne's jaw dropped in surprise, and for several moments she was speechless. It required a deep breath for her to regain her composure. "How could you possibly know?"

"The signs are clearly there," my wife replied. "First is the morning sickness which Lady Charlotte spoke of. She has not yet made the connection, but she will soon enough. And then you now exhibit the blush of pregnancy, with your rose-colored cheeks that project a glorious sheen which cosmetics can neither produce nor conceal."

The young woman nodded at my wife's assessment. "And there is now a noticeable bump in my abdomen."

A period of silence ensued, with the only sound coming from the wind blowing through the trees, but even that abruptly came to a halt.

"You will have to make plans," Joanna advised. "There are alternatives, as I am certain you are aware."

"I plan to keep this baby," Anne said in a most determined voice. "And I will love it as much as I loved my dear Hugh."

"Perhaps you should discuss it with your grandparents."

"They will not deter me."

"At least, you should hear them out."

"The decision is already made, and if the baby is a boy I shall name him Hugh."

"Which would be most appropriate," Joanna had to agree. "But again, please take your time in reaching a decision, for you must keep in mind that it is not a simple task to raise a child without a father. And on this matter, I speak from personal experience."

"My poor Hugh will never have the chance to see his baby," Anne uttered softly, whilst tears welled in her eyes and spilled onto her cheeks. She dabbed at them with a lace handkerchief as the wind gusted and the sky darkened even further, indicating the storm was imminent. "I must leave you now and speak with my grandparents."

"Whatever the circumstances, I am certain that Sir William and Lady Charlotte will stand by your side."

Anne nodded appreciatively and departed, with her head held high.

Once she had disappeared into the mansion, we strolled over to the grove of trees which separated the adjoining estates. Peering through the thick shrubbery, we had a clear view of Eric Halderman's massive mansion. It contained numerous windows, with the largest ones being located on the first floor. Joanna used a long stick to stir a mound of manure which had obviously been expelled by a very large animal.

"This is the spot where Halderman spied and continues to spy on Sir William's estate," she said.

"And where he undoubtedly waited for Anne Atwood to make an appearance," I added.

"No doubt," she agreed and took my arm as we walked back to our waiting taxi. "I think Anne stood up to the disclosure of her pregnancy rather well, all things considered."

"She showed herself to be a quite strong woman," said I. "And I suspect that with the passing of time the memory of Hugh Marlowe will fade."

"It will not fade, but only grow stronger," Joanna predicted.

"Based on what, may I ask?"

"Her plans to have Hugh Marlowe's baby, who will remind her constantly of the man she once loved so dearly."

"How in the world will this poor girl deal with such overwhelming heartache?"

"With dignity, I suspect, for the blood of Sir William runs through her veins."

24

THE EXPERIMENT

E mmett Mullins had the appearance of a welder, with his thick frame
and heavily muscled arms. He was a man of few words, and when he
spoke each word seemed to count. Standing back and using his practiced
eye, he silently measured the width and depth of our fireplace before
searching the bricks within for crevices which he marked with chalk.

"Your apparatus will fit nicely, ma'am," he announced and began assem-
bling the strange contraption he had constructed for my wife.

First, he brought forth a small metal table, with four legs, which stood
no more than two feet tall. Its top was flat and contained three round
holes which were well separated and equidistant from one another. Then
he reached for three slender metal poles, each of which fit tightly into the
aforementioned holes. But the most curious items were the doubly layered
metal squares which were welded into the top of the poles.

"There you have it, ma'am, and I must admit I do not have the slightest
idea of what purpose it serves," the welder said.

"We are about to conduct an experiment in the art of fireproofing,"
Joanna explained. "The table you constructed so well now supports three
poles, which hold the metal sheets to be tested. Each of the small sheets

consists of two layers of steel you welded together, but only after inserting the fire retardants I requested."

"I was sure to follow your orders to the letter, ma'am," he assured. "The retardants of asbestos, gypsum, and a mixture of the two were placed separately in their enclosures."

"Very good," she approved. "I shall now insert three candles into the crevices within the wall of the fireplace and we can begin."

My wife forced the candles into position, then instructed the welder to move the apparatus into the fireplace, making certain that each metal square was facing, but well separated from, its opposing candle. "Now, Mr. Mullins, be good enough to ignite your blowtorch and apply the flame to the outer surface of each sheet individually, keeping it there until directed to move on to the next sheet."

Joanna watched with interest whilst the welder reached for the blowtorch that consisted of a brass cannister with an elongated spout from which the flame could be discharged. As the flame was lit and brought to maximum intensity, my wife's attention went intermittently from her wristwatch to the blaze and metal square, then to the opposing candle before returning to her wristwatch. She called out the passage of time for the benefit of my father and me. It apparently took seven minutes for the first candle to melt.

"Move on to the next square," she said, and requested the same procedure. Again, seven minutes were to pass before the second candle began to drip. "And now on to the third."

The intensity of the flame remained the same, but the final metal box seemed to resist the heat better than the others, for over ten minutes were to elapse prior to the candle beginning to melt. "Thank you very much, Mr. Mullins," my wife said, bringing the experiment to a close.

"We should wait a while for the apparatus to cool before removing it, ma'am," the welder advised, as he switched off the blowtorch and placed it aside.

"Please leave everything as is, for there will be further experiments," she requested.

"Very well, ma'am," he said. "When shall I return?"

"You will be notified," she replied. "But within the week, I would think."

"I should like to leave the blowtorch behind as well, for it remains quite hot," the welder said. "Once cooled, please hand it to Miss Hudson, from whom I will retrieve it later."

"A fine plan," Joanna said. "Please present us with the fee for your service."

"It is somewhat expensive, ma'am, for steel is in short supply during wartime."

"Understandably so."

"It comes to four pounds, five."

"A most reasonable charge," she said, and reached into her purse for the correct amount. "Now, be on your way and expect a call in the near future."

Mullins nodded appreciatively and departed with his tool kit in hand.

"Well, well," Joanna said, obviously pleased with the results. "What does your keen eye tell you?"

"That the metal sheet containing a mixture of gypsum and asbestos was the most fire resistant," I replied.

"Which one might have expected, for the gypsum contains hydrates, which when sufficiently heated release a water vapor that the asbestos traps," she elucidated.

"Do you believe your findings will assist in producing a more fire-resistant tank?" my father asked.

"It may well, if one can insert a thick asbestos lining which holds densely packed gypsum."

"You should pass your findings on to Sir Anthony."

"I plan to, but first I must call Eric Halderman and arrange for our meeting tomorrow."

"This is dangerous business, Joanna," my father worried, having been apprised of our visit to Sir William's estate. "You will be walking into the lion's den."

"I am aware, but fear not, for I will have my dear husband at my side."

"Armed, I would hope."

"There is no need, for Eric Halderman knows we lack the evidence to have him charged of any criminal activity," said Joanna. "He will behave like an innocent man and watch his every word."

"Then why bother with the meeting?"

"For a number of reasons," she replied. "First, there is only the slimmest possibilities he will agree to a final payment to stop the blackmailing, all the while denying any guilt. Nevertheless, I will try my best to this end."

"What will you use to entice him?"

"The loss of the things he values the most."

"His wealth and its trappings, then?"

"Along with his status in society."

"But to do so might necessitate making his criminal activity public, which would do great harm to Sir William's family."

"I am aware."

"You will be treading on a very precarious tightrope here."

"But it is the straightest road to resolution, and thus worth attempting."

"Let us hope for all concerned that your effort proves to be successful," my father said, then reached for his cherrywood pipe and carefully lighted it. "There is another matter in this case I find most concerning."

Joanna sighed audibly, for she shared the same worry. "It is the pregnancy of Anne Atwood."

"It goes beyond shame and humiliation for the family," he went on. "We must consider the possibility that she will do something foolish to bring her childbearing to an end."

"That has crossed my mind as well."

"Then, pray tell how do you propose to deal with the situation?"

"The first order of business is to finally resolve this case, one way or the other," she replied. "Once that is accomplished, I plan to have a long conversation with Anne and suggest a path out of her dilemma."

"May I know the suggestion you will propose?"

"I will only say that it involves her mother who is currently a patient in an isolated tuberculosis sanitorium," said Joanna and, ending the conversation, began to inspect the starting mechanism of the blowtorch. For some reason it merited her curiosity.

The telephone rang loudly which broke Joanna's concentration and caused her to place the blowtorch aside. She stared at the phone, which drew all of our attention, for late evening calls usually carried troubling messages.

I reached for the receiver. "Yes?"

It was Harold Markham, the director of pharmacology at St. Bart's, who apologized for intruding into our evening, but thought it important to inform us on the results of the test we had requested. He had repeated the analysis in triplicate to make certain the measurement was accurate. After thanking him, I replaced the receiver into its cradle.

"The test on Hugh Marlowe's saliva was strongly positive for cyanide," I reported, shaking my head in disgust. "What sort of man so callously murders his own brother?"

"Only the evilest of the evil would do so," my father replied.

Joanna returned to her study of the blowtorch, saying, "To Eric Halderman, his brother was simply a loose thread that had to be snipped off."

"Let us hope, my dear Joanna, that this most evil man does not consider you to be a loose thread as well," my father cautioned.

25

THE MEETING

Lady Charlotte's description of the Halderman mansion was spot-on, with rich furnishings that lacked taste. We were ushered through a marbled vestibule which was a replica of Sir William's except for the frescoes that were obviously of lesser quality. Above, we heard heavy footsteps which quickly came and went before silence returned. The butler opened a mahogany door for us and we entered a most spacious and ornate library. Its walls were lined with shelves that contained row after row of leather-bound volumes. On a nearby table were scrolls of ancient parchment that had an eye-catching glow about them. But the hanging tapestries were overly colorful, and the few paintings appeared modernistic, with odd-shaped forms. Close to the tapestries was a rottweiler of immense size who watched our every move. Eric Halderman was seated behind a massive Victorian desk which made the small man seem even smaller.

"This is a most unexpected visit, but you are welcome nonetheless," he said, barely rising from his chair.

"I come at the request of Sir William," Joanna stated in a formal tone.

"Ah, Sir William," said Halderman. "Pray tell, how may I be of service?"

"You may wish our conversation to be private," my wife encouraged, glancing over to Bruno who stood motionless next to a strange-looking safe. It was square shaped and held up on four thick legs which were bolted to the floor. "My words are meant for your ears only."

"I trust my manservant implicitly," he said, waving away any concern.

Despite Halderman's casual tone, one could feel the tension rising in the library. Even the monstrous hound at Bruno's side sensed it, as evidenced by its ears being pinned back on its huge head.

"Then let us come to the purpose of our visit," Joanna continued on. "I am here to demand you stop blackmailing Sir William."

"Wh—what are you referring to?" Halderman asked, obviously caught off guard.

"Your criminal activity," she replied matter-of-factly.

"This is absolute nonsense and I will not allow it to go any further," he asserted. "Should you persist, I shall ask you to leave."

"I would strongly suggest you put your theatrics aside, for I am not only aware of your current blackmailing activities, but of similar evil deeds in your past."

"You have been badly misinformed, madam," he said, keeping his voice even, but the scowl on his face indicated that my wife had touched a nerve.

"To the contrary, I have excellent sources in the underworld who were happy to tell me of your notorious past," she retorted. "There are a few you have crossed who would not hesitate to slit your throat. Shall I name them?"

Halderman's silence spoke volumes.

Joanna reached into her purse for a Turkish cigarette and, after lighting it, began to pace the floor of the expansive library. "I trust you do not find my smoking offensive, but I insist, for it sharpens my mind when facing a worthy adversary."

"If you had any proof to back up your contentions, Scotland Yard would be at your side," he said finally.

"That may well come later if we fail to arrive at an acceptable accommodation," my wife replied. She strolled over to a large window and gazed out at the stand of trees which separated Halderman's estate from Sir William's.

Something caught her eye, but only for a moment. "The amount of harm you have caused is beyond measuring and, were it up to me, I would hound you night and day until I brought about your finish. But the decision is not mine, and thus I find myself here as a negotiator. Sir William of course does not know the identity of his blackmailer, and it will remain so if we come to an agreement on a final payment which will end the blackmailing once and for all."

"This is a total fabrication which I refuse to be part of."

"You are what you are, and your words of denial have no substance, but, for the sake of discussion, permit me to ask the questions which you can respond to in a third-person perspective and thus avoid any self-incrimination." Joanna paused to allow him to bring the meeting to an end which he chose not to do. "Shall I continue?"

"If you must."

"Shall we not come up with a final agreement, I will bring the hand of Scotland Yard down on you with full force, despite not having nearly enough evidence to charge you. You see, they owe me a favor or two, and with your background in blackmailing, I will make certain your evil doings find their way into all of London's newspapers. Of course, Sir William's family, and Anne Atwood in particular, will be embarrassed and humiliated, but you, sir, will be destroyed." She took a long, final draw on her cigarette, before extinguishing it in an imitation Chinese dish. "Just imagine the public's response on learning you were blackmailing the Chancellor of the Exchequer. Here we have an honorable and decent man, a pivotal player in our war effort, being extorted by the likes of you. You would be detested throughout the whole of England. All of your wealth and trappings would disappear. Why, even your medallion as a member of the Marcus Society would be stripped away, for they would not wish to have your putrid stench associated with them."

Halderman's face seemed to narrow into a mean stare, with his penetrating eyes showing no fear. "I cannot speak for this blackmailer with confidence."

205

"Only tell us what you would demand in his stead, knowing that his last call was for ten thousand pounds."

"May I know the item under consideration?"

"Salacious photographs, of which there are more than a few."

Halderman leaned back and tapped a finger against his chin, like a man carefully considering a highly priced purchase. I wondered if he was tallying the number of future demands he could make on Sir William before bleeding the elder statesman dry. "I would say twenty-five thousand pounds should satisfy the blackmailer."

"Is that a firm and fast number?"

"In all likelihood."

"That response will not do," my wife insisted. "We require an absolute final demand."

"Then twenty-five thousand pounds it is."

"I shall so inform Sir William, but time will be required to gather such a large sum," said my wife. "There are paintings which must be auctioned off at the highest possible price, for Sir William also has loans to be paid and bank accounts to be replenished."

"That would be understandable to the blackmailer, I would think."

"Ten days, then?"

"Ten days."

"Before we depart, allow me to state one final, firm warning," Joanna cautioned. "Once the last payment is made, the blackmailer may be tempted to insist on further demands once a suitable period of time has passed. Were this unpleasant event to occur, I can assure you the blackmailer would face a most dismal future. Not only would he lose all his possessions, but he would be stalked to no end until all of his evil deeds come to light. Given enough time, sufficient evidence would be uncovered to charge and convict this individual, who no doubt would find himself imprisoned at Pentonville, where an extra piece of stale bread is considered a luxury. Let me assure you this is not an idle threat."

"I shall see to it that message reaches the individual involved," Halderman said, unmoved.

"Then our business here is finished," my wife said, turning for the door. "We will find our way out."

We departed without further words and walked through the marbled vestibule which was now quiet as a tomb. The entrance door was opened by an expressionless butler who did not bother to give us even the courtesy of a nod, much less a respectful bow. I wondered if he was yet another of Halderman's hired henchmen. Outside, the sun was beginning to break through a dreary Sunday afternoon.

"Do you believe he will live up to the agreement?" I asked in a low voice.

"He will as far as the payment of twenty-five thousand pounds is concerned," Joanna replied. "But, as Watson predicted, I fear he will bide his time until the current happenings have faded, and then he will strike again."

"Even with your warning of what the future holds should he do so?"

"It is much like a gambit in the game of chess which is now underway," she said. "And Eric Halderman is a supreme egotist who foresees himself having the last decisive move."

"How will you respond?"

"By removing the opportunity for him to have that last decisive move."

"But how will you go about accomplishing that feat?"

"In a manner which Scotland Yard would not approve of," she said, as dark clouds began to move in.

26

THE ACCIDENT

Joanna's experiment was of such interest to Sir Anthony that he paid a visit to 221b Baker Street the following Monday morning. He was particularly impressed with my wife's apparatus for testing the various fire retardants.

"Quite ingenious," said he, examining the small metal shield which contained both asbestos and gypsum. "Of course the mixture outperformed the others."

"That was to be expected," Joanna concurred. "But the question remains whether it can be used to fireproof a tank."

"Only to a limited extent, for the flames would be far too intense," Sir Anthony said. "Please keep in mind that your candles, which are made of beeswax, will melt at a hundred and fifty degrees, whilst the temperature within a tank on fire will quickly reach eighteen hundred degrees."

"And no human being could begin to survive at that hellish temperature," my father noted.

"It is a matter of timing, Watson," Sir Anthony said. "As the temperature rises above a hundred and ten, the tank crew has only seconds to climb out of the vehicle if they are to survive. Thus, were we to allow them just a few extra seconds using a fire retardant, it could make the difference between life and death."

"So Joanna's mixture of gypsum and asbestos could truly be of some assistance," I interjected.

"But there is where we encounter a problem," Sir Anthony went on. "Tanks move very slowly, at approximately the speed of a walking pace. If we add hundreds of pounds of fire retardant, it slows the speed to a virtual crawl, which makes the vehicle an easy target for armor-piercing shells."

"And gypsum can be quite weighty," said my wife.

"It weighs a hundred and eighty-five pounds per cubic foot to be exact," he informed us. "Thus, it would not be possible to coat an entire tank with that material. But strips of asbestos might be the answer, for they would be far lighter than gypsum."

"I take it you are currently working on such a project," my wife surmised.

"We are indeed, and it is showing some promise," said he. "But do not let my words dissuade you from performing further experiments, for any new data you gather could prove to be of importance to us."

"Then we shall carry on," Joanna pledged.

"Please do," said Sir Anthony and, with a fond wave to my father, departed.

We waited until his footsteps on the stairs faded before hurrying to the window overlooking Baker Street. Below, a military escort came to attention and opened the rear door of an official vehicle for Sir Anthony. It clearly showed the vital role the esteemed scientist played in Britain's war effort.

"Perhaps we should have invited Sir Anthony to lunch," I suggested. "It would have given him a moment of respite from his heavy burdens."

"He does not partake of lunch, for he believes the ingestion of food causes the blood flow to rush to the digestive tract and away from the brain, which diminishes one's thinking," my father said.

"That sounds like a quote from Sherlock Holmes," I remarked.

My father smiled at the notion. "It may well be."

"So then, what is next in our fireproofing experiments?" I asked my wife, as we returned to our comfortable, overstuffed chairs.

"I think we should now concentrate on strips of asbestos, which are less weighty and easier to install," she replied. "But more thought is needed before proceeding."

"You must keep in mind that such strips may be difficult to come by during wartime."

"That should not present a problem, for Sir Anthony could surely supply us with the limited amount required," my father said.

"Please see to that, Watson," Joanna requested.

The phone nearby rang. Instead of lighting his cherrywood pipe, my father reached for the receiver.

"Yes?" he answered cordially, but a moment later his expression turned most serious. "Yes, I am Johnny's step-grandfather and his physician . . . She is seated by my side." My father pressed the receiver to his ear, intently listening to every word of the call which seemed to go on and on. "No broken bones, then?"

Joanna gasped audibly.

"We shall be on the next train to Windsor," he said and quickly placed the receiver back into its cradle.

"What has happened?" Joanna asked breathlessly, as she tried to maintain her composure.

"There has been an accident," my father replied, taking her hand and squeezing it reassuringly. "A runaway carriage came up on the footpath and struck your son and his friend. Fortunately, the carriage brushed by and they sustained only bruises, with no broken bones. Both lads were thoroughly examined by the infirmary doctor."

"No head injury, then?"

"None."

We grabbed coats and hats and, on reaching Baker Street, were able to immediately hail a taxi and arrived at Paddington station in a matter of minutes. Whilst Big Ben was striking the noon hour, we boarded a train to Eton.

An hour later we disembarked at Windsor and hurried across the bridge and up High Street to Eton. Despite the report that Johnny's injuries were minor, we were worried, for infirmary doctors are not known for their diagnostic skills. Furthermore, superficial bruises are at times the covering of more serious internal damage. Both Joanna and I found comfort in having my father at our side, for he was a most talented physician, with a gentle, knowing hand. Although his love for Johnny was every bit as deep as ours, he showed no emotion, for that was the mark of an excellent physician with over thirty years of practice to his credit. He was accustomed to being the calm in the storm.

We were met outside the infirmary by Dr. Samuel Morse, an elderly physician who was more than gracious to us. He reported with great precision each of Johnny's bruises to the upper thorax and right hip area. X-rays of the chest and hip showed no abnormalities, with Johnny having a normal gait and clear breath sounds. What he found surprising was the lad's response to the accident. Whilst his friend was badly shaken, Johnny appeared unaffected and seemed more interested in the runaway carriage than his superficial, but nevertheless painful, injuries.

Once inside, we found Johnny seated on the edge of an examining table, obviously in good spirits as he smiled at our approach. "It is a pleasure to see all of you again, but please defer any embraces, for my chest remains somewhat sore."

Joanna ignored the warning and, placing her arms gently around him, kissed his cheek. "Are you well?"

"I am fine," he said.

"I was so worried."

"Mothers have a habit of doing so," he said warmly and gave her a reassuring nod. "The bruises are not severe, for they barely brought blood to the surface."

"Which is a good sign," my father asserted. "But I must inquire if there is any pain when you walk."

"None whatever, but I should ask that you not push down on my hip area if further examination is required. It remains quite tender."

"Which is to be expected, but it will pass," my father said.

"It might be wise for you to rest at home whilst awaiting a full recovery," I suggested. "Should any unexpected complications arise, you would be under the careful eye of Dr. Watson."

"I would advise that as well," said Dr. Morse. "For we now have several cases of severe influenza in the infirmary, and it appears to be quite contagious."

"Is it the Spanish flu?" my father inquired at once.

"I am afraid so."

A collective chill swept down our spines, for the Spanish flu was an exceptionally vicious form of influenza, with a high mortality rate for all afflicted. It was currently spreading across Europe at a speed never seen before for an infectious disease.

"Will Eton close down?" my wife asked.

"It is a distinct possibility, madam."

"Then my son will convalesce at home."

"A wise decision," I said.

In short order, we raced to Johnny's dormitory where he gathered his belongings and quickly packed a single suitcase. We hurried to Windsor station, wishing to separate ourselves from the outbreak of Spanish flu as rapidly as possible. The disease was known to have a horrendous course, with patients turning blue whilst they struggled for air and perished. Fortunately, the station was in thin attendance and there was no difficulty obtaining a private compartment for our journey back to London.

My father, who was seated next to Johnny, gently patted the lad's shoulder and remarked, "You are holding up very well indeed after experiencing such a frightful accident."

"It was no accident, Dr. Watson," Johnny said in a neutral tone. "That hansom meant to do us harm."

"We were told it was a runaway carriage," Joanna interrupted.

"No, Mother, it was clearly a hansom, with a driver who was seated at the rear in control."

"Can you describe him?"

"Of course," he said, and reached into his jacket for a cherrywood pipe, which he slowly lighted whilst gathering his remembrance. At 17 years of age, his remarkable resemblance to Sherlock Holmes now seemed much more striking, with his long, narrow face and heavily lidded eyes. Even their hair was the same, being dark in color and combed back neatly, with every strand in place. "The driver was a very large man, whose height and girth stood out despite his position at the rear of the hansom. He was broad-shouldered, with a remarkably big head if one went by the size of his derby. I did not catch a good view of his face as the hansom raced by so rapidly."

Bruno, Eric Halderman's henchman! we all thought simultaneously.

Joanna's facial expression remained unchanged, but I could detect a sudden coldness in her eyes and knew that inwardly she was fuming. Now, in addition to the criminal business at hand, there was a score to be settled. "Did the driver make any attempt to rein in the so-called runaway horse?"

"Again, Mother, it was surely not a runaway, for there was no attempt to bring the animal to a halt," Johnny said, then added, "Moreover, the driver did not bother to shout out a warning to those on the footpath."

"And I would think he made no stop to lend assistance to those on the footpath," my wife surmised.

"He disappeared as quickly as possible, which the police attributed to the fact the hansom was stolen."

"Stolen, you say?"

"Quite so," the lad continued on. "According to one of the constables, the hansom went missing from a nearby estate that morning. It is yet to be found."

"It will be in short order, for the hansom has served its purpose," Joanna predicted.

"And its purpose was to bring severe injuries or worse to either me or my good chum Jeremy," Johnny concluded. "Now, Jeremy is a quiet, nice chap who spends most of his time reading Shakespeare's plays and the Bible. He believes both were written by the two greatest writers the world has ever known. Furthermore, his family is equally as gentle, with his father being an assistant to the Archbishop of Canterbury. That leaves me as the most likely target, does it not?"

"I am afraid so," his mother said unhappily.

"So, with me being a primary target, I wonder if this somewhat awkward attempt on my life is related to my dear mother, who has made her share of enemies and who also happens to be the daughter of Sherlock Holmes." He paused to light his pipe before giving Joanna a humorless smile. "You no doubt have brought an angry enemy to our doorstep."

"And a most clever one," she said, and narrated a concise, yet complete summary on the blackmailing activities of Eric Halderman. She made a particular mention of the manservant Bruno, who her son had so aptly described, but her emphasis was on Halderman and his merciless greed.

"He appears to be much like a leech, who will only disengage once the victim is sucked dry," Johnny depicted accurately.

"With the face of a badger," I added.

"A narrow snout and a cold stare, then," Johnny said and slowly nodded to himself. "I find it remarkable how much the human face tells of the person within. Surely you have deduced the characteristics of a given individual by studying their facial expression. This holds true whether it is kindness, gentleness, meanness, or what have you. In the case of Mr. Halderman, the face of a badger may well be a warning sign, for bad-gers can become fierce, malevolent creatures, particularly when cornered. In certain species, such as the honey badger, they are vicious through and through, and will kill for the pure joy of it."

"Pray tell, how does one determine when an animal finds joy in killing?" I asked out of curiosity.

"In the matter of the honey badger, it will enter a cage containing dozens of chickens and slaughter them all, but only eat one or two," Johnny elucidated. "Thus, it is believed their killing is driven by a sense of pleasure."

"To our knowledge, not only has Mr. Halderman killed, he did so to his own brother without the least bit of hesitation," my wife said.

"So the cruelty is there, with the man appearing to have no soul," the lad went on. "He is both callous and cold-blooded, and it would be wise to believe that further murders are not beyond his scope. Do you believe he would have lost sleep had Jeremy and I been killed by the hansom?"

"Not a second's worth," Joanna replied.

"Thus, my dear mother, you are dealing with a nemesis of the first order and he will not allow you or anyone else to interfere with his stock-in-trade," he said, then cautioned, "You must be very careful confronting this man."

"I plan to be," she assured.

"You must look for his weak spot," her son advised. "For once found, it will bring down the strongest of men or beasts."

"It was easy enough to find, for it all revolves around his ill-gotten wealth," Joanna said. "And I aim to take full advantage of that weakness."

"Make certain you do, Mother, and make equally certain that when it's done you have destroyed his ability to ever regain what he has lost," he said and, leaning back, closed his eyes, no doubt devising ways he might assist.

27

THE EQUIPMENT

The clerk at Piccadilly Outdoors was most surprised by the list of items my wife wished to purchase. He carefully read and reread the particulars, as if to make certain all were available.

"I do believe we can accommodate you, madam," he said, gesturing in the direction of the items with his hand and leading us down an aisle which had numerous displays of camping equipment. "Is there one type of fireproof glove you require?"

"They should be thick enough to ward off intense heat, but not to the extent it interferes with one's agility," Joanna replied.

"What purpose would they serve, if I may ask?"

"They would protect a chef from a large, outdoor fire," she replied.

"Ah, yes," the clerk replied knowingly, "for he would be dealing with large pots and pans which had been exposed to considerable heat."

"Precisely."

He reached for a pair of gloves made of a tightly woven material and passed them on to my wife. "These are quite popular, madam, and are known to protect against both heat and flame."

Joanna tried the gloves on for size, but they were obviously too large for her hands. On returning them to the clerk, she said, "Our chef is not of great stature, so I will require a somewhat smaller size."

"Here you are, madam," he said, handing her a smaller set of gloves, which Joanna tested and found to be a snug fit. "Will those suffice?"

"Quite nicely," she approved. "I shall require two pairs, for there will be multiple chefs in attendance. The second set should be a size larger."

"A medium, then?"

"That should do."

After placing the gloves aside, the clerk asked, "Will protective goggles be in order as well?"

Joanna considered the proposal at length before nodding her response. "There could be sparks flying about."

"Shall I include a small and medium size?" he asked.

"Please do."

The clerk glanced at the list once again before guiding us to an adjacent aisle which housed canvas tents and the like. "Is there a particular variety of knapsack you have in mind?"

"One that is sturdy, with thick straps and capable of carrying a sizable load."

"How sizable?"

"A medium should do, but allow me to measure," Joanna said, as the clerk presented her with a brown knapsack that carried a price tag of two pounds. Much like the other items, I had no idea of the purpose they would serve, but my wife assured me I would be informed in due time. She was now using a tape measure to ascertain whether the size of the knapsack was correct. "These are the perfect size," said my wife. "And again, two will be required."

"Very good, madam," stated the clerk, placing them into a large basket beside the gloves and goggles. "Now, as to the last item, you are most fortunate, for we have only recently received a new shipment of cellophane which remains in short supply. We must therefore limit the sales to one roll per customer."

"What area will a single roll cover?"

"A large lamp."

"That is ideal for our needs," said Joanna, then tapped a finger against her chin as she considered yet another matter. "Ah, yes, there is one final item which comes to mind. Might you have a rubber suction bulb with a large mouth?"

"We do indeed, madam," he replied and reached to an upper shelf for a fist-sized suction bulb.

Joanna tested the device against a glass counter where it produced a forceful pressure that made it difficult to disengage. "Be good enough to add this to the other items," she said.

We paid a rather expensive bill for the unusual collection and, after having them loaded into our leased motor vehicle, continued on our shopping spree. Unlike her usual self whilst on a buying tour, Joanna remained most secretive about the strange list of purchases she was making, only informing me there were several more stops in store. She even refused to discuss our need for a leased motor vehicle, which would be required for only a day. But I had learned long ago that my wife's mind worked in curious ways and for reasons which were often beyond my grasp. Initially, I thought the gloves were to be used in the fireproofing experiment, but why two pairs of differing sizes? And what possible use could we have for two canvas knapsacks? I sighed to myself, knowing there would be even more questions coming, for our next stop was a chemist shop. And the chemist was certain to ask for specifics regarding the prescriptions I ordered.

"You must give me some information on the larger dose of phenobarbital I prescribed, for the chemist will no doubt inquire about its quantity," I said. "The amount is tenfold that used for sedation."

"Inform him that a friend has a dog which is having seizures and the drug will be administered in varying doses to control them," she replied.

"Which, of course, is a fabrication."

"But a believable one."

"I must insist that you at least give me a hint of what I am about to involve myself with," I demanded.

"It is for a good cause," she said evasively.

"Is that all you will disclose?"

"For now, but prior to our departure from Baker Street, you will be apprised of more detail."

We found the chemist shop quite busy and the chemist himself occupied, which was fortunate, for he would have little time for questions about my oversized prescription.

Joanna's attention was briefly drawn to a display of facial cream which promised to remove lines and restore luster. She carefully studied the ingredients listed on the container before returning the cream to the shelf.

"Not very encouraging, then?" I queried.

"It causes peeling, but the crow's feet will remain."

"I was unaware you had those."

She smiled at my compliment and nudged me with a playful elbow. "You obviously need spectacles."

"Ah, Dr. Watson, your prescription is prepared," the chemist greeted me from behind the counter. "But I am curious as to the use of such a large request. I rarely dispense a gram of phenobarbital for a single patient."

"It is for the dog of a family friend who is having recurrent seizures," I lied. "The animal detests the taste of phenobarbital, and thus the drug must be given by injection at varying doses."

The chemist nodded at my explanation. "That accounts for your need of needles and syringes, and for the saline which will be used as a dilutant."

"Right you are."

"Very good, then," he said. "Your total is one pound six."

After paying the bill, we continued on to our last stop which was the neighborhood butcher who made it his business to care for everyone's wishes, but who paid particular attention to Miss Hudson's orders, always providing her with the best and freshest cuts. I hoped we were not about to involve him in some nefarious scheme.

"I should tell you that I truly dislike telling falsehoods to other professionals," I said.

"Are you referring to the chemist?"

"I am."

"Well then, be comforted by the fact you told him a half truth."

"Regarding what?"

"The use of the drug."

"But we are not familiar with a friend's dog who has seizures, for only Halderman's rottweiler is so afflicted."

"That was the half truth."

Our butcher, Archie Andrews, limped over to welcome us. He once worked as a delivery man for a local brewery, but an accidental fall ruined his knee and caused him to lose his position. "This was a most unusual order," he said. "She rarely puts in a request for such a large, single steak."

"The order is not for our household, but meant as a gift for a friend who is now down on his luck," Joanna explained.

"This cut should keep him in good stead, for it will be the centerpiece of more than a few suppers."

"Excellent, for he will have more than a few days to enjoy it," she said. "I trust it contains a good, thick bone to be the basis of a hearty soup."

"Oh, I can assure you this cut will be much to his liking." The butcher went behind the counter and returned with a large steak which could easily feed a family of three. In its center was a thick bone that measured nearly an inch in width. "And what do you think of this, then?"

"Perfect," Joanna approved. "Please add the cost to our account."

"It is already done," said he. "And my best wishes to Miss Hudson."

We departed with the heavily wrapped steak, but placed it in the boot of our motor vehicle rather than on the rear seat next to our other purchased items. My wife gave no reason for this arrangement, nor did she explain why she packed the fireproof gloves, suction bulb, and roll of cellophane into one knapsack, whilst leaving the other empty.

On the short drive to our rooms, Joanna informed me, "We shall enjoy an early supper of Miss Hudson's most excellent stew, then be on our way, for there is more business to be done."

"What business is this, pray tell?"

"You shall hear more at the supper table, for Watson and Johnny will be asking the very same question."

"But knowing young Johnny, I suspect he will not allow you to be so vague and evasive about your plan."

"He will see through it."

Twilight was falling when we reached 221b Baker Street and locked the doors of our motor vehicle to secure its contents. The large wrapped steak remained in the boot as well. On entering the first floor, we were met by the strong aroma of beef stew which we followed into the kitchen. Miss Hudson was carefully tasting the delicious stew, and did so once again before adding more pepper.

"Ten minutes more should suffice," she estimated. "And its gravy will be quite thick, just as you requested."

Which came as another surprise to me, for my wife was not fond of the dish and, in particular, did not favor gravy, for she believed it masked the taste of the entrée.

"Has my son been of good appetite?" Joanna asked.

"Quite good indeed," Miss Hudson replied. "He and Dr. Watson enjoyed a most hearty lunch of smoked salmon and roasted brussels sprouts."

"Sharp as ever, then?"

"He is far more than sharp, Mrs. Watson," our housekeeper said. "I could not help but overhear the lad explaining some new hieroglyphics to the senior Dr. Watson."

My wife was not simply making idle chatter, but rather checking on Johnny's mental acuity, for at times a daze occurs after what appears to be an insignificant blow to the head. Obviously, her son had no such post-traumatic effect.

"Oh, and by the way, Emmett Mullins called to inform you that your order has been placed and can be picked up at the smoldering shop any time before seven."

"Very good, and now up the stairs we go to await your splendid supper."

As we ascended the stairs, I asked, "Are there to be more tests on fireproofing?"

"One of real importance," Joanna replied.

"May I inquire why you chose not to have the new equipment delivered to our rooms?"

"My! My! You are curious about this venture, aren't you?"

"It is a simple question."

"Then I shall give you a simple answer," she said. "There was no need to have the equipment delivered here, for the experiment will be done away from Baker Street."

"Ha! A mystery within a mystery."

"Which you, dear heart, will help me unravel."

Our parlor was nicely heated by a blazing fire, which countered the evening frost that was now setting in. My father had brought in a blackboard from our storage room, upon which Johnny was now scribbling Egyptian hieroglyphics. He wrote the graphics in an easy, rapid fashion, much like he would do if signing his name.

"This is the symbol for the sun, Dr. Watson," he was saying. "But it might also represent Ra, whom the Egyptians believed to be the god of the sun."

"How does one differentiate?" asked my father.

"By reading on and determining which is the best fit for the sun itself or for the god," he replied. "And on further deciphering, one can see there may be a third, hidden meaning as well."

"Quite a crafty bunch, I would say."

"More than you will ever know, sir," Johnny said and, catching sight of us, waved fondly. "I will make an Egyptologist out of Dr. Watson yet."

My father smiled at the lad. "I am having enough difficulty deciphering Shakespeare."

"As is the rest of the world," said Joanna, and walked over to kiss her son's cheek. "You look well."

"I am feeling well, Mother, but my chest remains a bit sore when I sneeze."

"It could be a minor fracture which was not detected by x-ray, or simply a deep bruise," my father said.

"How does one distinguish between the two?" Joanna asked.

"Time," my father replied. "A bruise heals in a matter of days, a fracture may take weeks."

"Which do you believe is the most likely?"

"A deep bruise."

There was a quick rap on the door and Miss Hudson entered carrying a full tray, with the bowls of beef stew still steaming. The table was already set, so we quickly took our places and unfolded our napkins, with appetites whetted by the savory aroma. Miss Hudson stood near and waited for us to sample the carefully prepared dish.

"Delicious!" my father praised.

"Superbly seasoned," I noted.

"Well worth getting hit by a hansom," Johnny said in a neutral voice, which brought smiles to our faces.

Miss Hudson was delighted with our responses and departed, leaving us to enjoy the delectable supper, which captivated Johnny's tastebuds. He could identify the seasoning ingredients the landlady had employed and made particular mention of the sweet, peppery taste of the paprika whose flavor indicated it had come from Hungary. But our conversation soon drifted away from food to that of blackmailing, with an emphasis on how blackmailers gained possession of the items to be used in their trade.

"In most instances they are bought," Joanna said. "The blackmailer allows it to be known that he is prepared to pay considerable sums for letters or photographs which compromise people of wealth and position. He will receive these items from treacherous valets or maids, but on occasion from genteel personages who have come on hard times or seek revenge. Blackmailers, such as Eric Halderman, do not deal in petty demands, for I have heard of a thousand pounds being paid for several lines written in a most compromising letter."

"Do they play their blackmailing item all at once?" Johnny inquired.

"Not necessarily, for they may hold back their cards for months or even a year when the stakes will be even higher," Joanna replied.

"But Halderman wasted no time in this instance," my father noted.

"There was no need to do so, for the stakes would never be greater," she said. "Here we have the granddaughter of the Chancellor of the Exchequer soon to marry into a well-known aristocratic family with close royal connections."

"The entire scheme had the most perfect timing," Johnny commented.

"Much like a conductor leading an orchestra, with the first note struck when Halderman arranged to meet Anne Atwood in the garden adjoining their estates, perhaps by enticing her dog over with treats, much like he had done in the past," my wife continued, as though she was reading from a script. "From that moment on, each step was carefully planned and carried out by a master blackmailer. He took notice of Anne's acting aspirations and set up her backstage introduction to the handsome Hugh Marlowe who happened to be his half-brother. He correctly predicted Marlowe would eagerly participate, for it would provide the young actor with the funds to look after his poor, ill mother. What was unexpected was that the planned brief affair would turn into love. It was at this point no doubt that Hugh Marlowe demanded the blackmailing be brought to a halt."

"That cost him his life," my father interjected. "The younger brother may have actually threatened to expose Halderman if the blackmailing continued."

"That is undoubtedly so," Joanna concurred. "And the stage provided the perfect backdrop for the killing. Halderman had agreed to send a horse-drawn carriage to transport the lovers around West London again. Instead, he sent Bruno to dispose of his troublesome brother. With that matter resolved, Halderman could persist with the blackmailing and even raise his demands."

"Which was the reason for the more salacious photograph being directed to Sir William," Johnny reasoned.

My wife nodded at her son's rationale. "It is a simple equation. The more salacious the photograph, the more embarrassment and humiliation it will elicit, which brings along a higher demand."

"He is a very clever fellow," my father said disparagingly. "And he will continue to be so, as long as he possesses the damning photographs."

"Could you not set a trap for him, Mother?" Johnny suggested.

"It could be done, but to no avail," Joanna replied. "For even if Halderman was caught and convicted, the photographs would be released and Sir William and his family ruined."

"A sad situation," he said.

"Quite," I said. "But allow me to lighten the conversation by telling you of a strange shopping spree which I participated in earlier today. I accompanied my dear Joanna to a number of stores where we made the most unusual of purchases. My wife refuses to tell me what use they will be put to, but perhaps the excellent minds of my father and young Johnny can unravel this puzzling mystery."

"We shall give it our best," Johnny said, obviously eager for the challenge. "You must describe each item in detail, including their size, make, and where they were purchased."

I began with our stop at Piccadilly Outdoors where we bought two pairs of fire-resistant gloves in small and medium sizes. Then I described the two protective goggles, again of small and medium sizes. Next came the two canvas knapsacks which my wife measured to make certain they were of the correct dimensions. The final two items consisted of a roll of cellophane which could cover a large lamp, and then a rubber suction bulb.

"Tell us more of the suction bulb," Johnny requested.

"It was the size of a clenched fist and made of sturdy rubber, with a large mouth."

"It carried some force, then."

"I would say so."

"Pray continue," he said, appearing to make a mental note.

"We then traveled to a chemist shop to obtain a large dose of phenobarbital powder, along with saline, syringes, and needles."

"For what purpose?"

"To treat a friend's dog suffering with seizures, but of course no such friend exists."

Johnny smiled humorously at my answer. "What next?"

"Off to the butcher's we went for a large steak with a thick bone, then home," I replied. "You may also wish to know that, except for the steak, all those items were placed in one knapsack whilst the other knapsack remained empty. And there are two final, unexplained occurrences. First, my wife insisted we lease a motor vehicle for only a day, and lastly there was Miss Hudson's instruction for us to remember to stop by a smoldering shop to pick up an order Joanna had made earlier." I sat back in my chair and said, "There you have it."

After giving those at the table an adequate amount of time to solve the riddle, I asked, "Does anyone have an answer?"

No responses were forthcoming.

"Perhaps Joanna will be good enough to place all these unusual pieces together for us," my father encouraged.

"It is in your best interest that I do not," my wife replied.

"Do you not trust our confidence?"

"I trust you implicitly, Watson, but if events go awry, you will be glad not to have known." She glanced at her wristwatch and said, "Now we must take our leave from this splendid company."

We arose from the table and adjourned to the fireplace, except for Joanna who briefly went to our workbench to obtain another item. I did not have a good view, but the item had the appearance of a small instrument. As we donned our topcoats, Johnny came over to kiss his mother farewell. His lips barely moved whilst he whispered, "Be careful, Mother, be very careful, for this is most risky business."

"I am aware," she whispered back.

28

THE FIRE

In the darkest part of the night I parked the motor vehicle off the road outside Sir William's estate. I raised the bonnet of the vehicle to give any passersby the impression that its engine had failed. I paused for a long moment to make certain the road remained deserted, then hurried back to the rear door to assist Joanna. It required the two of us to lift the knapsack which contained the blowtorch we had purchased from the smoldering company. Once it was secured on my shoulders, Joanna slipped the other, less heavy knapsack onto hers, and off we went, following a trail which separated Sir William's estate from that belonging to Eric Halderman. My wife held the cellophane-wrapped steak in her outstretched arm to keep its aroma well in front of us. Earlier, we had injected the steak with such a large dose of phenobarbital it would beyond a doubt put to sleep the monstrous rottweiler guarding Halderman's library.

"What if the hound detects our scent along with that of the steak?" I asked quietly.

"You raise an excellent point, for dogs can easily detect dozens of scents simultaneously and distinguish between them," Joanna replied and reached into her purse for a small vial that had a screw-on top. "I managed to steal a portion of the gravy from Miss Hudson's beef stew which will overpower the other nearby aromas. As you may recall, a dog lives by its stomach, and the intense smell of food will capture its entire attention."

"Will you simply unscrew the top and allow the scent to drift to Halderman's manor?"

"I shall shortly, but as we approach the mansion I will douse the steak with Miss Hudson's gravy, which will elicit a most enticing aroma. The only sound the hound will make is that of its tongue licking its chops."

We could see the lights on in Sir William's manor, whilst Halderman's was dark, as expected, for he retired to his bed at seven sharp. The clouds separated briefly and the moonlight allowed me to check the time on my pocket watch. It was near the nine hour, which should find Bruno dancing the night away at the Polanski in Whitechapel. In order to assure Bruno was away, Joanna had instructed Wiggins to station himself at the dance hall and await the thug's arrival. If Bruno did *not* appear at seven sharp, Wiggins was to phone Baker Street and alert us whilst we were having supper. No such call was received. We hurried along the path, for an individual peering out from Sir William's manor might see two shadows racing across the grounds and mistake us for thieves lurking in the night.

Once we reached the stand of trees between the two estates, Joanna removed the top from the vial of beef stew gravy and allowed the aroma to ascend into the chilly air. She next busied herself quickly arranging the items within her knapsack in the sequence they were to be used. *The items*, I thought for the tenth time. How in the world did the ever-clever Johnny put the list together and determine precisely the purpose each would serve?

"I heard Johnny warning you of the danger ahead," I said.

"I told you he would see through it," my wife reminded me.

"What was his major clue, may I ask?"

"The empty knapsack."

"But what of it?"

"It had to be measured to accommodate a quite large item, yet it remained empty when we returned to Baker Street," Joanna elucidated. "Thus, he reasoned it would be filled after we departed."

"Yet he had no idea where we were going."

"Oh, but he did," Joanna went on. "You told him we had to stop at a smoldering shop along the way. Pray tell, what device of such large size would a welder require?"

"A blowtorch, of course."

"And then the rest of the pieces fell into place, particularly when he noticed me removing a glass cutter from our workbench."

The heavy cloud cover returned and caused the moonlight to dim which brought back the black darkness. It was our cue for our dangerous adventure to begin. Joanna quickly soaked the steak with the gravy from Miss Hudson's beef stew and gave it a moment to penetrate through and through.

"The deepening scent will shortly reach the rottweiler, and the hound will be at the window awaiting its arrival," said my wife. "Can you approximate the time required for the phenobarbital to take full effect?"

"I would anticipate the animal would be heavily sedated within thirty minutes, assuming normal absorption."

Joanna rapidly checked her wristwatch. It was half-past nine. "If your calculation is off by as little as fifteen minutes, we are doomed."

"Let us hope Bruno fed the dog a hefty dose of the medication before departing."

We inhaled deeply to fill our lungs with oxygen, then raced across the wide lawn to the window which looked into Halderman's library. In a matter of seconds, the giant rottweiler stood on its hind legs and pawed at the window pane as it eagerly awaited its next meal. The hound made no sound. Joanna handed me the rubber suction ball which I applied to the center of the pane, whilst she employed the glass cutter to carve out a circular section from the glass. With a gentle pull I removed the round section and, looking in, found myself staring at the head of a massive dog whose dark eyes remained fixed on me. My wife quickly pushed the large steak through the opening and the rottweiler instantly disappeared from sight. The only sound we heard was the hound's teeth and jaw clamping down on the bony meal.

"You do realize that we are not only trespassing, but about to commit the crime of unlawful entry, with the intent of destroying property," I said in a whisper.

"I am aware, and it is for that very reason I chose not to divulge my plan to Watson and Johnny," she disclosed in a quiet voice. "I did not want them to become accomplices."

"But they would have attempted to dissuade you," I argued.

"Initially so, but they would soon point out the flaws and offer advice on how to overcome them," she said. "That would be considered aiding and abetting us to commit a criminal act, which would make them complicit and thus guilty of felonious conduct."

"Is that not stretching a legal point?"

"Not if we are apprehended and charged."

"Can you begin to imagine the headlines in all of London's newspapers?"

"I choose not to."

A light fog began to set in and I hoped it would grow stronger, for the murkiness could provide excellent cover for the escape back to our motor vehicle. I heard the dog's teeth crush into the steak bone, which made me even more aware of the damage the giant rottweiler could do to an intruder. My thoughts were interrupted by the sound of an approaching motor vehicle on the road outside the estate. Several moments passed before I saw the beam of headlights and I could only hope the occupants would not stop to lend assistance to the disabled vehicle. Even worse would be a patrolling police unit, for they would not only stop, but investigate and question those residing in the nearby estates. But the beam of lights passed and disappeared.

"The dog seems quiet now," I noticed.

"That is the behavior of animals after a large meal."

"Perhaps he is drowsy."

"That may be so, but we should wait until we hear the sounds of sleep."

There was sudden activity at Sir William's mansion. It seemed as if all of its lights had been turned on, whilst a limousine came out of the garage and went directly to the front entrance of the manor. A number of individuals—it was difficult to determine how many in the fog—appeared in the driveway and hurriedly entered the limousine which sped away.

"Do you believe Sir William has been called away on official business?" I asked.

"Most unlikely, for were that the case he would not be accompanied by others," Joanna replied.

"What then?"

"That is impossible to tell, but I can assure you it is an extremely urgent matter," she said and glanced at her wristwatch. "Twenty-five minutes have passed since the dog ingested the steak."

"Sedation should come shortly," I estimated. "But there are so many variables at play, such as the rate at which the drug is absorbed."

"I know, I know," Joanna said, her voice now showing concern.

The limousine carrying the group from Sir William's manor was now turning onto the main road outside the estate, as its tires squealed loudly before the vehicle accelerated again. Overhead, an owl hooted at the disturbance in the night. Time seemed to drag by in the silence, with each passing minute increasing the danger we faced.

I watched Joanna place the glass cutter at the bottom of the knapsack beneath the brass blowtorch, for it, along with the goggles and gloves, would be used next. As I gazed at all the items my wife had assembled, I could not help but be amazed by her son's deductive brilliance, for he had accurately predicted every step of our plan to invade the Halderman mansion, by simply being made aware of the purchases his mother had made. The glass cutter would allow us to enter, the phenobarbital would sedate the dog, and the gloves and goggles would protect her whilst a flame torched the safe. But one critical hurdle remained, for which I had no solution.

"Yet a singular problem stands," I said in a quiet voice. "A flame from a blowtorch will not gain us entrance into a sturdy Chubb safe."

"We don't have to enter," she said. "The evidence we seek are photographs which are made of celluloid. You will no doubt be interested to know that celluloid will melt at one hundred and fifty degrees, which is the melting point for candles made of beeswax."

"So the photographs in Halderman's safe will be destroyed if such a temperature can be reached within the safe."

"But that will depend in part on how well the safe is fireproofed."

I shook my head in wonderment. "Which explains why you constructed the fireproofing experiments in our parlor. You were attempting to simulate Halderman's safe."

"And if it helps our military, so much the better." Our conversation was interrupted by the owl perched above making a high-pitched shriek. At that very moment the giant rottweiler began to snore at high volume. It seemed to swallow involuntarily between the boisterous snores.

"Now!" Joanna commanded.

She reached in through the circular aperture and unlatched the window, then quietly opened it to the fullest extent. My wife climbed into the library and, after relieving me of my heavy knapsack, helped me in whilst motioning to avoid the sleeping hound. The moonlight remained dim and gave us an obscured view, but I was able to perceive the huge Victorian desk and the sturdy safe behind it. Just above the safe was a hanging tapestry, which my wife pushed aside so that the sparks could not reach it.

Joanna quickly donned protective gloves and goggles before switching on the imposing blowtorch. She applied the intense flame to the side of the safe, holding it steady at a distance of no more than a foot. Sparks flew into the air, but the metal of the safe seemed to resist the intense heat. My wife moved the flame even closer which caused an even larger shower of sparks to erupt, but she held her position. Ever so slowly the exterior of the safe began to take on a reddish glow that produced stifling heat. Joanna paused to mop the perspiration from her brow with her forearm as the temperature around her rose and clearly exceeded a hundred degrees.

"Say when you wish me to have a turn at it," I volunteered.

"I'll have at it another minute or two," she said, and moved the flame even closer to the wall of the safe.

In the light from the blowtorch, I could see the shelves behind the Persian tapestry, which were filled with scroll after scroll of tightly bound parchment. They were obviously ancient artifacts and came from a time that preceded the printing press. I doubted they had any religious connotation for an individual as evil as Eric Halderman. Suddenly, the light in the library brightened. It required only a moment for me to realize that the brightness was coming through the window. Then I heard the approaching motor vehicle which came to a screeching halt at the front entrance.

Joanna hurriedly switched off the blowtorch and dropped it, along with one glove, which had become entangled on the snout of the blowtorch.

"Who could it be?" I asked in a rush.

"Bruno," she replied without hesitation. "And for some reason he has returned early."

"How can you be so certain?"

"Logic," she answered and, grasping my arm, pushed me to the open window. "Jump out and stay put!"

We flew through the window, Joanna first, me after, and crouched down beneath the window sill. The silence was broken by the sound of loud voices which grew closer and closer.

"Should we make a dash for it?" I asked, as a chill ran down my spine.

Joanna shook her head at once. "They will turn on all the lights and see us running across the grounds, and then the chase will be on in hot pursuit."

"What then?"

"We wait for the opportune moment and sprint for the trees."

We heard the door to the library open, followed by the sound of heavy footsteps. Joanna pressed an index finger to her lips to reinforce the need for absolute silence. We moved in closer beneath the window sill for more cover and pricked our ears.

"See to the dog, Bruno," Halderman commanded.

There were more footsteps, followed by a brief pause.

"He is alive, but barely breathing, sir," said the manservant.

"He has been drugged."

"Perhaps he is sick."

"Do you not see the open window and detect the odor of kerosene?" Halderman asked harshly.

"Over here, sir!" came Bruno's rapid response. "There is a smoking blowtorch on the floor, with a glove atop it."

"The safe!"

We heard more quick footsteps, then a cry of pain. "Ow! Do not touch the safe, for it is hot as fire."

"Use the glove atop the blowtorch, sir."

There was a much longer pause, which lasted a half minute or so, before both men screamed out at the top of their lungs. Again, came more screams, equally as loud.

With great caution, my wife and I raised up ever so slightly, with our eyes just above the windowsill. To our amazement, a bolt of fire had erupted from the open safe and reached up to the hanging Persian tapestry which was now ablaze. The flames spread to the rolls of dried parchment on the nearby shelves, causing them to smolder and slowly ignite before they burst into a fiery inferno. Eric Halderman and Bruno were desperately patting at the sparks and smoking threads on their jackets.

"To the safe upstairs!" Halderman shouted to his henchman.

As they turned for the door, Joanna whispered loudly to me, "Run for the trees!"

We sprinted across the expansive lawn, knowing full well we were no longer dark shadows, but human figures that were clearly visible in the bright light cast from the burning mansion. The blaze was certain to be seen by neighbors who would alert the fire brigade. My wife and I wanted to be far gone when they arrived. We reached the stand of trees and paused to catch our breath before gazing back at the Halderman mansion. The entire first floor was now ablaze, with ascending flames that were licking at the second story and sending sparks up to the roof. The lights in Sir William's manor were still on and illuminated the trail back to our motor vehicle.

"Keep your head well down and race for our vehicle," Joanna said and pulled the collar of her topcoat up to cover the lower portion of her face. I followed suit and off we went, with me just a step behind my wife. We heard a muted female voice and the bark of their spaniel as we passed Sir William's manor, but paid it no attention. A horn sounded in the distance, which may have announced an approaching fire truck. We picked up the pace and, although nearly stumbling, reached our parked motor vehicle in short order. I closed the bonnet, switched on the motor, and, on making a rapid U-turn, sped away from the fiery scene.

Joanna waited until we drove past the oncoming fire truck before speaking. "That was a most interesting phenomenon, was it not?"

"I take it you are referring to the burst of flames from the open safe," I surmised, watching her light a Turkish cigarette without even a trace of tremor, whilst my heart rate was yet to slow down. "There must have been some highly flammable liquid within."

Joanna shook her head in response. "I suspect it contained only stacks of photographs which are made of celluloid."

"But you told me those would only melt with the application of high heat," I recalled. "Did you not say they would dissolve at a temperature of one hundred and fifty degrees?"

"I did indeed, but I am of the opinion that the temperature within the safe rose to a much higher level of three hundred and fifty degrees, which

236

is the ignition point for celluloid," she replied. "Thus, the photographs caught fire."

"Which should have simply burned and not caused them to behave like a flame thrower."

"Ah, dear heart, you must read up on thermodynamics as I did," Joanna said and gave me a mischievous smile. "It was a perfect example of fire chasing oxygen."

"I am still at a loss."

"It is rather straightforward actually," she continued on. "Once a substance catches fire in an enclosed space, it will use up all available oxygen and cease to burn. In this instance, Halderman opened the safe just as the photographs were burning their last, more or less smoldering as its supply of oxygen was nearly depleted. Suddenly, the safe was opened and air rushed in, which supplied abundant oxygen and gave the fire new life. The flames literally jumped out, seeking more and more oxygen, and caught everything in its path ablaze."

"Which included the hanging tapestry and scrolls of dry parchment, all of which set off the inferno," I concluded. "And thus, the downfall of Eric Halderman."

"I am not so certain about the latter."

"Why not, pray tell?"

"Because he was willing to rush upstairs to open a second safe, despite being caught in the midst of a blazing inferno," she said. "That safe must have contained something of immense value."

"Are you suggesting Halderman has even more damning photographs stashed away?"

"What else would be of such value to him?"

I had no answer to that question.

29

THE UNEXPECTED PATIENTS

I entered my office at St. Bartholomew's still pondering the outcome of the blaze which consumed Eric Halderman's mansion the night before. There were two questions of paramount importance: What was in the safe on the second floor, which was of such great value, and were its contents rescued before the flames destroyed the entire mansion? We had carefully read the newspapers at breakfast, but there was no mention of the blaze, which was to be expected, for it had occurred too late in the night to find its way into print the following morning. Our curiosity was such that Joanna considered reaching out to her deep-seated sources for the information, but decided against it for fear the inquiry might lead back to our involvement. Thus, all we were left with were our guesses, which my wife detested. Like her father before her, she believed guessing was a shocking habit, destructive of the logical faculty.

With effort I turned my attention to the mounds of paperwork stacked up upon my desk. I spent the next hour dictating letters of response, reading and signing numerous pathology reports, and reviewing applications for individuals wishing to become histology technicians. But my mind continued to drift back to last night's fiery adventure and our most narrow escape. The dire consequences of our being apprehended were too ruinous to contemplate.

My unpleasant thoughts were interrupted by a gentle rap on the door, which preceded the entrance of my young associate Jonathan Quinn. He brought with him the list of surgical specimens which had been submitted during the night. It always drew my immediate interest, for the specimens often came from patients who had conditions which required emergency life-saving surgery.

"What do you have for me, Jonathan?" I asked.

"Three cases," he replied. "For starters, there was a ruptured appendix, with an infection spreading throughout the peritoneum."

"Was there a delay in making the diagnosis?"

"The delay was in the patient seeking medical care," Quinn said, reading from the case report. "He was an alcoholic who tried to soothe his pain with several bottles of scotch."

"And next?"

"An intestinal obstruction caused by hemorrhaging into a large tumor mass which had the appearance of an adenocarcinoma," he replied, turning to a new page. "And the final case was a ruptured ectopic pregnancy."

"Within the fallopian tube, I take it?"

"Right you are, sir. The fertilized ovum had blossomed within the fallopian tube near the uterine opening. The rupture was relatively small, but quite symptomatic nonetheless."

"Well then, you may proceed with your scheduled autopsy on—"

Quinn quickly interrupted. "Hold on just a moment, sir, for there are two fascinating cases of carbon monoxide poisoning I should like to bring to your attention."

"Two cases, you say?"

The young pathologist nodded his response enthusiastically. "And they are both alive, with their skin colored cherry red. I managed to obtain blood samples from them, and those specimens are the brightest red imaginable. You should see them, sir."

"I should indeed," I said. "Lead the way."

As we hurried down the corridor, I recalled the biochemistry behind the bright red color seen in patients with carbon monoxide poisoning. The carbon monoxide molecules bind tightly to the hemoglobin in the individual's erythrocytes, which markedly reduces their ability to carry oxygen. This results in the formation of carboxyhemoglobin which colors the blood a cherry red.

"Are the patients recovering?" I asked, as my mind went back to the fire at the mansion the night before. Had Halderman and Bruno been trapped in its mist and exposed to a cloud of carbon monoxide?

"They are, but all too slowly, for they were admitted and remain in a comatose state."

As we entered the pathology laboratory, Quinn guided me over to a workbench that held a rack of test tubes, each containing blood that was astonishingly red. The carbon monoxide had apparently replaced the oxygen on the vast majority of circulating erythrocytes, which caused the patients to lapse into a coma.

"Striking," I commented. "The individuals were fortunate to survive."

"Indeed, sir," Quinn agreed. "But there is more than simple carbon monoxide poisoning to these cases."

"Oh?"

"They are under guard by Scotland Yard," he went on. "No one is allowed near the patients without being properly identified."

"Are they criminals, then?" I asked, now wondering why Scotland Yard was present.

"The police would not say, sir," he replied. "But victims of carbon monoxide poisoning have almost always been exposed to fire involving flammable materials. With Scotland Yard so close at hand, one has to wonder if these two were involved in some criminal activity."

"Such as arson," I reasoned, for Quinn's benefit.

"That would be my guess," the young pathologist concurred. "For the patients from whom I drew blood had their hands wrapped in bandages covered with petroleum jelly, which is customarily applied to burned areas. Their faces showed superficial burns as well."

"A most keen observation and deduction," I praised my colleague, as I attempted to think of other ways to identify the two scoundrels. "Were there other remarkable features of the two victims?"

Quinn furrowed his brow as he thought back. "What struck me, sir, was their relative size. The first patient I obtained blood from was a very small, thin individual, particularly when compared to his companion in the adjacent bed. The second man was huge, sir, with the broadest of shoulders and an oversized head. I must tell you that his frame was so immense it took up the entire bed, with his feet dropping over the very end."

All the pieces of Quinn's astute observations now came together. There were two victims of carbon monoxide poisoning—one small and thin, the other remarkably large—who were exposed to an intense fire, as witnessed by the burns on their hands and faces. I envisioned Halderman and Bruno racing through the flames to open a safe on the second floor.

"When you draw blood on the wards, you are obliged to obtain the names of the patients, are you not?" I asked, knowing the answer.

"Of course, sir," Quinn replied. "How else could one identify the donor?"

"Were you able to learn their names?"

"Scotland Yard would not allow it, sir," he responded. "But I insisted, informing them of the need to establish the source of every specimen."

"Were you successful?"

"Only partially, sir. They would not give the names, only initials."

"May I see them?"

"Here they are," he said, and pointed to the labels on the blood-filled test tubes. "One reads E.H., the other B.T."

The initials no doubt belonged to Eric Halderman and his manservant Bruno. Their names and faces flashed through my mind as I recalled them trying to extinguish the sparks on their jackets whilst they raced away from the fire. Was that the cause of their burns? Perhaps, I thought on, but more likely their hands were scorched whilst attempting to open the safe on the second floor.

"Is something amiss, sir?" Quinn asked, trying to read the expression on my face.

"Not at all," I said, quickly thinking of an excuse for my momentary silence. "I am mesmerized by the intense red color of the patients' blood. You may wish to have photographs taken and illustrative slides made for teaching purposes."

"A capital idea, sir," Quinn approved. "I shall have multiple sets made, which will suffice for the department and for our personal collections as well."

"You should contact our blood specialist to learn if he, too, would like a set."

Whilst Quinn was jotting down a reminder note, a side door opened for a technician who was pushing a metal cart toward us. Atop it were surgical specimens floating in large glass containers.

"Ah, Dr. Quinn, I have a quick question on the Atwood specimen," she said. "Should we section the fetus as well?"

The name *Atwood* resonated in my mind, much like a loud echo in a closed chamber. Was it Anne Atwood, the granddaughter of Sir William? It had to be, particularly with the word *fetus* attached to the name. "What type of specimen is that?" I asked, keeping my voice even.

"The ectopic pregnancy, sir," Quinn replied and pointed to the largest container. "As you can see, the small fetus remained intact."

I studied the specimen with my reading glasses and could clearly determine the shape of a tiny fetus, with its head and extremities just beginning to develop. It was now hanging loosely from the fallopian tube. The label on the container read A. Atwood.

"It is at best six weeks old," I remarked.

"If that," said Quinn and turned to the technician. "There is no need to section the fetus."

"Very good," the technician said, obviously relieved at not having to do so.

As the cart was wheeled away, Quinn waited until the technician was well out of hearing distance before speaking in a low voice. "Sir, we have been instructed by the director of the hospital to place this case in the sensitive file. The pathology report is to be dictated by you and only you, then sent to the director's office straightaway. No copies are to be given to the surgeon or others who participated in the surgery."

"I will see to it," I said, fully aware of the guidelines for sensitive files which were to be strictly enforced. I had experienced such a case several years ago when a member of the royal family took his own life. There was no doubt that Sir William had requested the listing for his granddaughter and it would be carried out to the letter. "It would be wise to remove the patient's name from the glass container."

"Done," Quinn said and disappeared to perform the task.

My mind went back to the night before when Joanna and I were hiding in the stand of trees between the two estates. It was then that we witnessed the sudden commotion at Sir William's mansion. All of the lights had been abruptly turned on, followed by a group exiting in haste and entering a limousine which had sped away. Anne Atwood must have developed acute abdominal pain as a result of a ruptured ectopic pregnancy.

Quinn returned and guided me over to a table which held several Zeiss microscopes. Beside them were multiple boxes of slides from prior autopsies awaiting our study. I allowed Quinn to review the majority of the slides, for the cases were straightforward, which was fortunate because I continued to be distracted by the remarkable earlier findings that were associated with the blackmailing of Sir William. It now seemed most likely that Halderman and Bruno had reached the second floor of the mansion where they succumbed to carbon monoxide poisoning. The burns on their hands indicated the pair had attempted to open the safe. But had they succeeded? If so, the documents and photographs within would have been destroyed.

If not, the items might still be intact, assuming the fire brigade arrived in time to save part of the upper mansion. All well and good, I thought on, but why was Scotland Yard at their bedside, guarding the two?

It required several hours for the endless boxes of slides to be reviewed and the reports dictated, after which I participated in the autopsy of a visiting dignitary who had been stabbed to death whilst resisting a late-night robbery in Westminster. Then came a lecture to medical students and a prolonged committee meeting on contagion prevention. Finally, in the last rays of the afternoon, all was done and I decided to visit the surgery ward and learn of Anne's condition prior to leaving St. Bart's. She was young and to the best of my knowledge in good health, and thus should have an uneventful recovery. But then again, the loss of a wanted baby could be most heart-wrenching to an expectant mother.

On the elevator ride up to the ward, I planned to make my visit brief and only consult the chart to be informed of Anne's postoperative status. It was my intent to avoid any encounter with the surgeon who would no doubt ask of my interest in the granddaughter of the Chancellor of the Exchequer. The entire hospital knew of my close association with the daughter of Sherlock Holmes, and my appearance at Anne's bedside might raise unwanted suspicions.

As I approached the surgery recovery unit, I saw Sir William and Lady Charlotte standing by a closed door. Both looked haggard and drawn, with dark circles beneath their eyes.

"I hope I am not intruding, but I have learned of Anne's condition because I am director of pathology at St. Bart's," I explained my visit. "How is she, may I inquire?"

"Physically, she is recovering nicely," Sir William replied. "But I am afraid a deep depression has set in."

Lady Charlotte sniffed back her tears and tried to swallow them away. "She just lies there and will not utter a single word."

"Let us pray her condition is temporary," I consoled.

"The doctor believes so, but in the interim we are faced with a sadness beyond measure," he said in a soft voice. "Our beautiful granddaughter appears almost moribund, with no will to live."

Lady Charlotte leaned on her husband for support. "She has only spoken once since the surgery, and that was to inquire about the baby. When told it was too young to survive, her sad response was 'At least the child is now with her father.' And since that moment, she has laid listless and stared into space."

"Of course this event has in a small way lifted a burden from the family's shoulders," Sir William said. "But the cost was far too great, and it will be unbearable if we lose our precious Anne."

"You must be patient, for healing takes time, but it will come," I reassured him.

"So we have been advised," the elder statesman said, pausing as if to pick his next words carefully. "We of course would very much appreciate this matter being held in the strictest of confidence."

"It shall be," I responded. "All matters related to Anne will be placed in a sensitive file, never to be disclosed."

"Thank you for your consideration."

"Not at all, and if I can be of any assistance, please do not hesitate to call upon me."

After our collective nods, I departed the hospital as twilight approached, and hurried to Baker Street where I knew my remarkable findings would be met by most eager ears.

CLOSURE

O n my return to our rooms, I was surprised to find we had an unexpected visitor. Inspector Lestrade was seated in our parlor and had everyone's complete attention.

"Ah, John, you have arrived at a most opportune moment, for the good inspector is just now bringing one of our earlier cases to a final resolution."

"Which case?" I asked.

"That of John Morton Harrington," she replied. "You may recall him as the banker at Lloyd's who pilfered the accounts of Lady Jane Wellesley."

"I do indeed, for he committed suicide when confronted by his guilt," I said. "But the stolen money was never recovered."

"It has now, for it found its way into the safe of Mr. Eric Halderman."

"What!"

"Quite astonishing, is it not?" Joanna asked, sending me a subtle smile. "I should allow Inspector Lestrade to give you the details, for it was Scotland Yard who gathered the rather startling evidence."

"It was mainly happenstance which came our way in a most unusual fashion," Lestrade recounted, not concerned with Johnny's presence for he knew of the lad's involvement in prior cases. "A fire had broken out at a mansion in Hampstead Heath last night and a fire brigade was immediately dispatched to the scene. The first floor was totally destroyed, but the second story only partially so. When the fire was extinguished, Mr. Halderman and his manservant were discovered unconscious, with burn injuries, on the upper floor and rushed to St. Bartholomew's for urgent treatment. But once the blaze was finally put down, the firemen came across some very strange findings."

The inspector reached into his coat pocket for a notepad which he referred to before continuing. "In the library next to an open safe, they found a blowtorch and atop it was a fire-resistant glove. Of course they immediately considered arson and called in Scotland Yard. A thorough investigation was undertaken and the contents of a partially opened safe on the second floor proved to be most revealing. There were bundles upon bundles of hundred-pound notes that were evenly stacked upon one another. Behind the fortune was a leather-bound volume which contained the names of individuals being blackmailed, accompanied by photographs being used for extortion. Mr. Halderman was a most neat blackmailer, for he not only listed the names, but the dates and payment amounts. Amongst the names was that of John Morton Harrington and the sums paid, as well as their dates, which proved to be a quite good match for the dates and amounts stolen from Lady Wellesley's accounts."

"Halderman will say it was planted there, unbeknownst to him," Joanna said. "What with him being so clever, you see."

"Well, it *was* planted there, Mrs. Watson, by Mr. Halderman himself, for our fingerprint experts have detected his prints on that leather-bound volume," Lestrade said, with a self-congratulatory nod.

"Well done, Lestrade, well done indeed," my wife praised. "But pray tell, how will the blackmailing evidence be dealt with? Care must be taken so as not to embarrass those being extorted."

"We shall insist on absolute confidentiality," he replied. "Those poor individuals involved will be informed of our discovery, with the promise that the evidence will be either permanently locked away or destroyed once Halderman is tried and convicted."

"I take it this leather-bound volume was not merely a scrapbook of past successes," Joanna inquired.

"Of the past and present," he answered. "Some were obviously ongoing, with very recent dates. The most current victims were individuals of surprisingly good standing, and included a prominent doctor, a noted barrister, and a highly regarded architect."

"I hope no members of the royal family or personages of distinction in our government were involved," my wife probed.

"Fortunately not, but I must say the neighboring estates belong to the upper level of our aristocracy, including the Chancellor of the Exchequer. All will shortly be made aware of Mr. Halderman's evil doings."

"And bid him good riddance."

"Most assuredly."

The phone rang and my father answered. It was a call for the inspector who spoke briefly before placing the receiver back in its cradle. He reached for his derby and adjusted its position carefully prior to speaking.

"The manservant, who no doubt was an accomplice, has died," he reported. "He had struggled mightily for air because of severe lung damage from smoke and fire."

"From what you have told us, his loss will be of little matter, for it appears that Halderman was the mastermind behind the blackmailing enterprise," Joanna said.

"True enough, for it will be Mr. Halderman who faces the sternest of British juries," the inspector said and readjusted his derby once again. "I shall of course keep you apprised."

We waited for his footsteps on the stairs to disappear before gathering around the fireplace to which my wife added a log that brought the blaze back to life.

"Well now, it would seem that Scotland Yard has overlooked a straightforward case of attempted burglary," said Joanna.

"What brings you to that conclusion?" my father asked.

"Because Lestrade failed to observe or mention the circle of missing glass which was removed from the window in the library," she replied. "That, together with the blowtorch and glove, clearly indicate an illegal entry took place, with the intent to open the safe."

"Perhaps it will come to him later."

"That is most unlikely, for the blackmailing is the low-hanging fruit that will garner all their attention and provide the most publicity."

The phone beside Joanna rang and interrupted our conversation. To a person we wondered if it was yet another call for Inspector Lestrade to inform him that Halderman had passed away as well. This would have been most unfortunate, thought I, for a dead man, although obviously guilty, can be neither tried nor convicted in a British court of law, and thus the evil blackmailer would have escaped the prolonged imprisonment he so richly deserved. On the third ring, my wife reached for the receiver.

"Yes?" she said and listened without expression before repeating the caller's message for our benefit. "Sotheby's has called with an option of dates for the auction of your Turner, you say."

Joanna smiled to herself before passing on the good news. "Well, Sir William, you may inform the auction house that you decided to hold onto the Turner for the foreseeable future."

"How will you come up with the demand, then?" she repeated his question before answering. "There is no need, for the photographs no longer exist."

"Ah yes, that unpleasant fellow will shortly be removed from society as well."

There was a lengthy pause before my wife spoke again. "I shall not go into detail other than to say the matter is done and finished forever, and that you and your family should sleep well tonight."

"There is no charge, Sir William, for our only wish was to relieve you of this heavy burden during these most trying times."

"You are most welcome," she said and placed the receiver down. "And so the case is closed."

"Not quite," I interjected. "For I have more news which you will find most interesting. You will recall that whilst on our adventure last night, there was a sudden disturbance at Sir William's mansion, with a group departing in haste and entering a limousine which sped away. It was a true emergency that came to my attention at mid-morning. Anne Atwood was rushed to St. Bart's where she underwent immediate surgery for a ruptured ectopic pregnancy. I am pleased to report she is recovering nicely."

Joanna took a moment to explain the ectopic pregnancy to Johnny who was not aware of the medical term. One could see the lad's incredible brain absorbing every word.

"Is that a dangerous condition, Mother?" he asked.

"One can die as a result of the rupture," she replied. "But even with successful treatment, such a diagnosis is often accompanied by sadness, which at times can be extreme."

"Is there hope for recovery then?"

"There will be emotional scars, which take time to heal," my wife reminded us.

"No doubt," my father agreed and reached for his cherrywood pipe which he slowly packed with Arcadia mixture. "But let us return to the death of this fellow Bruno, who succumbed to massive lung damage from smoke and fire."

"Surely you do not grieve for him," I said at once.

"No, I do not, but another thought comes to mind," he went on. "I know it would seem of little consideration, but since you and Joanna did in fact set the fire, you bear some responsibility for the manservant's death. He was a scoundrel, but a human life nonetheless."

"True enough, but the actual cause was Halderman's greed, for he had every chance to escape the fire with Bruno by his side, but he chose not to," Joanna asserted.

"But still, a life was lost."

"Allow me to place Bruno's death in context," she said. "With the demise of this murderous scoundrel, Sir William, a much needed and distinguished statesman, has been spared public humiliation, and thus I believe we had made a fair exchange."

"That is particularly so when one considers the pivotal role Sir William plays in England's war effort against a most powerful enemy," I added.

"Moreover, Bruno was the driver of the carriage which attempted to kill my Johnny," Joanna said, as a flash of anger crossed her face. "If you are seeking even a hint of remorse, you'll have to look elsewhere."

My father permitted himself a brief smile. "You two drive a hard bargain."

"But one which is undeniable and with that in mind, my dear Watson, I can assure you that Bruno's passage from this world to the next will not weigh heavily upon my conscious," she said and reached for the bell to inform Miss Hudson that we eagerly awaited one of her sumptuous suppers.

ACKNOWLEDGMENTS

S pecial thanks to Victoria Wenzel, for being an editor par excellence, and to my superb publicist, Julia Romero. And as always, a tip of the hat to Scott Mendel, an extraordinary agent, who has guided me so well along the literary path.